Easily Amused

Easily Amused

A Novel

Karen McQuestion

MARINER BOOKS
HOUGTON MIFFLIN HARCOURT
BOSTON   NEW YORK

First Mariner Books edition 2011

Text copyright © 2010 by Karen McQuestion

www.hmhbooks.com

First self-published, in a slightly different form, in 2009
Published in 2010 by AmazonEncore

Library of Congress Cataloging-in-Publication Data is available

ISBN 978-0-547-74502-2

Printed in the United States of America

DOC 10 9 8 7 6 5 4 3 2 1

For Charlie, who gave me the title
and who is also easily amused

Easily Amused

1

When I saw a group of my neighbors clustered on the sidewalk in front of Mrs. Cho's house, I was sure they were talking about me.

It was a sunny spring evening, and I was heading out to meet my friend Piper at a local bar. After work, I'd changed out of my office garb and into a lacy tank top and short skirt, then slipped my feet into a new pair of strappy sandals. A quick look in the mirror to touch up my makeup and I was set.

Despite my efforts, it was a sure thing Piper would look better than me, no matter what she was wearing—ironic considering she's the one who's married with a baby, while I, on the other hand, am currently and constantly unattached. Not her fault, of course, but still annoying.

I'd pictured a brisk walk to burn a few calories and hoped I might even collect a few admiring glances on the way, which would have done my poor ego a bit of good. But springtime in Wisconsin doesn't necessarily mean warm weather; thirty seconds out of the house I realized it was a little too chilly to be without a jacket, and my hair was getting windblown. Worse yet, I sensed I was about to get waylaid by the four neighbors halfway down the block.

As I approached the group, Crazy Myra, who'd been leaning forward to whisper something to Brother Jasper, straightened up abruptly, like she'd been caught snooping in someone's medicine cabinet. The other two ladies—Belinda, the dog woman, and Mrs. Cho—took a sudden, suspicious interest in a lilac bush adjacent to where they stood.

My plan was to smile and nod, and then circle around them, but I was stopped by Mrs. Cho, who grasped the fabric of my top with her bony fingers. "Pretty," she said. For such a tiny lady, she had one hell of a grip.

"Mighty fine," Brother Jasper said. And then he added, "Lola, you look like springtime."

Before I could say thanks and press onward, Crazy Myra got into the act. "Where are you headed to, missy, all dressed up?"

"I'm meeting a friend for dinner." The part about dinner was a lie. We were really meeting for drinks, but I hated to say that because it sounded trashy. I suddenly wished I'd taken Piper up on her offer of a ride. "Don't be ridiculous," I'd told her. "It's like three blocks. I'll meet you there." Now I shifted awkwardly and glanced down the street, hoping to spot Piper in her silver minivan so I'd have an excuse to break away from the group.

At the office I'm known for having a take-charge personality, but socially I've always been a little unsure of myself, and these neighbors put me on edge. They were a little too eager and a little too Stepfordish, always stopping by to offer me cookies or invite me to the latest neighborhood gathering, none of which I attended. If they noticed a candy wrapper on my front lawn, they stopped to pick it up. If I struggled with heavy grocery bags, they were right there to help. I'd lived in the house for four months and still wasn't used to it. Growing up in the suburbs, we collected mail for vacationing neighbors or exchanged friendly waves as we drove past, but there was no door-knocking or favor-asking. Not that people in the burbs are standoffish. I don't mean to imply that at all—they just respect boundaries.

"Meeting a friend for dinner," Brother Jasper said. "How nice." He was my favorite of the bunch, not too intrusive but still friendly, always with a ready smile, his perfect teeth blindingly white against his mahogany-colored skin. Still I steered clear of him, always fearful he'd try to get me to go to his church-of-the-folding-chairs with the Styrofoam-cup coffee social they held afterwards. "We were just talking about our annual block party," he said. "I'm not sure if your aunt mentioned it? We raise money for the shelter."

"She might have," I said. I'd inherited the house from my great-aunt May, and everyone on King Street assumed we'd been close. In truth, I hadn't known her all that well; we'd crossed paths at family weddings and funerals, and that was about it. I was as surprised as anyone else when I found out I was her sole beneficiary. Not that I'd turn down a free house in a great location—just half an hour from downtown and blocks from the lake.

"It's quite an event," Belinda said, gesturing wildly. Without a leash or two to hold on to, her hands moved in spastic jerks, seemingly involuntarily. "We get bands to play and have carnival games, and there's lots of food. It's the high point of my summer."

Somehow I didn't doubt that. "How nice."

"Last year best year ever," Mrs. Cho said. "Two thousand dollars, we make. All the neighbors work together."

They looked expectantly at me. I was sure they wanted me to volunteer to make balloon animals or do face painting, but I wasn't biting. "When is it?" I asked, thinking that the date could exactly coincide with a trip out of town.

"See, that's the thing," Brother Jasper said. "We didn't want to plan it until we'd talked to everyone and made sure they were available. We don't like to leave anyone out." He grinned again, the kind of smile God must give you when he welcomes you into heaven. A person would have a tough time resisting the warmth and goodness of that smile. "Especially," he added, "since you're new to our neighborhood family. We want to make sure to include you."

He patted my arm, and I had to look down or I would have promised anything. I'd wind up *running* the block party, when in fact all I really wanted to do was extricate myself from the whole damn thing. "That's really nice," I said in the direction of my toes. "But I'm still waiting to hear about my vacation time from work. Can I get back to you?"

I peeked upwards and saw all four of them nodding.

"Just let us know as soon as you hear," Belinda said.

"Once we know," Mrs. Cho said, "then we plan."

Apparently the very existence of the block party hinged on my availability.

* * *

Piper was already sitting at the bar of Tad's Dry Dock when I arrived. With her white pants and navy blue halter top, she looked perfectly in keeping with the place's nautical theme: bar built to resemble the hull of a ship, porthole windows, and fake seagulls hanging overhead. I, on the other hand, looked like I was trying too hard.

"Guess what, Lola?" she said by way of a greeting, "Those nice guys bought me a drink." She pointed across the bar where three guys in their early twenties sat hunched over frosted mugs of beer.

Seeing her gesture, they raised their glasses as if to toast her. "Hey, Piper and Piper's friend!" yelled the one in the middle.

Piper waved and then leaned toward me. "I told them I was married but that my friend was single. They seemed interested."

I glanced sideways and sized them up. They had the un-shaven, unshowered look of frat boys just coming off a bender. "Good God, Piper, they look like college students. I'm not that desperate."

She shrugged and sipped her white wine. "Younger is good. Women outlive men, you know."

I ordered a rum and Coke. When it was served, the curly-haired bartender flashed a grin in Piper's direction and told me it was on the house. Since high school Piper had created waves wherever she went, and I followed in her wake. There were benefits, of course, free drinks and the like, but it wore on me sometimes.

I steered the conversation toward the problem of my neighbors. "I have no idea how I'm going to get out of this block party," I said to Piper. "I just know I'm going to get sucked into hot dog duty or something. And that won't be the end of it. Before you know it, I'll be on the neighborhood watch commit-tee." I squeezed the lime into my drink and stirred it with the straw. "I thought when I got my own house I'd be able to have complete privacy, but these neighbors are unreal. I can't even sit on my porch without someone stopping by to chat. I'm starting to wait until dark to take my garbage out, and they still nail me sometimes. All this socializing is sucking me dry."

"Neighbors who like you," Piper said. "You *do* have problems."

"I know it sounds lame, but honestly, I feel suffocated. It's like if you live there you're automatically part of the King Street gang or something."

"Just tell them you're not interested in helping with the block party, but thanks anyway," Piper said.

"Easier said than done."

"Or you could always tell them you're twenty-nine years old, antisocial, don't have anything in common with them, and they should please leave you alone."

"But I don't want to be mean about it." I shifted on my barstool. Everything came easily to Piper.

"Well, you have to tell them something," she said. "Or you're going to wind up like your aunt May."

"Great-aunt May," I corrected. "And don't be talking trash about May. She was a fine lady and left me one fabulous house." I wiped a pretend tear from my right eye. "I miss her so much."

"Oh please, you hardly knew her."

"And yet, in our own way, we were very close."

"Did you ever figure out why she left the house to you?"

"Nope," I said. "But I'm sure glad she did."

"You don't get creeped out living alone in that big old place?"

"No." At least I hadn't yet. Now that she mentioned it, I probably would.

The three college guys got up from their stools to join a table of girls in the corner. I was relieved I wouldn't have to ward off any drink offers or attempts at small talk, but part of me wondered, *Hey, why not me?* What—I wasn't good enough for a bunch of hygiene-deficient, beer-saturated lunkheads?

"So have you decided what to do about the house?" Piper asked.

"What do you mean?"

"I just wondered if you're selling it, or what." With both hands she gathered her hair up into a ponytail and then pulled an elastic band off her wrist, twisting the whole thing into an elegant looking messy bun. It's a trick some women do effortlessly, but I've never been able to achieve the same effect without half a dozen tries and a mirror. Underneath the bar's dim lights, Piper's blond hair looked almost luminous.

"Why would I sell it?"

"I don't know. I just thought you might. It's kind of a lot of space for one person. And you hate the neighbors. You could probably sell it, buy a condo, and still have a huge lump sum to stash away in a retirement account."

"I like my house," I said. "I just moved in—I'm not moving out." I'd spent my entire life sharing space with other people— first my parents and younger sister, then various roommates. Most recently I'd shared an apartment with a girl named Andrea who talked continuously. And I mean continuously. About nothing. We became friends while I was working at my second job out of college—an ad agency made up mostly of men, except for the two of us. Thrown together in a testosterone-infested office, we bonded immediately, but it didn't last. When we first moved in together, I'd thought her obsession with Celtic music was her biggest shortcoming. Then I discovered that her poor taste in music was exceeded only by her relentless pursuit of casual sex. She rarely met a man she didn't want to bonk, as she so quaintly put it. And none of her pick-ups had their own place, judging by the fact that they always came to our apartment to do it. By the time I'd inherited Aunt May's house, we were barely speaking. At this point, I didn't miss her *or* her Celtic music CDs.

By comparison, living in this house, my very own house, was nirvana: my yard, my space, my garage. Mine, mine, mine. No one around to comment when I ate egg rolls for breakfast or opted to spend a Saturday home alone in my pajamas. No one to take my last yogurt out of the fridge and leave a note promising to replace it. (She never did—not to be petty or anything.)

I never could have afforded this house under normal circumstances. The day I found out Aunt May left it to me, I'd walked around as dazed as those people who buy a lottery ticket for the first time and find out they won the million-dollar jackpot. Even better was the look on my sister Mindy's face when she heard the news. "Why you?" she'd asked. To which I answered, "Why not me?" For once the family princess didn't get first dibs on something. Mindy came out ahead in the good-looks and outgoing-personality department. Not to mention her engagement to her high school sweetheart, Chad. But I got complete ownership of a cool, old house in a great neighborhood. This was my score, my victory. The universe *did* have a plan after all. And now Piper was suggesting I sell it. Leave my house? My haven from the world? Never.

"I don't think I'm a condo kind of person." I shrugged.

"I don't mean right away. I was talking about eventually. Mike has some great ideas for long-term investing. If you're interested, you can give him a call. I'm sure he'd be happy to spell out your options."

Piper's husband Mike ran an investment firm, Washington Financial. I liked him well enough, but not so much I'd give him total control of my money. Call me cautious.

"Thanks, but I'm staying in the house, so that won't be necessary."

"Suit yourself," she said. "It was just a thought."

We chatted about my work as editor of a parenting publication, a monthly magazine put out by the local daily paper. I could have talked all night about my job—the staff writer Drew, who routinely made up words (using "anticdote" when he meant "anecdote"), the temperamental heating system, and my boss, who was more interested in ad revenues than the content of the magazine. Drew, the doofus, was an especially good topic for storytelling. I'd inherited him when I took the job, and I found him to be totally inept. He didn't work in the *Parenting Today* office as much as skulk around it. He wanted credit for filling staplers, emptying wastebaskets, and keeping the fridge stocked with the little creamers he pilfered from restaurants. The writing was secondary in importance to him. Unfortunately, Drew was related to my boss, so letting him go wasn't an option. Piper listened attentively to my stories, but when her eyes started wandering, I knew to change the subject and ask about her baby. He was walking now, so technically he was a toddler, I guess.

"I have some new photos," she said, digging through her purse. She pulled out a fat envelope full of prints and dealt them out like playing cards. I took my time and politely gave each one the once over, even though they all looked the same to me. Judging by the multiple images, Brandon had a well-documented babyhood: Brandon happy, Brandon pensive, Brandon clapping, Brandon eating spaghetti, Brandon in the classic holding-a-book-upside-down pose. One picture would have sufficed as far as I was concerned. I could have imagined the different facial expressions on my own. "He's adorable," I said, which was true enough. Most toddlers are cute by virtue of being miniature, roly-poly grownups. The things that would make an adult ugly—disproportionate heads, rolls of fat, sparse hair—are appealing on little ones. Go figure.

"I have more," Piper said, sweeping the photos off the bar and taking out another stack. Before I could say, "That's OK," they were arranged before me.

I picked one up to get a closer look. "Hubert was at your house?" Holding Brandon in the picture was our mutual friend from high school, Hubert Holmes. I hadn't seen him in several months, but here he was grinning goofily with the baby on his lap. I'd tried to get together with Hubert recently, but every time I called or e-mailed he'd brushed me off, saying life was hectic, then promising we'd get together soon. Just last week he'd been too busy to meet for lunch, but he had time to go to Piper's house and have Brandon smear biter biscuit on his shirt? What was up with that?

"He comes over now and then," Piper said, scooping up the photos and then plucking the last one out of my hand and stuffing the stack into the envelope. "To see the baby."

"I guess I'll have to have a baby if I ever want to see him again." I knew I sounded grumpy, but what the hell? The three of us had been the best of friends since high school. In our teenage years, Piper had always been the one ditching us. Whenever she was in the beginning stages of a romance, Hubert and I were on our own, but as soon as things cooled off, Piper was back in the fold. Now, for some reason, I was the odd woman out. "You know," I said, "he hasn't even seen my house yet, and I've been there four months."

Piper took a sip of wine. I waited, but she didn't say anything.

"And he said he'd help me move." He'd called the day before and begged off, citing strep throat as the reason. I said I understood, and I did. I was only irritated in retrospect. "Did he mention me at all when he was over at your house? Ask how I was doing?"

She set down her wine glass and swiveled to face me. "Don't take this the wrong way, but it's not always about you, Lola. Other people have problems too."

Her words hit me with a wallop. "What are you talking about?"

"Hubert's going through some tough times with Kelly, and let's just say you haven't been real sympathetic in the past."

Oh, that again. Kelly was Hubert's on-again, off-again, live-in girlfriend. I'd tried so hard to like her, but my loyalties were to Hubert. Still, I'd put on a good front around her, even going to their housewarming party and pretending to be interested in her stupid paper sculptures. Piper hadn't come to the party, something about having just given birth, so I was basically on my own. All in all I felt I'd been a supportive friend. "What? Hubert knows I would do anything for him," I said defensively. "I'm always willing to listen."

"Listening is one thing," Piper said. "It's your little comments that put him off. Even when couples are in a fight, you're not supposed to badmouth the other one."

"I don't badmouth Kelly."

"He said you told him to 'dump the bitch.'"

When she phrased it that way, it sounded really bad. "That was more like advice than badmouthing."

"Uh huh," Piper said. "Listen, Lola, I don't like Kelly either, but for some reason Hubert loves her. If you want to keep him as a friend, you've got to learn to keep your advice to yourself."

2

The evening didn't go as planned. At ten o'clock, right in the middle of a dart game, Piper's cell phone rang. Even above the din of the bar I could hear Brandon's cry, an ugly howl, the kind that leads to a red face and snotty nose. "Mike is at his wit's end," Piper said, snapping her phone shut and gathering up her keys and purse. "I'm really sorry, but I have to go home. Brandon is going through this thing where he won't go to bed for anyone but me, and he's crying himself into hysteria. You understand, right?" She met my eyes, and I nodded. I understood all right. What I understood was that Mike was a complete imbecile. How was it he could manage other people's vast fortunes but couldn't put a one-year-old to bed? How hard could it be? He outweighed the kid by a hundred and sixty pounds.

I had Piper drop me off at the end of my block. The night air was still and a little clammy too, the moist air a promise of coming rain. I walked slowly and saw my street as a stranger would—the neat lawns, mature trees, and elegant older homes. Each house was two stories tall and most were brick, but no two were the same. Belinda had the only contemporary house on the block; southwestern in style, it also had the only attached garage. The garage had a flat roof, and in the evenings she often let her dogs exit a bedroom window onto the top. Two of them, a little ankle-nipper she called Baxter, and a larger husky mix whose name eluded me, were up there now. They barked as I walked by, a high-pitched yapping and a deeper howl. As I passed, I heard the window open and Belinda's voice as she cooed to the dogs, "What's all the fuss out here? What do you see? What do you see?"

I sped up before she could spot me and yell out greetings. It had happened once before, and I'd found it awkward carrying on a conversation with her disembodied head twenty feet above.

Next to Belinda's house was a duplex rented out to college students. Out for the night, judging from the dark and silence. The next one, Crazy Myra's house, was just as still. She was known as an early riser.

The house across the street from Crazy Myra's belonged to the mystery man. I knew this because Belinda had filled me in on all the neighbors the first time we met. The buzz on King Street was that the mystery man was movie-star handsome, traveled frequently, and lived alone. "He says he's a consultant," Belinda said in a tone that conveyed skepticism. "But no one can quite figure out what it is he does, exactly. And get this," she said, leaning in closer, "he never puts out garbage."

"Never?" Even *I* found that curious.

"Not once in the two years he's lived here. Tuesday comes and goes, and there's never anything at the curb."

"What does he do with it?"

She shrugged. "Nobody knows. And we've been watching, believe me."

The mystery man's house was dark. Next door, Brother Jasper's was too, except for the glow of a cigarette on his front porch. Last smoke before bedtime, by my calculations. When I first moved in I'd watched his house from my front window, trying to figure out the origin of the weird light. Smoking was the only bad habit he had left, he said. I knew he could see me, so I waved a hand in greeting and saw the glow rise in response.

Just ahead, my porch light beamed—*Welcome home, Lola!* Inside, the dining room light shone brightly. I'd never realized how much of the room could be seen from the sidewalk when the drapes were open.

Except.

I stopped, puzzled. I hadn't left the dining room light on. And I certainly hadn't left the drapes wide open.

An odd mixture of fear and confusion crept over me as I tried to make sense of the situation. Sure I'd been in a hurry to leave the house after work, but there were certain things I always did no matter what, and they included locking the doors and making sure the blinds were down and the drapes were closed. It was a paranoid routine I carried with me no matter where I lived. I could almost believe I'd left the lights on in error, but I never would have left the drapes open. Never.

Someone had been in my house in the last four hours. I felt my underarms grow damp and reflexively clamped my elbows to my sides. I didn't move. My feet felt as if they were caught on something sticky. I couldn't go in the house—what if the intruder was still there? I glanced up and down the street but saw nothing out of the ordinary. Mrs. Cho's front lawn was littered with the bikes and skateboards belonging to the grandchildren who lived with her. The ceramic gnomes between the bushes in Crazy Myra's yard were tacky, but not threatening.

Across the street Brother Jasper's cigarette still glowed like an ember from the depths of his covered porch. Such a reassuring presence.

I took a deep breath and turned to cross the street. Brother

Jasper was the go-to guy around the neighborhood. He'd know what to do. At that moment I thanked God for both Brother Jasper and the addictive property of nicotine.

"Well if it isn't Miss Lola," he said as I bounded up the porch steps. "Isn't this a gorgeous night?" He leaned back in his rocking chair and rested his hand on what looked like a tall spittoon.

"I need help," I said in response. "There's something wrong at my house."

He sat upright and listened while I babbled about the light and the drapes and my compulsive leaving-the-house routine. My voice became more high-pitched as I went along. I stopped to take a breath.

"Sounds to me like we need to call the police," he said calmly, dropping the cigarette into the spittoon.

The police? "Do you think they'd come?" I asked. "I mean, I don't have evidence that a crime was committed or anything." I rested my hand on the porch railing and glanced across the street, suddenly filled with self-doubt. Maybe I *had* left the drapes open. Anything was possible.

"Of course they'll come, Lola. That's what they do."

* * *

Ten minutes later a squad car pulled up to the curb. Brother Jasper and I stood on the sidewalk waiting. He was smoking another cigarette (*You don't mind, do you?*) while I held a can of Dr. Pepper in my right hand. Brother Jasper had given it to me after calling the police on my behalf, but I'd been too rattled to drink from it. Both police officers knew Brother Jasper—I got the impression their quick response had more to do with their regard for him than my situation. The older of the two,

Officer Stein, greeted my neighbor like a friend while his part-ner, the very young, slightly pudgy Officer Dodge, just nodded an acknowledgement. I somehow made my way into the circle of introductions; Brother Jasper held my elbow to steady my shaking.

Officer Stein whipped open a small notebook and jotted down notes: my name, address, the time I'd left for the evening, and when I'd returned. "You live alone?" he asked.

"Yes."

"Who else has a key to your house?"

"No one."

Brother Jasper cleared his throat, voicing an objection. I turned to look at him. "Actually," he said, "I have a key. Your aunt gave it to me for emergencies. I've been meaning to give it to you, but every time I see you you're rushing off somewhere."

A spare key. This was news to me. If it had been anyone else besides Brother Jasper it would have creeped me out com-pletely.

"I'll make sure to give it to you before the end of the night." He looked sheepish.

I nodded in response. I didn't find him the least bit threat-ening, but that didn't mean I wasn't going to have the locks changed.

I gave the officers my house key. When I started to follow them across the street, the younger one held up his arm like a crossing guard halting traffic and said, "Better stay here, miss, and let us check it out."

I watched them approach my front door, weapons drawn. I took a swig of Dr. Pepper and shivered, suddenly cold and tired.

Crazy Myra came out of her house and crossed the street to where we stood. "What's going on over there?" she called out.

Never one to worry about propriety, she wore a housecoat with buttons the size of coasters and a shower cap.

"Evening, Myra," Brother Jasper said. "Sorry if we disturbed your sleep, but it looks like someone's over at Lola's house uninvited."

Uninvited. That was an understatement.

I kept my gaze across the street as Brother Jasper explained the situation to Crazy Myra. At the exact moment the police officers entered my house, the light in the upstairs bathroom went on.

I gulped. "He's upstairs," I said.

"Who's upstairs?" Brother Jasper asked, interrupting Myra, who was going on about the importance of deadbolts. She herself had several.

I lifted my arm and pointed. "Upstairs. The bathroom light just went on." I felt a surge of dread, like witnessing a victim in a horror movie opening the wrong door. I stepped forward and stumbled off the curb, my Dr. Pepper sloshing onto the back of my hand. "We should warn them."

"Wait a minute, Lola." Brother Jasper pulled me back. "Let them do their job. Trust me, they can handle this."

"They're police officers," Myra said, as if imparting new information. "They've been trained."

I could hear the officers yelling inside my house. The words were muffled, but it sounded like they were warning the intruder. Or maybe ordering him to come out. My forehead throbbed with the onset of a headache. My neck and shoulders tensed as tight as a tug-of-war rope. The bathroom light went off, and then all was silent.

Oh great. Out of the corner of my eye, I spotted Belinda being pulled down the sidewalk by two of her larger mutts, the husky mix and some big wooly thing. How she'd managed to cross the street without me noticing was a mystery, but here she was.

"I saw the police car," she said as she approached, the dogs straining to join us as if they too wanted to know what was going on. "I thought you might need some help. What happened?" The wooly dog panted and drooled close to my feet. I took a step back.

"Someone's in Lola's house that's not supposed to be there," Brother Jasper said. "But I think the police have it covered."

"Oh, you poor dear." She patted my arm. "Did someone break in?"

"We don't know yet," Crazy Myra said before I could open my mouth. "She just came home and the lights were on and the drapes were open. And she *never* leaves the drapes open, you know that."

"I could tell someone was inside when I came home," I said. "I didn't risk going in."

"You really should get a dog," Belinda said. "For safety reasons. And they're also good company." She leaned over and rubbed behind the husky's ears. "Then you wouldn't have to go out at night at all."

"That's a thought," I said. Both dogs sat suddenly, as if knowing they would be there awhile. I took another sip of the soda and glanced down at my feet. The strappy sandals that had seemed sexy earlier in the evening were now slicing my toes and digging into my heels. I yearned to take them off and sink my feet into my fuzzy slippers. I looked toward my house for signs of new developments, but it was still quiet and I couldn't see anyone through the windows. "They've been in there a long time."

"It's only been a few minutes," Brother Jasper said. "It just feels long when you're waiting."

"I'm sure they're being very thorough," Belinda said, wrapping the slack from the leashes around her wrist. "The police in our district are top notch. And committed to helping the homeowners keep the neighborhood safe, too. Did you know we have a neighborhood watch committee? We're always looking for new people to help out, if you're interested."

"Hmmm." Where was the neighborhood watch committee this evening? They could have prevented my break-in, and I could be home in bed by now.

Our lapse in conversation was punctuated by the slamming of my screen door. Officer Stein came down the steps and called out, "Miss Watson?" He motioned for me, his fingertips scooping toward his chin. "Could you come here please?"

I crossed the street with Brother Jasper at my side. I was aware that Myra, Belinda, and the two dogs followed, but for once I didn't feel like swatting them away.

"He says he knows you," Officer Stein said as we joined him on the sidewalk. "He says he's a friend of yours."

The screen door creaked open, and I looked up to see Officer Dodge pushing a tall, familiar-looking man through the doorframe.

"Hubert?"

He stood barefoot on my porch wearing sweatpants and a T-shirt; the younger policeman gripped his arm to prevent escape. He blinked a few times, looking like he'd just walked out of a dark movie theatre into daylight.

"Please tell them we're friends, Lola. They wouldn't believe me."

"You know him?" Officer Stein asked.

"Yes." My brain was having trouble with the idea of Hubert and my house occupying the same space. After my talk with Piper, I'd assumed he never wanted to see me again. Seeing him on my porch without shoes was as startling as bumping into your minister in the red-light district in Amsterdam.

"Hubert, what are you doing here?"

"I didn't think you'd mind. You said to stop over anytime," he said.

"Yes, but I assumed you'd call first." OK, my voice was kind of pissy, but jeez—I hadn't seen the guy for months and suddenly he's inside my house? "And how'd you get in, anyway? I had the door locked."

"I know. I'm sorry. I thought it would be OK."

Before I had a chance to interrogate him further, Officer Stein leaned over and put a fatherly hand on my shoulder. "Does he have permission to be in your house? Because if not, we can—"

"No, no, it's fine."

Behind me Myra muttered something to Brother Jasper that I thought sounded like "lovers' spat." One of the dogs whimpered loudly.

"I can release him then?" Officer Dodge asked. Upon getting an affirmative reply, he loosened his grip. Hubert rubbed his left arm and did a few deep knee bends in appreciation of his new freedom. He smiled a lopsided grin, the right side of his mouth lifting higher than the left.

Officer Stein apologized to Hubert. "We had to treat you as an intruder. We had no way of knowing you were the young lady's friend."

Hubert brushed it off with a good-natured wave. "It's OK. I understand. You guys were just doing your job."

I told them I was sorry for the false alarm.

"It never hurts to check things out," Brother Jasper said. "Better safe than sorry."

"We prefer this kind of outcome, actually," Officer Stein said, and his partner nodded in agreement. What an incredibly affable group.

I wasn't sure what the protocol was in this type of situation, so I introduced Hubert to the sidewalk gathering as if we were at a cocktail party. Hubert, always a social guy, explained that he came to my house because he got locked out of his own, and then he went on to compliment Belinda's dogs and the neighborhood in general.

"You won't find a better block anywhere in the city," Myra said.

Hubert looked around appreciatively. "I can see that."

"You couldn't pay me a million dollars to live anywhere but here," she added for emphasis.

I followed Brother Jasper across the street as he accompanied the officers to their squad car. I felt compelled to apologize one last time. "I'm so embarrassed that you had to come all the way here," I said. "I had no idea it was my friend inside. I don't even know how he got in."

"He said he used the key hidden on the porch under the planter," Officer Dodge said.

"Ah yes, the hidden key," Brother Jasper said. "I'd forgotten about that." This was the first I'd heard of it.

"I hope your night gets better, miss," Officer Dodge said before climbing into the passenger side. I wasn't sure if he was mocking me or being genuinely friendly.

Officer Stein shook Brother Jasper's hand. "Good night, sir. Take care."

Brother Jasper held up one hand like delivering a blessing. "Good night and stay safe."

3

After the squad car pulled away, I said goodnight to Brother Jasper and left him fumbling in his shirt pocket for his pack of Marlboros. Probably going to smoke his *last* last cigarette of the night.

Hubert and company were still chatting in front of my house. Myra and Belinda and the canines were charmed by him, I could tell. He'd had that effect on everyone for as long as I'd known him. He was a big, goofy-looking guy who possessed as much curiosity as a preschooler. Hubert could spend hours listening to someone talk about their job or dog or years spent in the military. And he was genuinely interested, not just being polite. He always remembered names, and he had perfect recall of past events. "Remember the year neither of us went to prom so we went to a movie instead?" he once asked.

"Hubert, I *never* went to prom."

"It was junior year," he continued. "And I couldn't use my dad's truck because it was in the shop getting transmission work done, so you drove. We saw the sequel to that *Scream* movie. It was really hot that weekend, and afterwards we drove around with the windows open singing along with the radio. Remember?"

Only vaguely. I wished I had his memory for details, but my

high school days went by in a blur. College too, come to think of it. It was only lately that time seemed to drag.

Now he stood and listened intently as Myra spoke, her short arms gesturing vigorously. Hubert found whatever she said amusing. But then again, he was easily amused. He threw back his head and laughed, delighting both women and making the husky sit up and bark.

"I'm back," I said when I got within earshot.

My announcement had the desired effect—Belinda and Myra began to say the kinds of things that lead to a departure.

"It was so nice meeting you, Hubert," Belinda said. She added, "Maybe I'll see you around the neighborhood." Her tone was pretty flirtatious for a woman in her forties. She pulled the two leashes taut, and the dogs rose excitedly, anticipating another walk.

"Don't forget," Myra said, giving Hubert's arm a squeeze.

"I won't," he said. "Nice meeting you, ladies."

Myra walked slowly across the lawn to her house next door, while Belinda headed down the sidewalk to the end of the block.

"Good-bye, Roger. Good night, Muggles," Hubert called out after her. Both dogs paused and turned their heads.

"Buh-bye," Belinda said, waving and smiling, and then she continued on with a spring in her step I'd never noticed before.

Roger? Muggles? "You know the dogs' names?" I asked, dumfounded.

"Of course. Dogs are people too, you know."

It wasn't until we were settled in easy chairs on opposite sides of the living room that I heard the story of how Hubert came to be in my house.

"Kelly locked me out," he explained. "And I didn't have my

shoes or my cell phone or my wallet or anything." He rolled his eyes and held up his palms. "Wouldn't you know? As it turns out, my neighbor was leaving about that time. I flagged him down as he was driving away, and since he was going downtown and your house was on the way, he said no problem, he'd be glad to drop me off. It worked out perfect, lucky for me."

"She locked you out? On purpose?"

Hubert ran a hand through his thick brown hair, a gesture he made when uncomfortable. "Well," he said and shifted in the chair. "It's not all her fault. Kelly's been working a lot of hours lately, and she's under a lot of pressure. A lot of pressure. And she has an artist's temperament. When she comes home, she likes things to be a certain way. I know that, but I just wasn't thinking—"

"For God's sake, Hubert, what happened?"

He sighed and squeezed the arms of the chair like he was getting a tooth drilled. "After I cooked dinner tonight I missed cleaning up some marinara splatters on the back of the stove. It was obvious after she pointed it out, but I'd somehow zoned out and completely missed it. I said I'd clean it up, but she said that wasn't the issue. The issue was that she shouldn't have to follow me around pointing out my mistakes. Then later when I went outside to get the mail she locked me out. I knocked on the door, but she wouldn't open up. She said she needed some alone time and I should go for a walk. I waited a long time, but I was getting kind of cold, and that's when I saw my neighbor leaving."

"She locked you out?" I knew I was repeating myself, but the point seemed emphasis-worthy. "You do realize, Hubert, that this is not normal behavior?"

"Who's to say what's normal?" he said, looking wounded. "Everyone's different, Lola. Not everyone's like you."

I could tell by the look on his face that Kelly-bashing was off limits. Still, I couldn't resist one more comment. "You know, Hubert, true love isn't supposed to be this painful."

"Yeah, well," he said, pushing his hair back off his forehead. "Kelly and I just need to work through some things."

We sat without speaking; the clock on the fireplace mantel ticked loudly. It was a sound I hadn't heard before. "You wound up the clock?" I asked.

He grinned. "Yes, I did. I just made myself at home. I hope you don't mind. This place is great." His voice had regained its usual enthusiasm. "I love this old woodwork—the crown moldings, the arched doorways. Your fireplace is awesome, and that claw-footed bathtub upstairs rocks. The whole house is in terrific shape. All you'd have to do is get a few pieces reupholstered, refinish the hardwood floors, and paint a few rooms, and you'd have a showplace." His brow furrowed as he looked around the room. "And you might want to get rid of all those doily things that are under the lamps. What's that all about?"

"They're my great-aunt's," I said. "I haven't had a chance to do much to the place since I moved in."

He leaned forward and rested his chin in his palms. "I'll say. Nothing here reminded me of you. I almost thought I was in somebody else's house."

Which reminded me. "How the hell did you know how to get in the house? The cop said you got a key from under the planter."

Hubert sat up and cleared his throat. "Well, I started off waiting on the porch. I was there for all of five minutes when this little Korean lady came by on her bike and stopped to talk. Cute little lady—about so high." He held his hand about four feet off the floor.

Yeah, I could picture her.

"Really a sweetheart," he continued. "She was just coming back from the market; her basket was loaded with cabbage. I told her I was a friend of yours, and she said you'd gone out to dinner."

"I was with Piper."

"Ah, I should have figured as much. Anyway," he said, "your neighbor showed me where the key was and said I might as well wait inside. Actually what she said was, 'Too cold for porch sitting with no shoes.' So I let myself in. I tried calling your cell, but you didn't answer, so I figured I'd just wait for you. I was having fun checking out your house, and everything was going just fine until the police threatened to shoot me." He stuck out his lower lip. Always the jester.

"That had to be the woman next door, Mrs. Cho," I said. "I can't believe she showed a complete stranger how to get into my house. You could have been an ax murderer or a rapist, for all she knew."

"And yet, I am neither. Just a lowly fourth grade teacher at Eisenhower Elementary. Sorry to disappoint." He folded his legs and sat cross-legged on the chair, like a large swami minus the turban.

"I'll say you're lowly. No shoes and no wallet—there are homeless guys under the overpass doing better than you."

"Yes, but the homeless guys don't have a friend with a four-bedroom house. If they did, they wouldn't be sleeping under a bridge." He grinned at me, like I was in on a joke.

It dawned on me then. "Were you thinking you were going to sleep here tonight?"

"Well, yeah. That's OK, isn't it? You said I could come drop by anytime."

There it was again. My open invitation to visit anytime. Wasn't there a statute of limitations on such social blatherings? Surely it couldn't be endless, or you'd have people you knew in grade school dropping by for milk and Girl Scout cookies. "Oh, I don't know, Hubert. I'm not really set up for guests. Maybe if I'd known you were coming…" My voice trailed off, giving him an opportunity to jump in with an alternate plan. To tell me I could drive him to one of his poker buddies' houses or that he could crash at his parents'. It wasn't that I didn't want him to stay; it was more like I felt he'd been sprung on me.

It's an unfortunate quirk of my personality that I've always been easily overwhelmed. My parents had two daughters; me, the typical serious type-A older daughter who needs a lot of transition time, and my sister Mindy, who could throw a party on a moment's notice. I've tried in the past to go against type without success. The truth of it is, I'm rattled by things other people take in stride. Knowing this, I arrange my life to avoid stressful situations. An unexpected visitor, even a good friend, feels like an intrusion. My mind whirred with all the things I would have done with some advance notice: changed the sheets, bought groceries, scrubbed out the tub. "Besides, don't you think Kelly is over her snit by now? She's probably worried sick about you. I bet if you called her right now—"

"I already did call her," he said, not meeting my eyes. "While you were out. And she wouldn't pick up. I know her, and when she gets like this she needs her space. I'll try again tomorrow."

"It's your space too, you know."

"I know." He sighed and looked around the room. "I know how surprises throw you off course, Lola, and if I could have given you some notice, I would have. But I've got nowhere else to go at this hour, and you've got all this space. One night, that's all I'm asking." He stared straight at me, his eyes pleading.

"The extra bedrooms are all dusty. I wasn't planning on anyone using them."

"Whatever, Lola. I can sleep on the couch even. I don't care."

I suddenly felt ashamed of my hesitation. "No, no, the couch would be too short for you." For someone of his height, six feet tall, most couches would have been too short. "Don't worry about it. I can get a room ready. It'll be fine." I tried to remember where Aunt May kept the extra sheets. Probably next to the towels in the deep closet in the upstairs hall. I hadn't gone through any of that stuff yet. Just to be on the safe side, I'd have to wash the bedding before I set up one of the beds. "No trouble at all."

"Great." He leaned back in the chair, visibly relieved. "I really appreciate it, Lola. It could be fun even. You'll see."

Fun was a bit of a reach, but anything was possible. "Sure."

"This will be great. We can play Scrabble tonight if you want." He was really making an effort now. Scrabble was my thing; he hated board games. "And we could go to a movie tomorrow, if you're up for it."

"Or we could buy you shoes."

"I forgot about that," he said, wiggling his toes. "Oh!" He leaned forward in the chair and tapped his forehead with his fingertips. "And I totally forgot to tell you—we're both invited to your neighbor's house for dinner next week."

"What?"

"Well, it has to be next week because she's making kimchi and it has to soak for several days."

"You accepted a dinner invitation without asking me?"

"I wouldn't normally, Lola, but we're talking homemade kimchi, here. I couldn't imagine anyone turning *that* down."

Oh, just watch me.

4

The next day I woke up earlier than usual for a Saturday morning. It seemed like I'd just settled into a comfortable position when dawn arrived with a thud, like a subway car coming to a stop. Normally I'd let myself drift back for another delicious hour, but the knowledge that there was another person in the house intruded on my recreational sleep habits.

The night before, despite Hubert's protests, I'd frantically vacuumed the area rug in one of the spare bedrooms, then taken some extra sheets out of the hall linen closet and given them the sniff test, which they did not pass. It was another hour before I pulled them fresh and warm from the dryer. Hubert insisted on making up the bed himself and, groggy from fatigue, I let him. Then I headed off to my room to collapse into my own bed.

Now I lay there and listened for signs that Hubert was already up and about, but I heard nothing out of the usual. Above me the attic creaked like it did on windy days. When I first moved in I thought it was squirrels, but I never found any evidence of that, or any other rodents, thankfully. The rest of the house was quiet, but just knowing someone else was around gave the air a different feel.

I kicked off my covers, grabbed the day's clothes from my closet and dresser, and crossed the hall into the bathroom. Normally I'd have lounged for a few hours in my bathrobe, but good friend or no, I wasn't about to have Hubert see my chenille robe with the frayed sleeves and my sticky-up morning hair.

I emerged from the bathroom a new person. Or an improved one, anyway. Nothing like a hot shower to give the day a sense of possibility. Maybe some time with my old friend Hubert was just what I needed. I'd make breakfast for the two of us—at the very least I had the ingredients for cheese omelets and toast—and maybe I'd take him up on his offer to go to a movie. It had been ages since I'd seen anything not on DVD. Big screen, surround sound, hot buttered popcorn. I could be convinced.

I made my way down the stairs with a sense of purpose. The whole "stranger in my house/unexpected visitor" thing had made me feel like my life was out of control, but now I was the one in charge. I'd start with eggs, and then navigate the day from there.

Except.

I couldn't find Hubert. On my way to the stairs I'd passed the spare bedroom. The door was wide open, the bed as neatly made as those found in barracks. I assumed, of course, that he'd gotten up while I was in the shower and I'd find him downstairs. A logical conclusion, except for the fact that he wasn't there either. I walked through every room calling his name, like a concerned pet owner searching for a cat.

No Hubert.

I couldn't help but be irked. First he entered my locked house, scaring the bejeebus out of me and making me stand outside in the cold with my *neighbors*, no less, then he guilted me into letting him stay the night, and just when I got used to the idea he took off? Where the hell was he?

I stood in the middle of the living room looking for signs he'd *ever* been there, but with no suitcase there wasn't even anything he could have left behind. Seeing as I hadn't found a pile of ashes anywhere, I ruled out spontaneous combustion. That, at least, would have been excusable.

He went back to Kelly, that's what he did. Sure, old Lola was fine for emergencies, but at the first light of day he'd flown back into her fickle arms. Nice. Real nice. Whatever happened to consideration? Whatever happened to loyalty? Whatever happened to leaving a note?

Just thinking of Kelly made me livid. The red-haired demon. In another life she was probably one of those evil mermaids who lured sailing men to their destruction. Or maybe they weren't mermaids. Anyway, they were something, and they were bad news, but men, oblivious men, fell for their sweet songs and then crashed their ships on the rocks, which is what should happen to stupid people anyway. I sat down hard on Aunt May's courting couch and watched as a cloud of dust rose from the cushion. I really should vacuum the furniture more often. Or at all. But who had time to vacuum furniture, what with friends breaking in and then going off without notice? My schedule was pretty full.

I picked up the phone on the end table and speed-dialed Hubert's cell phone. When I got his voice mail, I left a message telling him exactly how I felt. I said he was irresponsible and rude and that I thought he owed me an apology. That felt good. But not good enough. I wanted to hear his voice on the other end of the line asking forgiveness.

I had to look up the number for what I thought of as Kelly's place. She'd lived there first, and I always called Hubert's cell rather than deal with the heinous one. But I'd make an exception this time. I pushed the buttons with shaking fingers and listened—one ring—two rings. I leaned forward and rapped my knuckles against the coffee table. *Pick up, pick up, pick up.* Three rings, and then the machine kicked in with Kelly's "I'm not home right now." I almost hung up, but as I was about to set the receiver in the cradle I heard, "If this is Hubert…" I lifted it up to my ear in time to hear the rest: "We're over and I never want to see you again. You can come and pick up your stuff anytime. It's in the hallway."

5

I was still sitting on the courting couch in the living room, the cordless phone in my cupped hand, when a car pulled up in front of my house. I heard voices, one of them Hubert's, and the sound of a car door slamming shut. Looking out the front window, I saw a rusty junker pulling away from the curb and Hubert coming up the walk carrying a white bakery bag. The driver gave a quick tap of the horn as he drove off. Hubert turned and waved at the sound.

"Oh, you're up!" he said when I met him at the door. "Perfect timing. I hope you didn't eat yet, because I've got breakfast." He swung the bag to show me. "Bagels and cream cheese. Life is good." Apparently no one had told him I was mad as hell and that he no longer had a girlfriend or a place to live.

I pushed the door open to allow him entry. "Where have you been?" As soon as the words were out of my mouth, I realized I'd channeled my mother circa my teenage years. Her "Where have you been?" was always followed by "I've been worried sick." But I couldn't follow that script because I wasn't worried sick, just really torqued off. "I had no idea where you were. You just up and left."

His face fell. "I'm sorry. Didn't you find my note?"

"I looked for a note. There was no note."

Hubert blinked and then broke into a grin. He set the white bag down on the coffee table and beckoned for me to follow him. One minute later we were in the kitchen, where he triumphantly pointed to a piece of paper located amongst the carryout menus on the front of the refrigerator. "No note, huh, Miss Smarty-pants? What do you call this?"

I'd call it a note. It said, "Lola, I went out with Ben Cho. I'll be back soon. Thanks again for taking me in on such short notice. I really appreciate it. Love, Hubert." Below his name he'd written the time in parentheses. I glanced at the kitchen clock to compare. "You've been gone for two hours? Who's Ben Cho?"

At the kitchen table over bagels and cream cheese, I got the lowdown. Hubert woke up that morning at six and was reading the paper when there was a tap at my front door. It was Ben Cho, who'd been sent by his mother to give a pair of shoes to my displaced friend. Korean-Americans always rally around the new person to help them get situated, Hubert explained, spreading a thick layer of pineapple cream cheese on his bagel.

"But you're not new," I said. "You're not even Korean."

He licked a stray dollop off his fingertips. "I know that. But it's the same concept. You see someone in need, and if you can help, you do. Kind of a nice philosophy. If everyone thought that way, the world would be a better place. Did you know Mrs. Cho's husband owns Tae Kwon Do World? Pretty cool, huh?"

I didn't even know Mrs. Cho had a husband.

Hubert continued. "He came here twenty years ago with nothing and brought the rest of the family over a few years later. Now they have a house and a business and are living the American dream. Pretty impressive." He raised his eyebrows as a thought hit him. "You know, I should really ask him to come and speak to my class. We're covering what it means to be an American citizen, and I'm doing a short unit on Ellis Island and immigration. He'd probably have tons of stories. And if he demonstrated some tae kwon do, all the better. The kids would love that."

Hubert had a tendency to go off on tangents. "So Ben gave you the shoes," I prompted.

"Oh yeah," Hubert said. He looked down at the sneakers on his feet. "And he waited until I tried them on. They actually fit, sort of. Then we started talking, and he said he was going up to Brother Jasper's church to set up some chairs for this thing they're having, and I went along to help. Then we stopped at the bread place. God, it smelled good there. Brioli's, about three blocks down. You know it?"

I shook my head.

"Oh, you really have to go. It's mostly a bakery, but they've got a few café tables, and they sell stuff to drink, too—coffee and juice and cappuccino." He lifted his mug and took a sip. "And then I came back here. That's pretty much it."

"But how did you pay for the bagels?"

He made a noise in his throat like he was trying to clear something out. "Well actually, I borrowed a few dollars from the money in the nightstand drawer in my room." I must have looked disapproving because he added, "I would have asked, but you were sleeping. I'll pay you back."

"You don't have to pay me back. It's just..." I tried to picture that particular room. A bed, a nightstand, a dresser with an oval mirror above it. I'd moved in during the winter months and had decided that instead of cleaning the house out one drawer at a time, I'd wait until spring and go through it all at once—every cabinet, drawer, and closet. But unfortunately once spring arrived, I'd lost my motivation. "There's money in the nightstand?"

He grinned. "A whole shitload of it. You didn't know?"

Apparently there was no end to what I didn't know. "Define shitload."

"The drawer's crammed full of cash. Mostly singles, but some fives and tens, too. And there's a bunch of change in the bottom. You didn't know this?"

"I keep meaning to go through Aunt May's stuff, but I haven't gotten to it yet."

Hubert looked incredulous. "You haven't gotten to it yet? I'd have done that first thing. It's like a treasure hunt around here. Who knows what else you'd find?"

Well sure, he could say that—he found money. The drawers I looked in had contained wool socks and tattered tablecloths. "It's on my list. It's just been real hectic with work and all." The words sounded lame, even to me. It made me wonder what I'd done with my free time the last four months. Could watching Netflix DVDs and surfing the Net account for that many hours?

"I only took twenty, but I'll pay you back as soon as I get home and get my wallet."

Home. The word jarred like a direct hit at Paintball Dave's. I'd forgotten to tell him that his definition of home was changing fast. "About that..." I paused while the words rearranged themselves in my mind. Better to tell him outright or do the soft-shoe shuffle?

He held up a hand. "Don't even say it. I insist on paying you back." There he was again with his lopsided grin. Such a big, happy doofus. How could Kelly be so mean? "It's the least I can do after you let me stay and everything. Although, nothing personal, I will be glad to sleep in my own bed tonight."

The last time I'd felt like this was in fifth grade when I said good-bye to Whiskers right before my dad took him to the vet's to be put asleep. I took a deep breath. "Hubert, you need to call home."

"Kelly called?" His eyes lit up like Christmas.

"No, I called over there looking for you, and Kelly had a message for you on the answering machine."

"And what did she say?"

"I really don't want to get in the middle of this. Just call and you'll hear for yourself."

His eyebrows furrowed in puzzlement, but he didn't push the subject, just picked up the receiver to Aunt May's old wall phone and pointed a finger. "Hey, a rotary dial! How trippy is that? I haven't seen one of these in ages." He turned to me with a smile, and I nodded. Then I gave a halfhearted wave and left the room. I didn't need a front-row seat to watch him get his heart torn out. Behind me I heard the *chut, chut, chut* of the dial rotating back to its original place. I kept going until I couldn't hear it anymore. To put even more distance between us, I went out to the front porch, shutting the front door behind me. If he started crying, I wouldn't be able to stand it. If it were me, I'd want some privacy and time to pull myself together.

I leaned against the porch railing so that my face was in the light and took a deep breath. It was the kind of warm spring day I'd yearned for all winter long as I shoveled my front walk and brushed snow from my windshield. The air had the after-rain smell I'd always associated with worms when I was a kid. Across the street a delivery truck pulled up in front of the mystery man's house; the driver hopped out and left a package on the front stoop. Next door to my right, Crazy Myra arranged wicker furniture on her porch and muttered to herself. Down the block I heard a chorus of dogs yapping.

Just as Myra headed inside, my outside door opened and Hubert appeared at my side. He stood next to me for a second and then leaned over and rested his elbows on the railing.

I couldn't read his face, but I could imagine his misery. "Hubert, I'm really, really sorry this happened. I know I wasn't always that supportive of you and Kelly, but I know you love her. This has to be really painful." I gave his arm a reassuring squeeze, but he didn't speak, just threaded his fingers together and kept his gaze downward. I continued. "I know it's devastating, but maybe it's for the best. Honestly, I never thought you two were a good match. A clean break will give you a chance to move on."

Hubert turned to face me and gave me a wide grin, the kind I always secretly thought of as his "happy monkey" look.

"Are you quite done?" he asked. "So much drama, Lola. You have totally misconstrued this whole thing. Kelly and I aren't breaking up. That's not going to happen."

"Didn't you hear her message?"

"Yeah, I heard it, but you have to know Kelly. She goes through these things and then gets over it. She's probably forgotten about it already."

"So this is a regular thing? She's done this before?" Who would put up with such lunacy?

"Not this exact scenario, no. But she's creative that way." He unlinked his fingers and ran a hand through his hair. "You really don't know her, Lola. I wish you could see her like I do.

Most of the time she's the most caring, charming person you'd ever want to meet."

I'd have to take his word for it.

"She just has this other side. It looks like meanness, but it really stems from insecurity. Kelly just acts out. She's getting better, though. Relationships aren't always easy, you know."

I didn't know, actually, having had only two serious boyfriends, one in middle school and one in college. Jon had moved away in seventh grade, and Danny, the guy I'd been with for two years and thought I'd be with forever, had moved on to a different girl. Since then my love life had consisted of a string of unrequited crushes and a few dates that never panned out. My mother insisted I was too picky; my father chalked it up to shyness; my sister Mindy said I was a social retard. They all had a point, but I tried not to think about it too much. "So what are you going to do now?"

Hubert sighed. "We'll work it out. We always do. And then things will be great for a while." He smiled again, this time without showing his teeth. "On the bright side, we seem to go longer and longer between episodes." He tented his fingers into a church and steeple.

I filled the awkward silence by saying, "Good luck, I guess."

"Thanks." He exhaled and then gripped the railing as if he were standing on the deck of a cruise ship. The *Titanic*, maybe. "I hate asking, but would you mind driving me home now?"

"Sure," I said. "If that's what you want."

"It'll be the last favor I ask of you. Promise."

6

Kelly's place was a first-floor apartment in a brick building. Two units up, two units down. Because Kelly's father was the landlord, she and Hubert had a choice apartment with window views of a seedy courtyard ringed with plastic benches and the kind of stand-up ashtrays usually only seen outside retail outlets. Kelly's dad owned the whole complex, as far as the eye could see from the middle of the parking lot. Charmingly known as Vista View Apartments, the property was comprised of several once-grand apartments, a freestanding party room building, and a separate little house labeled "The Laundry Hut."

As we drove through the complex's winding roads, Hubert directed me. All the buildings looked the same. I thought back to the housewarming party and how I'd wandered about in the dark after parking on the street. If it weren't for Hubert's balloons, I never would have found the place.

"You can drop me off at the door," Hubert said, indicating an entrance topped by a green and white striped awning.

But that didn't feel right to me. Leave a guy with no wallet, no cell phone, and borrowed shoes in hostile territory?

"I think I'll just tag along and make sure you can get in." I pulled the car up behind Hubert's yellow VW beetle, blocking him in, which was unavoidable since every other space had apartment numbers on them. I guess Kelly's dad never heard of having guests.

"Suit yourself," Hubert said cheerfully.

Crossing through the parking lot we passed several people: an older woman coming out of the Laundry Hut with a basket of towels, a couple getting into an SUV, and a young woman struggling with a stroller. Hubert bounded ahead to help. I heard her say his name in greeting, and then he folded the stroller and hefted it into her open trunk. She thanked him, and he returned to my side. "Amber Sorenson," he said, by way of explanation. "She has the cutest baby." As we approached the apartment, he waited for the woman with the towels; she used a key card to open the door while Hubert held the basket for her.

"Thanks, Hubert," she said, taking back the basket. "Sorry to hear about you and Kelly. You'll be missed around here." She trudged off without waiting for a response.

"I'm not going anywhere," Hubert called out after her, but she either didn't hear or didn't want to argue about it because she headed up the stairs without breaking stride.

"News travels fast in these here parts," I said.

"That's Mrs. Debrowsky. She lives right above us."

Between the thin walls and Kelly's loud, dramatic voice, I was willing to bet Mrs. Debrowsky had heard plenty.

We rounded the corner to find each side of the hallway lined floor to ceiling with boxes. I gave one a gentle nudge with the side of my foot. "This must be your stuff, don't you think?"

Hubert sighed. "It's going to take me all day to unpack this and put it back where it belongs." He gave a half smile. "Kelly sure has been busy."

"Should we start looking through the boxes for your keys?"

"Nah, Kelly's home. Her car is here. She'll let me in."

A few minutes later he didn't look so confident. I leaned against the tower of boxes and watched as my friend repeatedly knocked and called out Kelly's name. When he started with the begging, I put out a hand to stop him. "I don't think she's going to open up. Time for plan B."

"Maybe she's still sleeping," he said. "That would be good news, bad news. Man, she gets really crabby when people wake her up, but she gets over it pretty quick." He held a fist to his chin like Rodin's Thinker. "Maybe I should go outside and try knocking on our bedroom window."

"You don't have a secret key hidden somewhere? Or an extra with a neighbor?"

He shook his head. Great, keys to my house were scattered throughout the greater metropolitan area, but his apartment was locked as tight as a casino vault.

Our move to plan B was facilitated by the reappearance of Mrs. Debrowsky, who plodded toward us with an underwear load. "Kelly's not home," she said, resting her bosoms on the top of the basket. "So there's no point in you banging and yelling and disturbing the whole building. She said if I saw you to tell you your car keys and wallet are in this box and you should just take your stuff and go." She jerked her head toward a box on the top of the stack.

"Sorry about the noise," Hubert said.

"It's OK," she said gruffly. As she walked away she called out, almost as if to herself, "Like I said, Hubert, I'm real sorry to see you go. When I saw that crew from the moving company stacking your stuff in the hallway, I couldn't help but think you didn't deserve that. You're a nice boy."

As I watched her turn the corner to the stairwell, her words sank in. So Kelly had actually hired a moving crew? She'd planned this for some time, that was certain. I waited for Hubert to have the breakdown he deserved—a little anger would have been appropriate. Shock or despair would have worked too. Instead, he stood there straight-faced, arms at his side like a kid competing at a spelling bee.

"I'm sorry," I said, trying to meet his gaze, but he was staring over the top of my head.

"Maybe," he said, "I could call a locksmith. My name is still on the mailbox. If I tell them I've been locked out, maybe they would—"

"I don't think that's a good idea. It would just cause more trouble." I placed a hand on his shoulder. "Let it go, Hubert. She doesn't want you here."

We both stood for a second, Hubert looking like he'd been sucker-punched.

"It's just, I don't know what to do now," he said, in a voice so quiet I could barely hear him. He blinked quickly so that I wouldn't see his eyes welled up with tears, but it was too late. I saw. "Why is she doing this?" He sighed. "I feel like I'm caught in a bad dream. I just don't know what to do."

He didn't know what to do, but suddenly, I did. I grabbed a box off the top of one of the stacks. "No point in standing around here any longer. Why don't you come back with me to my house? You can give yourself a few days to sort it out."

7

It wasn't as simple as that, of course. Most things in life are more complicated than you'd anticipate. Like the first time I played a real game of tennis, which was in high school phys ed, embarrassingly enough. I'd seen tennis games before and even batted a ball around on the street with Hubert, but who knew playing an actual game would be so freaking hard? Apparently when I played with Hubert he'd been deliberately hitting the ball right to me, making me think I had this tennis thing down. After the first serve in gym class, I realized that tennis was far harder than I'd thought. It's a whole other thing when people aren't trying to make it easy.

And Kelly wasn't trying to make it easy, believe me. Because the boxes weren't labeled, Hubert couldn't just grab his clothes and toiletries and leave the rest for another time. Opening them didn't help either—the contents were a jumble: underwear mixed with yearbooks, CDs thrown in with belts and ties, a stuffed gecko mushed in between stereo speakers. One box even held an assortment of mustards. Not Kelly's condiment of choice, apparently.

"It'll take hours to go through all of them," I said after we'd rifled through half a dozen boxes. "I think we're just going to have to move them all to my house."

"OK," Hubert said. "If you say so." A teenage boy came by on a skateboard, narrowly missing a box we'd pulled away from the wall. Hubert paused to give the kid a high-five as he whizzed past. "Zach, my man. How's it goin'?"

"Pretty good, Mr. Holmes," the boy called out.

Hubert gestured with a wave of his hand and turned to me. "I've told him a million times to call me Hubert, but he won't do it. Says his mom thinks it's disrespectful to call a grown-up by their first name." He leaned against the door as if settling in for a long conversation. "He's really an exceptional kid. You know how they're always saying teenagers don't read anymore? Not Zach—he's a huge reader. And not just the Harry Potter books either. I'm talking about books you'd never expect a kid to read. Books like—"

"Hubert." My voice came out more sharply than I intended. "Any thoughts on how we're going to move this stuff?" Math wasn't my thing, but even I could see that the square footage of cardboard in this hallway would never fit in Hubert's VW Beetle and my Honda Civic. Taking several trips was an option, but the thought of shuttling back and forth made me tired.

"Move this stuff?" His forehead furrowed like he was doing long division in his head.

"You know. Like, move it from here to my house? Do you know anyone with a truck? Any really strong friends who owe you a favor?"

He thought for a moment and then smiled as a solution broke through. "Hey! We can call Piper."

Piper, with her 112-pound body and spaghetti arms, wouldn't have been my first choice, but as it turned out, Piper and her minivan were just what we needed.

She arrived within twenty minutes of getting Hubert's call on my cell phone. When she drove up and saw us waiting by the back door, she put the van in reverse and backed over the lawn to meet us halfway.

"I'm not so sure you should have done that," Hubert said after she climbed out of the driver's seat. He toed the muddy rut on the grass with the tip of his donated shoe. "Kelly's dad is kind of fussy about the grounds. He's not going to be happy when he sees this."

Piper pointed to the tread marks. "That?" She waved a hand dismissively. "Ach, that's nothing. That'll grow back before you know it. Now where are all these boxes? Brandon's halfway through a nap, and Mike's watching the game. I don't have all day." Some of the larger boxes required both Hubert and me to grab hold of an end and move crab-like down the narrow hallway. Piper, always the diva, put herself in charge of holding the door. By the third trip, I could feel beads of perspiration forming on my forehead. I'd always admired the fact that Hubert had such an extensive library of hardcovers. Now I found myself wishing he were the kind of guy who collected throw pillows or ping-pong balls.

"That's it. You're doing great!" Piper said, shifting into cheerleading mode as we passed through the door. "Three trips down, just a few more to go."

Hubert and I loaded our boxes into the back of the van, which was more spacious than usual since Piper had folded down the seats and emptied it of baby paraphernalia.

"We've barely made a dent," I said to Piper as we went back in. I pointed to a paving stone propped up next to the doorway. "Why don't you stick that brick in the door and come and help us out?" She grimaced but stuck her foot over the threshold to keep the door from auto-locking, and then she reached down to pick up the brick. I assumed she'd follow us, but when we returned the door was wedged open and she was nowhere in sight.

"Where the hell did she go?" I asked Hubert.

His eyes darted toward the stairwell. "I thought I heard her go upstairs, but I don't know what she'd be doing up there. Jeez, I hope she's back by the time we're done."

"She better be back sooner than that," I muttered as I headed outside.

When we returned to the building, Piper was holding the door for a stream of people carrying boxes. Hubert's boxes. I recognized Mrs. Debrowsky, but there were also two older men I'd never seen before. Zach, minus the skateboard, was behind them, followed by a younger boy. Zach's brother, judging by the resemblance.

"Where do you want these, Mr. Holmes?" Zach called out.

I turned to see Hubert's reaction. "You guys are the best!" he said. "Just the best." An expression of gratitude came over his face. "You don't have to do this."

"Me and Avery wanted to help," the taller man said. "We're really going to miss you."

"Yeah," added Avery, "it won't be the same without you, that's for sure. No one can get a Weber grill started like you, Hubert. You've got a knack with lighter fluid, like nobody's business."

"You're such a good guy," Mrs. Debrowsky added. "Always willing to give a hand. We appreciated it."

Zach's brother stepped forward. "I didn't understand about place holders in math at all until you explained it. Now I get it." The group nodded in unison, as if they'd all had trouble with place holders before Hubert came along.

"Aw man, don't get me started," Hubert said. "You guys are going to make me cry."

Mrs. Debrowsky shifted from foot to foot. "Do you want this in the back of the van? Or what?"

"Oh yeah." Hubert's head jerked toward the parking lot. "I'll show you. Either in the van or Lola's car or my Beetle." As they walked away, I could hear him yabbering on in appreciation. "Thanks, Fred. Thanks, Avery. This is great. You guys are unbelievable."

I glanced at Piper, who leaned against the open door, her arms folded in satisfaction.

"This is your doing?" I asked.

She grinned. "My dad always said to work smarter, not harder."

I had to hand it to Piper—she knew how to work it. In tenth grade she got me an extension on a paper by explaining to the teacher that my grandma was dying. I'd been far too shy and distraught to bring it up myself, and I would probably have accepted the markdown for being late. Senior year she got me a date for the homecoming dance with her boyfriend's cousin, a guy from another school. Piper knew how to get things done. Always planning, always doing. Meanwhile, I was like a leaf floating down the river to wherever life took me. So far, my strategy wasn't getting me anywhere. If I let Piper run my life, I'd probably be married now with a kid on the way. If it weren't for her taste in men—more status than substance—I might consider it.

It was amazing how quickly seven people could empty a hallway. Piper kept her station as door-holder and cheerleader, urging us on at every pass through. I overheard Zach ask Hubert, "Who is that lady?" When Hubert said she was a friend, Zach said, "Dude, she's really pretty. You should go out with *her*." If anyone at Vista View had any loyalty to Kelly, I didn't see it.

By the time we left, the sky was overcast and the wind had picked up. Ah, spring in Wisconsin.

We pulled out of the parking lot with Piper in the lead, Hubert right behind, and me bringing up the rear. Hubert's neighbors stood in a row and waved as we went by. I did a parade float wave, and Hubert tapped on his car horn.

8

When I pulled up in front of my house, Piper and Hubert were already unloading boxes. Halfway home I'd gotten snagged on a red light and was left behind while the two of them sped merrily away. It gave them a bit of a lead, but judging from the number of boxes on the lawn, I took a lot longer than I thought.

"I'm in a big hurry," Piper yelled as I approached. She was tossing boxes out of the van with the fury of a St. Bernard digging for avalanche victims. "I've got to get home pronto. Mike called and Brandon's up."

Oh, so that was it. Stop the presses. Alert the media. The baby is *awake*. God forbid Mike should have to deal with his own kid for once. His hands-off approach to fatherhood didn't seem to bother Piper—she relished being the only one Brandon wanted—but it annoyed me to no end. Wasn't parenting supposed to be a two-person job? Did Piper have to give up everything in her life just because she had a baby? When I tried explaining my frustration to my mother, she just laughed and said I'd get my friend back eventually. Babies were a full-time job, she said, as if I didn't know that. It just seemed to me that Mike could help out more.

Hubert pulled out a box and set it down on a stack adjacent to the curb. Further back, boxes were scattered haphazardly. Piper's work, no doubt.

"Some of those things might be breakable," he said after Piper lobbed a smallish carton over her shoulder.

"Piper, chill." I held up my hand in the universal sign for "Stop wrecking your friend's stuff."

"It's mostly books, I think." She paused and tucked a strand of hair behind her ear. "They'll be fine. If anything gets damaged, just let me know and I'll pay for it."

"Sure, just write a check," I said. "But what if it's the Waterford crystal that's been in his family for generations? What then?" The Waterford crystal line was a hypothetical. In all honesty, I doubted Hubert's family owned any priceless heirlooms. I'd been to his grandmother's house—she collected ceramic cows, and I was pretty sure none had been passed on yet. Still, it was the point of the thing.

"It's OK, Lola." Hubert placed a hand on my shoulder. "She's doing me a favor. Just let it go."

Piper gave me a sideways glance complete with eye roll, and then she turned back to the van. As a compromise, she climbed inside and pushed the boxes toward the back for Hubert and me to unload. We moved the rest in silence.

"That's all she wrote," Piper sang out when the van was finally empty. She clambered out and slammed the door shut. "You're good to go. And I am out of here."

"Thank you so much. I'm really grateful you came on such short notice." Hubert moved toward her with outstretched arms. His lankiness gave the hug an odd look—like a mother giraffe leaning over to nuzzle her baby. "I really owe you." He spoke to the top of her head. "If you need anything at all—a ride to the airport, a babysitter, anything—just let me know."

"Will do." Piper's voice was suddenly cheerful. She was good at departures. They moved apart, and she held him at arm's length. "And you make sure to call me and tell me how you're doing. I'll be thinking of you."

"Thanks. I will."

She turned to me. "See you later, Lola. Maybe we can do lunch sometime?"

"Sure." Sometime was a safe bet. We hugged and she drove off, waving as she went.

After Piper's van turned the corner and was out of sight, Hubert said, "By any chance, do you own one of those moving cart things? What are they called?" He snapped his fingers. "A dolly? Or maybe a wheelbarrow or something?" I shrugged a no, and we both stood a moment and surveyed the box explosion on the lawn. Hand-carrying them into the house would take forever.

Besides my Honda, I didn't own anything with wheels, but my next-door neighbor made up for my circular shortcomings. Mrs. Cho's lawn was littered with more axles than you'd find at a NASCAR race: roller skates and bikes and a coaster wagon. While Hubert surveyed the scene, I could tell his own wheels were turning.

"I'm going to ask Ben if they have anything," Hubert said. "If nothing else, we can borrow that kids' wagon."

Normally I wouldn't have encouraged getting my neighbors involved, but my shoulders ached and I was starting to get a headache. Even if I wanted to object, I didn't have time— Hubert was knocking on the Chos' door before I could even have found words. I watched him talk to someone through the screen door. He pointed in my direction, and I waved in case they could see me. Then the door opened and a hand beckoned him in. Oh great. Now that he'd been absorbed into the Cho clan, there was no telling when he'd be back.

I left the boxes and went into my own house to use the bathroom. If Hubert came back and I was still inside, he'd figure it out. He was smart that way.

On the way back through the living room, the blinking light on the answering machine caught my eye. Four messages? Sometimes I went a week and didn't get a one. We hadn't been gone *that* long.

I stopped to push the button and heard, "Good afternoon, Lola. This is Brother Jasper from across the street just calling to tell you there's been a change in plans. The block party is now on Saturday, May seventh. We had to make it earlier because it's going to be a fundraiser for a little boy from the church. His name is Derek, and he has leukemia. We hope you can make it then, but even if you can't, please include Derek in your prayers. I appreciate it. Thanks."

My first thought was for poor little Derek. Leukemia, what a bite. My second thought was that date was my birthday, which was a fine reason to skip the block party. I would write a nice check for the little guy and be done with it.

Message two revealed my younger sister's voice: "Lola? This is Mindy. If you're there, pick up." Long pause. "Well, I can't imagine where you'd be on a Saturday afternoon." Another long pause and a sigh. I pictured her perfectly glossed lips forming an exasperated O. "Look, I was wondering if you'd want to go to the Wonderful World of Weddings at State Fair Park with me and Jessica today. I thought we could check out the bridesmaid dresses and flowers and stuff. I'm going to try your cell. Call me if you get this message in the next fifteen minutes."

Message three: "Lola, this is Mindy again. Jessica's here and we're leaving now for the wedding thing." I heard her muffled voice through the hand-covered receiver saying something to her maid of honor, Jessica, and then she was back. "I'm thinking because your cell is turned off that you're probably home and just pulling that antisocial crap you do, so we're swinging by to pick you up. Wear flat shoes because the hall is enormous and we've got a lot of ground to cover." The voice after the beep said she'd called at 12:43.

I winced at the thought of Mindy and Jessica showing up at my door. Frankly, I didn't want to be involved in the decision-making part of Mindy's wedding-o-rama. I'd told her to pick whatever bridesmaid dresses she wanted—I didn't care. She'd asked my opinion on everything from champagne toasts to place cards, and I told her repeatedly that anything she picked out was fine by me, but she refused to believe my apathy was genuine.

I compared the time of the call with my watch. Phew. They would have come and gone by now. Who'd have thought Hubert's crisis would have saved my day?

Message four: "Um, Lola? This is Drew." Shoot, I knew where this was going. "I'm really sick." He cleared his throat, and then his sick voice officially began. "I know you said you need those articles first thing Monday morning, but I'm thinking there's no way I'll have them done by then. I probably won't even be in to work on Monday. Because I feel really terrible." Big coughing fit. "OK, well if you need anything, you can call. But I might not answer if I'm sleeping. And if you pass by my apartment and my car is gone, that's because I let my brother borrow it. Since I wouldn't be using it anyway. Because I'm so sick." Got it. Not coming in to work on Monday due to fake sickness. But really out of town. "OK then. Bye."

Drew was one of two staff writers at the parenting magazine where I was the editor. His very existence gave me tension headaches. The other staff member of our little parenting magazine was Mrs. Kinkaid, and yes, she wanted to be called Mrs. Kinkaid. She'd worked for the newspaper in one capacity or another for thirty years, being passed around from department to department, wherever she could do the least damage. When the newspaper created this spin-off parenting tabloid (mostly for additional advertising opportunities), the newly installed editor inherited Mrs. Kinkaid. And when *I* got the job, the first person I saw when I walked through the door was Mrs. Kinkaid, welcoming me with a platter of brownies and a lot of chatter.

Most of the time I didn't mind her too much. She had a chipper disposition and was a halfway decent writer who came up with some snappy headlines, but her lackadaisical attitude toward work was another thing. She yakked on the phone with her daughter and balanced her checkbook on company time. I suspected she had the dirt on someone higher up because every time I complained, my boss did the equivalent of patting me on the head by telling me Mrs. Kinkaid was part of the deal. Take her or leave it.

With Drew out on Monday, it would be just Mrs. Kinkaid and me. Not such a bad deal, as long as I ignored her phone chattering and concentrated on my own work. The funny thing was that, despite the idiosyncrasies of my staff, I really loved my job. The magazine came out only once a month, so there was no great pressure. Much of the content was advertising disguised as articles, but I didn't mind that much. I got the final say in the layouts, graphics, and cover photos, and every now and then we did something fun like a photo or essay contest.

My predecessor had quit because our office was in the basement of the daily paper, our parent company. She had some kind of subterranean claustrophobia and hated being so removed from the hubbub upstairs. I didn't share her feelings. Except for the spiders, working in the basement suited me fine.

My family joked about the irony of me, a single female with no prospects, working for a parenting magazine. I was a little hurt that at age twenty-nine they'd already written me off. I joked back about how much I liked being independent, even as I wondered if they were right.

As I was pushing the delete button, Hubert came through the door, followed by Brother Jasper, Ben Cho, and two other young Asian men. They all carried boxes. I was beginning to see a pattern here.

"Hey, Lola," Hubert said, setting his box down in the corner of the living room and gesturing for the others to do the same. "Look, I got help."

"I see that," I said. "Hey, Brother Jasper. Hi, guys."

"Miss Lola," Brother Jasper said, smiling. "This is turning out to be a fine weekend. First I get to eat some of Mrs. Cho's delicious cooking, and then I get to be one of the first to welcome Hubert to the neighborhood. And," he said, extending an arm in my direction, "how good of you to take your friend in during his time of need. You have a very giving spirit."

I hoped that wouldn't get around. I said, "Well, it's good of you all to help with the boxes. It would have taken us hours. Thanks a lot."

The guys responded with a chorus of "no problem" and "you're welcome."

Brother Jasper grinned. "Glad to help. What comes around goes around."

Now was my chance. "Brother Jasper, I got your message, and I just wanted to let you know I won't be able to make the block party. It's my birthday, and my folks have this thing planned." He looked so understanding—why did I feel the need to explain further? "Otherwise I'd love to help out, but they'd be so disappointed. I'll certainly donate to the cause, though." I sneaked a glance at Hubert, hoping he wouldn't blow my story, but he was busy talking to Ben Cho.

"Don't worry about it, Lola," Brother Jasper said. "Attendance is strictly optional. You'll be missed, though."

"Thanks."

Hubert paused in the doorway as the rest of group filed out the door. "You don't have to help anymore, Lola. We're pretty well covered now." He made a shooing gesture with both hands. "Go along and take that bath you've been yearning for. Leave the rest to us."

I hesitated. Back at Vista View when I'd been sweating up a storm I'd mumbled something about wanting a good soak once I got home, but I hadn't realized he'd heard me. I felt a flush of shame at my own selfishness, but that didn't stop me from wanting to take him up on his offer.

"We'll be fine. And if you leave your keys," he added, "I'll even put your car in the garage when we're all done."

I knew in that moment I'd lost control of my house and my life, but I was tired and his offer sounded good. As I headed upstairs, I couldn't help but think of the old cliché: what a difference a day makes.

9

A good long soak in a tub full of warm water is one of life's greatest pleasures, as far as I'm concerned. Bath time is a serious business, and I've invested in an assortment of bath oils, crystals, scented soaps, and loofahs to ensure it goes well.

When I took a bath, I lit candles and sometimes played CDs. I skipped the music this time, but I still opted for the other niceties, arranging my towels for easy access and lighting some purple soy candles before climbing into the tub.

Once immersed I leaned back, careful to drape my hair over the edge, and then I closed my eyes. I wondered how long Hubert would stay. In the meantime, his boxes would take up most of the living room. Thank God he didn't have any furniture to move. When he'd moved in with Kelly she was already set for furniture, so he gave all his away to a family who'd lost everything in a house fire. Piper said his generosity was good-hearted but foolish (*What if they break up and he needs it back?*), but I thought it was sweet. This was before I knew Kelly's other side. Turned out Piper was right. As usual.

I heard the guys talking downstairs but couldn't make out what they were saying. They must have finished the hauling and now were just shooting the breeze. I picked up a net-covered sponge, drizzled liquid bath wash on it, and squeezed until it produced a froth of suds. The scented candle was in full force now, and the room smelled of lavender. My bathrobe hung over a hook on the back of the door, like in a movie.

Below me a door slammed, and I heard the men's voices trail outside before subsiding completely. It was nice of them to help. I considered baking some muffins for Brother Jasper and the Cho boys as a thank you and then decided against it. Better to send Harry & David pears and let the UPS man do the delivery. A personal gift without getting too personal.

I ran the wet sponge over my left arm leaving a streak of suds, switched hands to do the other side, and then sank down so only my head protruded. Usually I stayed in until my toes resembled albino raisins or the water cooled, whichever came first.

I was so relaxed I was almost dozing when I heard a clattering of footsteps. Startled, I recognized voices: my sister Mindy and her cohort Jessica. Every muscle in my body went from limp to clenched in an instant.

I heard Hubert call up the stairs, "I don't think that's such a good idea."

"Don't be ridiculous," Mindy said, outside the bathroom door. "I'm her sister. If I can't barge in on her, who can?"

I held my breath as if that might make me unreachable. Oh, why couldn't Hubert have told her I wasn't home?

"Hey, Lola," she yelled. "It's Mindy—open up." She rapped on the door: shave and a haircut, two bits. "Come on, Lola."

"Just a minute," I said, scrambling out of the tub.

"Let me in," she said and banged with her fist.

Like hell. Frantically I grabbed my luxury towel, wrapped it around my middle, shimmied inside of it, and then lowered it to get my legs.

"Lola, what, are you drowned?" She tried the knob. Thank God I'd locked it.

"I said, *just a minute*."

"Oooh, she's cranky," Mindy said, presumably to Jessica.

Mindy could push my buttons like no one else. I tried never to lose my cool around her because seeing me riled was one of her greatest pleasures. Staying calm in her presence was a perpetual challenge.

"Hey, Lola, come on out. I have a surprise for you."

I groaned. A surprise from Mindy was never a good thing. One year she gave me a one-month membership to her fitness club for my birthday, for the sole purpose, I'd concluded, of drawing attention to the fact that she was a size two and I was a size eight. On my good days.

One Christmas she gifted me with a session at Glamour Shots. Apparently she thought I could only achieve glamour with the help of a soft focus and some photo retouching. Another time she asked me to meet her for dinner, just the two of us, and then she showed up with her boyfriend and his much older, never-married, *Star Trek*–loving cousin. A sort of impromptu double date, she explained in the bathroom after the salad course. All of her gifts were designed to surreptitiously point out my shortcomings.

"Jessica took pictures at the wedding show. We can download them on your computer," she called now, as if that would lure me out.

"Go downstairs," I ordered as I slipped on my bathrobe. "I'll be down in a minute."

I heard Hubert's voice from below. "Ladies. Come on down and have a glass of wine with me. Give Lola a chance to get herself together."

Wine? It was a little early in the day to be drinking. Not to mention that there wasn't any wine on the premises. What was he thinking?

"All right," Jessica said. "Party at Lola's." I could picture her pumping her fist in the air. She was the original good-time girl, the kind you see waving a lighter at concerts and hanging out the back of convertibles. Guys noticed her for her long legs and big bazongas. The combination made her look like such a knockout that they never seemed to notice that she was only pretty in a horsey-faced kind of way. Mindy, with her curly chestnut-colored hair, button nose, and big doe-eyes, was the prettier of the two, but her petite build couldn't compete with Jessica's Amazonian height and porn-star proportions.

"We're going downstairs now to talk to Hubert," Mindy yelled through the door. "Hurry up."

I pulled my bathrobe off the hook. "OK, see you in a bit," I said, but I wasn't sure they heard me over the clomping of their feet as they headed downstairs toward Hubert's wine.

I took my time dressing, making Mindy wait in retaliation for having invaded my bath time. I only realized that was a mistake when I followed the sound of laughter downstairs and found Mindy and Jessica on either side of Hubert on the couch, looking at an open book on Hubert's lap. Jessica held a half-full tumbler of what looked like grape juice. She leaned forward in such a way that her scooped-neck top barely covered her scoops.

"What's so funny?" I asked as I came into the room and sat down in a wing chair. I felt like I was crashing a hot-tub soiree between Hugh Hefner and a couple of his bunnies. "What have you got there?"

"I just came across one of our old yearbooks when I was

opening some of the boxes," Hubert said. "I thought the girls might get a kick out of seeing it."

"You were so skinny in high school," Mindy said, tapping the page and then pointing the same finger at me. "Wow, what a difference."

Hubert looked up, puzzled. "She looks the same to me."

Mindy tilted her head to one side and appraised me. "Her hair's the same—that's why you think she hasn't changed. She's kept it in that just-hanging-down style forever. For my wedding, we're all getting updos. Lola will be *forced* to look good that day."

"So glad you found that yearbook," I said. "Good going, Hubert."

"He found wine, too." Jessica held up her glass as if toasting me. "Fat Bastard!"

"Excuse me?" I said.

"The brand name is Fat Bastard," Hubert explained. "Kelly and I bought a few bottles at a wine tasting." At the mention of Kelly's name, his face clouded up. The wench sure had a hold on him. "Kel wanted to buy it because of the name, but she didn't actually like the taste."

"Too bad for her," Jessica said and laughed, her mouth so wide I saw the fillings in her back teeth. "More for us."

"How much did you guys drink?" I asked.

"Oh! My wedding!" Mindy jumped off the couch and grabbed a large plastic bag off the floor. "We absolutely have to show you all the stuff we got at the wedding show." She slid my stack of magazines off the coffee table and then spread brochures on the newly cleared surface. "Most of this I already have set up for my wedding. Jess and I really just went to get hyped up."

I was able to feign interest through the floral and photography sections of the talk, but when she started describing her aisle runner, her voice took on the muted-cornet sound of Charlie Brown's teacher. *Bwah, bwah, bwah, bwah, bwah.*

"When are you getting married?" Hubert asked, breaking the tedium.

Jessica tapped the coffee table with her fingernails. "Are you going to tell them?" She looked from me to Hubert with raised eyebrows.

"That's my surprise," Mindy said.

Clearly they'd had too much to drink. Mindy and Chad's chosen wedding day was no surprise; it had been set three years ago. The date was burned into my brain.

"It's the third Saturday in August," I said to Hubert. "Because they met the third weekend in August right before their junior year of high school." I was sure Hubert had heard this story before. Mindy and Chad were five years younger than us, so we'd already graduated by the time they'd become a couple, but he'd been around my family enough to have heard of their fateful meeting at the local pool that summer.

"Correction," Mindy said. "The wedding *was* scheduled for the third weekend in August, but there's been a change. The reception hall double-booked, so they offered us an alternate date."

"With a big price break too," Jessica added.

"Luckily Father Joe had a slot at the church available on the very day, so it worked out perfectly." My sister grinned like she could barely suppress the news. "You won't believe it. Wait'll you hear."

The suspense was getting tiresome. "So when is it?"

"Get this." Mindy leaned forward. "I'm getting married on *May seventh.*"

"May seventh?" I asked.

"Hey," Hubert said, "that's Lola's birthday."

My heart sank. "Oh no, not on my birthday." To turn thirty on the very day my younger sister got married? How loser-ish was that?

"Why not? You got something better to do that day?" Mindy asked. "It's so perfect. You'll never forget my anniversary, and you'll always know how many years I've been married—just take your age and subtract thirty."

"It's really May seventh?" I could barely get the words out. Oh please, let her be joking. I'd even forgive her for my spike in blood pressure if this whole thing turned out to be a ribbing at my expense.

"I know what you're thinking," Mindy said. "How in the world am I going to get this whole thing put together in the next three weeks? I've thought of everything. We'll just have to get the bridesmaid dresses off the rack." She shrugged as if to say, *What are you gonna do?* "Luckily I've had my dress forever." She'd been making payments on it for the last two years. "With everything else, we can cut corners or pay extra. Jessica here called all the guests already, and most of them can still make it. We've got it all figured out."

"We've been working like dogs to pull this off," Jessica said. She rested a hand on the yearbook on Hubert's lap.

"How long have you known?" I wondered if I could bow out of the wedding completely. I racked my brain for a legitimate excuse for missing my own sister's wedding. The block party? No, thanks. Emergency surgery? Impossible to plan. Car crash? Would involve wrecking my car. Sequestered jury duty? If I knew how to manage that, I'd sign up ahead of time. It would be ideal—no pain and an extended hotel stay. Sorry, Mindy, I'd love to be in your wedding, but I'm too busy doing my civic duty.

"Oh gosh," Mindy said. "I've known for about two weeks, but I wanted to spring the news on you in person. Mom didn't tell you then? I told her not to."

"No, Mom didn't say anything." I thought back to my last phone conversation with our mother and the way she kept asking if I'd seen Mindy lately. I'd thought it was another attempt to encourage us to be friends, when actually she was in on this whole thing.

Mom was a traitor.

"You don't look so happy about this," Jessica said. "Not too many brides would want to share their special day with their sister."

"I'm just—" I struggled to find the right word. "Surprised."

"And here's the best part," Mindy said, beaming.

More? I steeled myself.

"I've talked to the woman at the bakery. Wonderful little German lady named Hilda." This she directed to Hubert, who nodded as if he knew Hilda. "And she agreed to make us an extra cake." She held up both hands—*ta-da!* "Chocolate cake with chocolate frosting."

The room was silent as she waited for a reaction. Finally I made a guess. "For those who prefer chocolate?"

"No, silly," Mindy said. "For your birthday. Chocolate with chocolate—your favorite. I thought we'd have them wheel it out on one of those carts like they have for room service, with the candles lit ahead of time. Then Chad will announce that it's your thirtieth birthday, and I'll lead the singing."

"Oh no," I said, the blood rising to my cheeks.

"She's always so shy," Mindy said to Hubert. "But once she's in the spotlight, she'll love it."

"No, I won't love it," I said. "Do not do this."

"It'll be great," Mindy said, as if I hadn't spoken. "Everyone will get such a kick out of it."

I gritted my teeth. "This is a very bad idea, Mindy. Cancel the chocolate cake, and forget about the singing. Not going to happen."

Mindy turned to Jessica. "I knew we shouldn't have told her about the cake ahead of time. I just *knew* she'd get this way." She sighed and folded her hands primly in her lap, and then she gave me a studied look. "You don't really want to ruin this for me, do you, Lola? You said I could plan my wedding any way I wanted, and this is what I want."

"Yes, it's your wedding," I said. "But this stops being about your wedding once you drag my birthday into it. Then it's about me, and I do have definite ideas about that. I have no intention of having two hundred people, most of whom I barely know, singing to me."

Mindy twisted her hands and exhaled dramatically. "Oh, why is it always so hard for you to just go along? This is my plan: I get married, we have a nice dinner, we sing 'Happy Birthday,' we cut the cake, we do some dancing. The birthday song lasts like one minute. How embarrassed can you be? It's not like I can just ignore the fact that it's your birthday. That wouldn't be very nice, would it? And a dual celebration, how cool is that? The relatives would love it, you know they would."

I folded my arms and gave a glare that silenced her.

Hubert raised his hand like a fourth grader not quite sure of the answer. "I think," he said, turning to Mindy, "that your heart is in the right place, but maybe if it makes Lola uncomfortable, you could work out a compromise. Maybe a cake, but no singing?" He looked from Mindy to me.

"I could still announce it's her birthday, though," she said.

"And if everyone just starts singing, that's up to them. I won't even suggest it." She brightened at the thought.

"How about this for a compromise," I said. "If at any time during the wedding day I hear the words 'Lola's birthday' coming from your mouth, I leave and never talk to you again." It was all I could do to keep from shouting the words. "And if I hear the birthday song, preannounced or otherwise, someone's getting hurt." I stood up. "How's that for a compromise?"

The three of them regarded me with wide eyes.

"Party pooper," Mindy said. "No-fun Lola strikes again."

"Whenever you don't get your own way you resort to name-calling," I said. "Grow up, Mindy."

"Oh, I am grown up, thank you very much." She held up her left hand and wiggled her ring finger so the light glinted off the diamond. "I'm the one getting married, remember?"

I'd heard enough. "I don't want to be rude," I said, grabbing her wedding brochures and stuffing them back into the bag, "but you really have to go now."

"I'm not done with my wine yet," Jessica protested, holding up a full glass. Somewhere during the cake debate she'd refilled it without me noticing.

I jerked the glass out of her hand and took a long swig of the Fat Bastard. It was surprisingly delicious: flavors of stone fruit like plums and cherries combined with cedar and toasty aromas. Kelly didn't know squat about wine. I looked down to see Jessica staring at me, mouth agape.

Mindy stood up and looped the bag over her arm. "Come on, Jessica. When she gets like this, there's no talking to her. We might as well go."

"She drank my wine," Jessica said, incredulous.

"I'm sorry you have to rush off," said Hubert. "It was nice seeing you again. It's been a long time."

"Maybe now that you two are living together we'll see each other more often," Mindy said, helping Jessica to her feet.

"We're not living together," I said, setting the story straight.

Hubert smiled. "Oh no, I'm not going to be living here. Lola's just letting me stay until I get things worked out."

"Whatever," Mindy said. "Staying. Living. Call it what you want. Either way, you're both sleeping under the same roof." She pulled Jessica's arm in the direction of the door. "I think I better drive. You've had a little too much of that Fat Bastard." I heard Jessica giggling even after the door was shut behind them.

"Well," Hubert said. "That was interesting. Hard to believe Mindy's getting married. I still think of her as that little kid who was always pestering us."

"Hubert, would you excuse me for a little bit?" I said. "I need to make a phone call."

10

I brought the cordless phone upstairs with me and threw my-self back onto my bed, the way I used to when I was a teenager. It was the closest thing to pole vaulting I'd ever done. During my high school years, my mom, hearing the frame bang against the wall, would shout up the stairs, "Whatever you're doing, stop it. It sounds like the ceiling's going to cave in." But Mom wasn't here to yell at me now. It was my house, and I could wreck it if I wanted to.

I dialed Piper's cell, but only got voice mail. Drat. I was hoping to avoid calling her home phone. Mike usually answered, which was always a problem for me. But I had no choice. I called the landline and braced myself when Mike picked up after the second ring. "Hey, Lola, how are you?"

I hate it when people check caller ID and answer using my name. It seems both intrusive and know-it-all-ish at the same time. I was tempted to hang up and call back from someone else's house just to throw him off. Instead I answered, "Great, Mike. And yourself?"

"Never better. Work's keeping me busy, Brandon's growing by leaps and bounds, and my lovely wife gets more beautiful every day." Mike had a salesman's enthusiasm for everything. I'd been hearing that line about Piper getting more beautiful ever since they'd started dating. Once Hubert and I had a lengthy debate about the plausibility of that statement. I thought it was ridiculous—Piper was exceptionally pretty, but come on, no one was infinitely beautiful. Clearly it was just more of Mike's hyperbole. Hubert took a more philosophic view, that Piper became more beautiful to Mike the longer they were together. When you really love someone, he said, their flaws melt away. Clearly I'd never really been in love.

"Good to know, Mike," I said. "Listen, is Piper around? I was hoping we could talk."

"She's giving Brandon a bath. If you hang on, I'll see how far along they are." He set down the phone, and I heard his footsteps click across the hardwood floor. He was going to check how far along they were? How about taking over so she could have an important conversation with an old friend?

Piper came to the phone a few minutes later. "Hey, Lola, what's up?"

"Is this a good time?"

"Sure. I have a few minutes." She covered the mouthpiece and said something to Mike. How aggravating. "OK," she said, "shoot."

"It's just," I said and took a deep breath, "I mean, Mindy and Jessica stopped over to talk about the wedding." I paused to swallow the lump in my throat. "You know how evil Mindy can be. It didn't go well."

"What did she do?"

"She wants to humiliate me at her wedding. She's going to—" Suddenly I was at a loss for words. Despite my intention to play it cool, I felt tears come to my eyes. Then to make it worse, a sob escaped. Oh, why did I always cry when I was mad? Luckily Piper knew the score. Thank God for old friends.

"Oh no." Her voice was sympathetic. "Just a minute. I want to go in the bedroom. It's too distracting here." I heard her say to Mike, "You'll just have to watch him. I need to talk to Lola." Maybe it *was* possible to get her attention after all.

"So," she said when she returned to the phone, "tell me all about it." I pictured her sprawled on her back on the bed, one knee raised and the phone clutched to her ear. There was a nice symmetry in the thought of each of us situated identically.

I told her about Mindy's evil plan to shine the spotlight on my thirty-year-old unmarriedness at the wedding. Like the good friend she was, Piper responded with appropriate outraged gasps. "She is such a piece of work," she said when I was done with the story. "This is almost as bad as the time she used your identity at the gynecologist's." I'd almost forgotten about that one—at age sixteen Mindy had gotten birth control pills from the family ob-gyn by using my name and social security number. Apparently, from the doctor's gynecological vantage point, we looked remarkably the same. When the paperwork from the insurance company arrived at my folks' house, I could tell from the look on Mindy's face what had transpired, but of course she denied it. To this day I wasn't sure my parents believed that it wasn't me. I was in college at the time and used the clinic on campus for all my personal needs. Not that I'd told them that. "What a piece of work," Piper repeated. "It never ends with her, does it?"

"She just loves to embarrass me in public. I threatened her, but I just know she's going to do the cake thing anyway." I pressed the phone tighter to my ear. Downstairs I heard Hubert vacuuming. "And then what am I going to do? If I walk out, I look like a bad sport. She wins no matter what."

"She's really got you in a tough spot." Piper tsked sympathetically. "You can't walk out, that's for sure. But what if you do something unexpected and one-up her? Beat her at her own game?"

"Yeah, that's a good thought," I said bitterly. I had never attempted anything like that, mostly because Mindy was so underhanded I never got wind of her maneuvers until it was too late. I was always the one sitting on the metaphorical whoopee cushion, the one with the big fake smile on my face pretending that yes, a session at Glamour Shots was just what I wanted! A membership at your health club? Really, what a thoughtful gift! "Maybe someday I'll figure out a way to top her."

"Someday? How about now? No time like the present." I recognized the edge in Piper's voice. She had an idea.

"What do you have in mind?"

"Let's think this through," she said. "The reason Mindy wants to make a brouhaha about your birthday at the wedding is to point out that you're thirty, unmarried, and growing older every day with no prospects on the horizon, right?"

Talk about depressing. "Right."

"But what if," and here Piper's voice reached a crescendo, "you countered her measly little cake plan with a plan of your own? What if you stand up and make an announcement that just blows everyone away? And what if *your* announcement steals the show?"

A show-stealing announcement? I couldn't imagine. "Like I say I'm dying of a brain tumor?"

Piper laughed. "No, no, no. See, that's your problem. You have to step up your expectations for yourself. Try thinking positively for once."

"Tell them I won the lottery?"

"Better than that. Make a speech announcing *your* engagement. Produce some gorgeous guy and an enormous diamond ring. Make it twice as big as Mindy's. And have the guy be a knockout—a James Bond type."

Above me a fly buzzed loopily in the corner of the ceiling. "Sure, I'll just order one from the James Bond catalog, Piper. Good plan, except for the part where I have to meet some hot guy and get engaged in the next three weeks. Other than that, completely doable."

"Oh, you have no imagination. You don't actually have to be engaged. We'll find someone who will play along. After the wedding, when it doesn't matter anymore, you can say you broke up."

Trust Piper to come up with an *I Love Lucy* scheme as a solution.

"Well," I said, "even if I managed all that, I'm not sure I could pull it off. Lie to my parents and relatives? I'd never be convincing. Even if I could, there's no way I could come up with a guy. How often do you *see* a really handsome guy, much less one who would do a favor for a complete stranger? The whole thing is just too dicey."

"Are you kidding? I see good-looking guys all the time. They're everywhere. And any guy who has family issues—and really, who doesn't?—would be happy to help out. This is going to be great. Just think of the look on Mindy's face. She's going to die. And it will serve her right too, after everything she's pulled."

"It would be great." In theory, anyway. I smiled at the thought.

"And we'll make sure your guy is really tall, since Chad is short. Oh man, would that burn!" Piper was just getting started. "And you can have some of those 'reserve the day' cards printed up with your wedding date on them and pass them out. We can totally pull this off, I'm sure of it."

"It does sound good." I wasn't completely convinced though. Daydreaming about revenge was fun, but no one actually did these kinds of things except in movies. Did they?

"Now, who could we get to play the fiancé?" she said, as if casting a play. "Not Hubert. You know I love him to pieces, but he's a bit goofy looking and lacks that 'wow' factor. And you've known him since seventh grade, so that would just be pathetic. Are there any guys where you work?"

"Just Drew." Piper knew all about Drew. His shortcomings were the source of most of my work rants.

"Is he good looking?"

"Eh. Average." I felt a little guilty saying it. Who was I to cast judgment? I was pretty average looking myself.

"How about in the other departments?"

"I don't mix with the other areas. I work in the basement."

"Oh, that's right. I forgot you're the Phantom of the Opera over there. Well, don't worry about it. I'm on the case. I'll think of something."

As usual, talking to Piper was the right thing to do. She always came up with the right sympathetic response, whether that meant letting me vent, giving me a different outlook, or dreaming up a ridiculously outlandish plan for revenge. This time around she'd managed all three. By the time I'd hung up the phone, I felt much better.

11

When I got downstairs, Hubert was squatting next to the vacuum cleaner winding up the cord. "The guys tracked in some dirt when we moved the boxes," he said apologetically. "I wanted to get it before it got ground in. Hope you don't mind." He stood up and brushed off the front of his jeans.

"Why would I mind?"

"Because I'm using your stuff without asking?"

"Feel free. *Mi casa es su casa.*" It was practically the only Spanish I knew. I'd waited my whole life to use that line.

"OK, good." He rested a hand on the handle of the vacuum. "Hey, that Mindy's really something, isn't she? When she gets an idea in her head, she just doesn't let go. Kelly's kind of like that too. They feel so strongly about things they don't always realize how they affect other people."

"Mindy's a little bitch." I blurted it out without thinking; Hubert looked shocked. "She's happiest when she's making me look bad."

"Well, I don't know about that," he said slowly. "I mean, you two have never gotten along well, but it's not like she hates you or anything."

"You don't understand, Hubert. It's a sister thing. Life is

a competition for her." His only-child status made the concept impossible to grasp. Anything I said was apt to sound petty. "The whole birthday cake at her wedding thing was supposed to look nice but actually point out to everyone there that I'm five years older than she is and still not married. It's her way of showing that she won."

"No." His face scrunched in disbelief. "I can't believe that."

"I'm telling you, Hubert, I know how she operates, and that's exactly why she's doing it."

"But that's just so mean. And plus, who cares if you're not married? You're smart and pretty and kind. You have a terrific job and a great sense of humor. And you're a good friend."

"Thanks. Write that down and when I'm forty and desperately filling out my profile for Match.com, I'll give you a call and you can help me with the wording."

We stood silently for a moment, facing each other as if about to pace off for a duel. Hubert gave the vac a little push with one finger and then grinned. "Are you as hungry as I am? Because I'm starving."

Half an hour later Hubert returned from the Chinese place with six times the amount of food I usually got for myself. I guess that's what I got for opting not to go with him and telling him anything he picked up would be fine. "It all sounded so good—I couldn't decide," he said, pulling the white containers out of the bags and lining them up on the kitchen table. "I figured this way we could try it all."

"It smells wonderful." It had been hours since the bagels and cream cheese. I could feel my stomach rumble.

I poured water into glasses; we piled food on our plates and sat down to eat.

"I ran into Belinda when I was picking up the food." Hubert opened a packet of soy sauce and doused his rice.

"Belinda?"

"Your nice neighbor with all the pups?"

Oh, that Belinda.

"She was leaving as I was walking in. I almost invited her to join us, but we haven't done anything together in a long time, and I thought it would be more fun just the two of us."

We ate quietly for a few moments, until Hubert said, "While I was sitting waiting for the food order, I called Kelly's sister." The statement hung in the air for a second until he cleared his throat and continued. "Kelly's not taking my calls, and I thought Rachel might know something."

"What did she have to say?"

"Not much. Mostly that she was sorry it didn't work out, that she always liked me. She thought it sucked that Kelly hired a moving company to move me out without giving me any notice."

"Notice? Did you tell her that she locked you out with bare feet and no wallet?" He looked so pained I regretted the words as soon as they left my mouth.

He sighed. "Anyway, Rachel seemed to think this is permanent."

You think? I bit my tongue so I wouldn't say the words out loud.

"I'm finding it hard to understand." He looked weary and sad.

"I'm really sorry, Hubert." What else was there to say?

"If only I knew where this came from. Not knowing is the hardest part."

"I'm sure it's not anything you did." I reached across the table and patted his arm. "She's just not the one, Hubert. You'll get through this."

He opened his mouth as if to contradict me, but then he seemed to think better of it. To change the subject, I asked about his job.

"Don't you ever get tired of having twenty-six kids looking at you?" I asked. "You always have to be in charge, always one step ahead."

He looked startled at the question. "Gosh no, I don't get tired of it. I love it. The kids are great. I love their enthusiasm and hearing their take on things. I love knowing I'm making a difference in someone's life. It's never boring. Sure, some of the job sucks—the lesson plans, making sure I've covered everything that will be on the standardized testing. And I'm on the curriculum committee, which is a pain, but if I'm not involved, other people make decisions about my job. Overall though, I wouldn't trade it for anything." He clicked his chopsticks together and then picked up a chunk of sesame chicken and skillfully maneuvered it into his mouth.

"Wouldn't it be more fun to teach high school kids?" I asked.

"No way," he said. "Elementary, my dear Lola, that's where I belong."

"I give you a lot of credit. I couldn't do it."

"How about you?" he asked. "You still like your job?"

Hubert was the only one who ever expressed interest in my work. "Most of the time," I said. "I get a lot of satisfaction in putting together the magazine from scratch every month. I try to balance it so there's a good mix of information and entertaining articles. My boss wants the ads featured prominently, but I try to keep them from overriding the content." I stabbed at a chunk of chicken with my fork; unlike Hubert, I'd never mastered chopsticks. I was too modest to tell him my favorite part of the job—the periodic e-mails of praise from readers. The general consensus seemed to be that the magazine had improved since I took over. One article I wrote on toxic toys even won an award. "I can't think of anything else I'd rather do."

"So, life is good," he said.

"I guess so." I didn't have a husband or even a boyfriend, but I had my house, my health, my job, my friends. I couldn't quibble. Much.

By the time I pushed my plate away, I'd consumed more than I'd thought possible. "I can't eat another bite."

"Oh, but you have to," Hubert said. He reached into the bag, and I heard the crinkle of cellophane. "Fortune cookies!" He presented them on outstretched palms. "You pick first."

I chose one and waited while he opened his. His eyebrows furrowed. "Mine says, 'Out with the old, in with the new.' What kind of fortune is that?" He looked up, and I shrugged. "Now it's your turn."

I tore the clear wrapper, split the cookie in two, and smoothed the piece of paper on the table. "You'll find treasure where you least expect it." I gave him a quizzical look. "That doesn't tell me much. I don't expect treasure anywhere. Ever."

"Except in your nightstand drawer," Hubert said. He leaned back in his chair and balanced on the back legs for a few seconds, and then he came down with a thud. "Hey, that's what we should do tonight. We should start going through your aunt's stuff. Wouldn't that be fun?"

I gave him an exasperated look. "Cleaning is never fun, Hubert."

"Don't think of it as cleaning, think of it as exploring. Did anyone go through any of her stuff before you moved in?"

I shook my head. "Her attorney gave me the key, and when I went through the house, everything was exactly as it was the day she died. She was having coffee with Brother Jasper on a Sunday afternoon when she felt some pains in her chest. He called 911, and the paramedics came right away. They said her heart gave out in the ambulance. They tried to revive her, but weren't able to. She was old—in her late eighties, eighty-seven, I think."

"Wow," Hubert said. "You never told me that story."

I resisted the urge to remind him that he hadn't really been around much the last year or so. "The coffee cups and the sugar were still on the table when I first walked through the house."

"That's kind of creepy." He looked around the kitchen. "Did you ever find out why she left it to you? Instead of your folks or the other relatives?"

There was that question again. "No. I barely knew her. I only saw her at family functions maybe once a year or so, and we didn't talk much." The memory made me feel guilty. I never used to know what to say to Aunt May. She was fairly pleasant to talk to, but her oldness made me feel uncomfortable. In retrospect, I wished I had taken an interest in her life. "But the neighbors said Aunt May talked about me all the time. She told them when I graduated from college and when I got the job at the magazine. Kind of weird to think about it now."

"Maybe she just admired you."

"Yes, of course. Because I'm smart and pretty and kind, with a good sense of humor."

Hubert grinned. "Don't forget the part about how you're such a good friend."

"I have so much going for me, it's amazing more people aren't leaving me houses."

"There's the right attitude." He looked amused. "So, do you want to go through the bedrooms first, or the downstairs?"

"We really have to do this?"

"Gosh yes, this is going to be fun."

12

I was hoping we'd find more money, but the ninety-eight dollars and forty-seven cents Hubert found in his nightstand drawer seemed to be the extent of it. We didn't find any antiques either, unless you count a few pieces of carnival glass and a half dozen ancient pewter mugs. Hubert thought the mugs were a find and offered to take them after I put them on the discard pile. "You're getting rid of those?" He was incredulous. "But they're so cool. I could put them in the freezer and use them for beer when I have the guys over for poker night."

"Sometimes old mugs like these are toxic. I wouldn't take any chances," I said, pulling a stack of plates out of the built-in china cabinet. "I wrote a piece for the magazine on lead poisoning. It's not just from paint chips, like most people think."

"I remember that article." He blew the dust off a serving platter and turned it over to read the back. "That was a really interesting one. I liked where you quoted the forensic guy. My mom has some ceramic dishes she got from an artist in Spain, and after I read your story, I told her to stop serving food in them. She had no idea."

"You read a parenting magazine? You don't even have kids."

"Are you kidding? You're my friend—I read all your stuff. Besides, I hope to have kids someday. I *think* I'd make a pretty good dad."

I looked up and watched him sitting cross-legged on my dining room floor, helping me clean my house on a Saturday night. "I think you'd be a most excellent dad."

He looked sheepish. "Really? Well, thanks. You too." He paused as if processing his own words. "I meant a mom—you'll be a great mom."

"I knew what you meant."

We continued the project on Sunday, going through the kitchen cupboards and the first-floor bathroom. Hubert was right. With every bag taken out to the garbage and every box dropped off at the Goodwill, I felt a psychological load lifted.

"We can start on the upstairs next weekend," Hubert said. "And after that the basement and the attic. Then we can paint." He was as enthused as a television host for one of those home makeover programs.

"Whoa there." I crossed my fingers in front of me like warding off vampires. "It's not that I don't appreciate the help, I really do, but we don't need to tie up every weekend from now on. This is all stuff that can wait. Why don't we spread it out a little? Start up again, say maybe, next fall?"

"Next fall? Man, you weren't kidding. You really do hate deep cleaning." He snapped his fingers. "I have a thought. What if I do it myself? Take care of everything. All you'll have to do is wander in from time to time and tell me what stays and what goes."

"Oh, you don't have to do that."

"I'd be glad to, really." His face had a sincere, wanting-to-please, puppy-dog look. "Think of it as my rent. As long as I'm staying here, I might as well do something to earn my keep."

Even as I told him that wasn't really necessary, I did a bit of internal cheering. I hadn't realized how much the crammed closets and drawers weighed me down emotionally. My life was a closed-up space, and Hubert was opening windows and letting in the light.

* * *

On Monday when Mrs. Kinkaid asked me about my weekend, I had more to tell than usual. I rarely mentioned my personal life, but with Drew out with his pseudo-sickness, the atmosphere in the office was different. A just-us-girls kind of feeling, which made me uncharacteristically chatty. Within minutes, though, I regretted being so open.

"So you have a man living with you now," she exclaimed, leaning back in her chair. She was wearing the black cardigan today. As opposed to the white one. She wore cardigans year-round to ward off the bone-penetrating dampness, a side effect of working in a basement. I was never quite sure how the cardigan magic worked, but I didn't question it. "Just the two of you, sharing a house."

"No. Well technically, yes. But he's just an old friend who needed a place to stay because his girlfriend Kelly kicked him out." Why did everyone want to assume there was a subtext to this story? "We're not involved or anything." Our office was one big room with Drew and Mrs. Kinkaid's desks on one side and mine on the other. Usually I didn't mind the shared space, but the look she gave me now reminded me why having my own office would be so much better.

"Hmmm." She peered over her Ben Franklin glasses. "This takes me back to my own days as a single young lady. Did I ever tell you that Mr. Kinkaid and I started out as friends?"

When I shook my head, she started in on a very long, convoluted story about her husband, Jim, which basically boiled down to the fact that Mr. Kinkaid had actually been dating Mrs. Kinkaid's best friend, Dottie, at the start. When Dottie cast him aside, Jim came to Mrs. Kinkaid seeking an explanation and some consolation. One thing led to another, she said, "And the next thing I knew, we were quite the cozy couple." She clasped her hands together to illustrate cozy coupleness. No space between the fingers. "The best part of the story is," she said, and then waited a few seconds for the suspense to build, "that I asked Dottie to be my maid of honor, which I thought was quite big of me, considering. But she refused to do it. Wouldn't even come to the wedding, she was so mad. She'd changed her mind, you see, and wanted him back. But it was too late. By the time she figured out what she'd given up, he was all mine." A satisfied smile spread across Mrs. Kinkaid's face. "And Mr. Kinkaid and I were happy every day of our married life, right up until he died."

Yes, that would put a damper on things.

"So maybe this girlfriend of Hubert's will see the error of her ways, but by then it will be too late. He'll be in love with *you.*"

Now she was really spinning stories. "I don't think so," I said. "I've known Hubert for seventeen years. If he hasn't fallen in love with me yet, it's not going to suddenly happen now."

"Miss Lola Watson," she chided. "You just got through telling me he's one of your very best friends. And what do you think a husband is, but a best friend? That's the trouble with you girls nowadays. You're so caught up thinking about what you want that you don't even see what you have. Do you want to be married, or don't you?"

She had more to say on the subject, I had no doubt of that, but luckily for me the phone rang at that moment. It was Mrs. Kinkaid's daughter calling with a child-related crisis. I listened as Mrs. K. changed lanes as easily as the lead car at the Indianapolis 500.

The rest of the morning we were busy—me with putting together a magazine and Mrs. Kinkaid with taking care of her personal finances via her checkbook, a task she could justify since officially she was waiting for two different people to call her back.

My strategy for replacing Drew's missing articles included updating a similar story that had run last year and inserting a personal piece on the same topic. That was the joy of *Parenting Today*—we had our annual birthday party issue, summer vacation issue, back-to-school issue, et cetera, and so on. I'd taken to writing personal essays on these topics as backups in case I encountered a gap close to press time. Most of them were nostalgia pieces with a humorous bent. Sometimes I got positive feedback on these stories. Almost all the flattering comments came in the form of e-mails, which I printed and kept in a file folder for those days when I needed a boost.

By late afternoon I'd made great headway on my work while Mrs. Kinkaid kept busy laboriously sharpening pencils at her desk using one of those plastic handheld jobbies commonly used by grade-schoolers. We had an electric sharpener, but that required a trip across the room. Plus, Mrs. K. found the noise it made grating.

When the phone rang at four o'clock, she looked up. "Are you getting that?" she asked, continuing to rotate a pencil in even strokes. Even from my desk eight feet away I could smell the fresh wood shavings.

"Certainly." God forbid we interrupt the pencil project. "*Parenting Today*. Lola Watson speaking."

"Lola, hey, it's Piper."

I scooted my chair so that my head would be partially obscured by my computer monitor, away from Mrs. Kinkaid's curious gaze. "Hello, how can I help you?"

"It's Piper."

"If you wait, I can look that up."

She laughed. "What's the deal? Is Mrs. Kinkaid listening?"

"Yes, that is correct." I wedged the phone between my ear and my shoulder and put my hands over my keyboard. "Would you mind repeating that information?" I tapped on a few keys.

"Oh, Lola, please. Just tell her you're talking to a friend. Who cares? You said she takes personal calls all the time. And you're the one in charge. It's not like she's the boss."

I knew Piper was right, but there was a part of me that needed to maintain a show of professionalism. Just because Mrs. Kinkaid had the work ethic of Paris Hilton didn't mean I needed to follow suit. "Could you spell that?"

Piper sighed. "OK then, we'll play it your way. I'll just tell you the reason I called, and you can call me tonight from home if you have any questions."

"Yes?" I held my hands expectantly over my keyboard. I'd opened up a new document and was going to pretend to type whatever the caller said. That kind of thing bored Mrs. Kinkaid to distraction. With any luck she'd get up to fiddle with the radio station or water the plant. Once she started humming, I'd be able to talk freely.

"Remember my plan?" Piper said. "The one for getting back at Mindy?"

"Uh huh." I dutifully typed, "Plan for getting back at Mindy."

"Well, Brandon and I had to stop at Mike's office today to drop something off. Just a minute." She put the phone down. "No, no, honey. Not in the mouth." I heard the sounds of a skirmish and then Brandon's wail.

Across the room, Mrs. Kinkaid waved to get my attention and held up some change. She pointed to the door to indicate she was going out to the vending machine and mouthed, "Do you want anything?"

I shook my head.

Piper returned to the phone. "Here, have a graham cracker." I assumed she meant Brandon, not me. "OK, I'm back."

"I can talk now," I said. "Mrs. Kinkaid went for a candy bar."

"Good, and Brandon should be fine for a bit. Boy, has he been a stinker lately." She exhaled loudly. "So where were we? Oh, I remember. So, I'm at Mike's office waiting for him to be done with a client, and who walks into the reception area but this absolutely gorgeous guy. Tall, with dark wavy hair, and brown eyes you could drown in. I'm talking handsome, but not in a pretty-boy way, you know what I mean? And he was dressed smart casual. Not everybody can pull *that* off. So, I'm waiting and this guy sits down because he has an appointment to meet with Mike's partner and he's a little early and we start talking. And man, is he easy to talk to—charming and personable like you wouldn't believe."

I had a sudden funny feeling. I hoped this wasn't heading where it seemed to be heading.

"Before long, Ryan and I—that's his name, Ryan—are talking like old friends. He thought Brandon was really adorable, so I knew he was smart." She laughed. "And get this: I told him about Mindy and the wedding and the cake and everything, and he's totally on board for playing your fiancé."

"Oh, Piper," I said. "No. Please tell me you're kidding."

"Nope, I'm not kidding." She sounded downright gleeful.

"This is unbelievable."

"Oh, you better believe it." She was just winding up now. "And it gets better. This guy is loaded. He's a consultant for an international company and travels all over the world. And here's the topper—he lives right in your neighborhood, so you can tell everyone that's how you met."

My stomach lurched as if I were in the front seat of a roller coaster after it just made a sudden drop. "Piper, that plan was just talk. Like when we used to dream about hitchhiking to California and becoming movie stars? We both knew we were never going to go to Los Angeles. Planning it was as far as it was going to go." How could she have thought I'd actually go through with this? It was like some cheesy movie of the week. "I can't believe you asked some guy to do this."

"Lola, I know you're not that adventurous, but just let me finish. This guy is so cool, and he was totally sympathetic to your situation."

"He probably thinks I'm the biggest loser in the world. I'm embarrassed to even think about it."

"No, no, no," she said. "He understands. It turns out he has this older brother who started his own software company and is now a bajillionaire and owns his own jet. His parents think this brother is the second coming. No matter what Ryan does, he doesn't measure up. Trust me, he feels your pain."

I did have pain, that was true enough. In fact, it was worse now that I was having this conversation. "I can't go through with it," I said. "You need to talk to him, Piper, and call the whole thing off."

"What would you have me tell him?"

"Tell him it was a joke. Or say that you're delusional and don't actually have a friend. I don't care what you tell him, just make it go away."

"So you're OK with Mindy making a fool out of you at her wedding? You're fine with that now?"

"Of course not," I said. "But there has to be another way around it." I tried to think of a solution that didn't require subterfuge. "You know what? I'll just talk to my parents and explain my feelings. I'll have them ask her not to make a big to-do with the cake." Mindy would listen to them. Maybe.

"Sure, that would stop her," Piper said, not a little sarcastically. "She'll just switch gears. Hire a mariachi band to play 'Happy Birthday.' Or give you a male stripper for a gift when you're on the dance floor. She'll up the ante, just for spite."

There was some truth in what she was saying. Mindy wasn't known for giving up easily.

"Piper, I just don't think I can pull it off. The whole thing feels wrong."

"Lola, slow down. Take a few deep breaths and relax. You're already picturing being at the wedding. You're panicking prematurely." She knew me so well. "Here's a thought: why not just meet Ryan, have a few drinks, talk to him, and then decide. He's very nice. If you want, you can tell him I got the whole thing screwed up, that you were just joking. It wouldn't kill you to go out with him once. He's totally hot."

"How hot?"

"Mindy would *die* if she saw him with you. He's head-turning gorgeous—I'm not kidding. If I weren't already married, I'd go out with him in a minute."

Despite the alarm going off in my head, I was curious.

"How old would you say he is?"

"Early thirties, max. Never married, engaged once. He was the one who broke it off. It just didn't feel right."

"He told you that?"

"Sure, it's amazing what people will tell you if you just ask."

Wow, another fifteen minutes in Mike's waiting room and she probably would have found out this guy's social security number and the PIN to his ATM account. I mulled over everything Piper had said until her voice in my ear interrupted my thoughts. "Lola, are you still there?"

"Yes, I'm thinking." I moved the phone to the other side to give my neck a break. "OK, you know, you're right. It wouldn't kill me to meet him for coffee or drinks. I'll do it." When was the last time I'd had a date with a totally hot guy? As far back as never and even before that. "Give him my home number. No wait, give him my cell, that's better."

There was a long silence, but I knew we were still connected because I could hear Brandon babbling on the other end. "Piper? Did you hear what I just said?"

"I heard you," she said. "It's just that I already—"

I didn't catch the rest of the sentence because at that moment Mrs. Kinkaid burst through the door calling my name. "Lola, Lola, look who I found." She'd flung the door open so forcefully it ricocheted against the wall and bounced against her elbow. I looked up to see her pull a man into the room by his shirtsleeve. I caught the amused look on his face right before it registered that he was tall with dark, wavy hair and brown eyes you could drown in. And dressed smart casual. Not just anyone can pull that off.

13

Piper was still talking, though her words weren't registering. I said, "I have to go. I'll call you back later." I set the phone in its cradle and stood up. The dark-haired stranger broke free of Mrs. Kinkaid's grasp and crossed the room to my side of the desk. I stood up to greet him.

He held out a hand. "Hi, I'm Ryan Moriarty. Your friend Piper suggested I stop by."

He gripped my palm firmly and then did this really smooth thing. Without hesitating, he reached over with his free hand and clasped my forearm. The intimacy of the gesture made me breathless. He held it for one spine-tingling second before letting go.

Mrs. Kinkaid, who stood behind him, broke the silence. "I was trying to get my Kit Kat bar out of the machine, like I've done a million times. I put my money in, and the spiral thingy twisted around, but the candy bar didn't drop down—just hung there like it was caught on something." Both Ryan and I gave her our full attention. "I banged on the glass, but it just wouldn't budge. I was just about to go get the custodian when this gentleman here came along." She paused to take a breath and looked up at him admiringly. "He just took his fist and hit the side of the machine once, like Fonzie with the jukebox." Here she illustrated, swinging her arm with closed fingers. "And the Kit Kat bar practically jumped down."

"That was so nice of you," I said.

"It was nothing." He waved dismissively. "I like to be available for any and all vending machine emergencies." His grin made me feel like we shared an inside joke.

"I'll keep that in mind."

Mrs. Kinkaid moved closer, so that the top of her head aligned with his shoulder. "Then he says he's looking for Lola Watson, and I said, 'Lola's my boss. Come right this way.'"

I stared at her, amazed to hear her say I was the boss. If only Drew weren't out for the day. He could have used the news himself.

"Lola and I have a mutual friend," Ryan said to Mrs. Kinkaid. "And she thought Lola could help me with a problem I'm having." His smile revealed beautiful, perfect teeth. Nature doesn't give out those kind of teeth; only a highly skilled cosmetic dentist can. He turned his attention toward me. "I don't know what time you get off work, and I know this is last minute, but if you could join me for dinner, I'd be so grateful. I know it's a lot to ask."

It was the oddest experience—Ryan Moriarty was a stranger to me, and yet, as if in a dream, I felt as if we had an understanding. I glanced at my watch. "Our office hours are until six. Maybe I could meet you somewhere in an hour or so?"

"Oh, pish posh," Mrs. Kinkaid said. "Why don't you just go? I can handle things here and lock up when I leave."

I hesitated, looking around the office. I always thought of it as my domain, my own little corner of the universe. But looking at it now, it really wasn't much. Three desks, a mini-fridge, a few filing cabinets, and a large, leafy plant in the far corner.

The only windows were at ceiling level, revealing the shuffling feet of newspaper employees venturing outside for a smoke. Above us, one of the florescent bulbs stuttered.

"What do you say?" He held out a hand as if inviting me onto a dance floor.

"OK." I nodded. "Just let me shut down my computer and get my things together. It'll take a few minutes."

When he left to pull the car around, I busied myself locking desk drawers, turning off my computer, and checking my teeth in my compact mirror for remnants from lunch.

Mrs. Kinkaid chattered as I prepared to go. "My dear, that is one handsome man. When he came over to the machine and I looked up and saw him, I about died. It was like having James Bond come to my rescue. How do you know him again?"

"He's a friend of a friend." Funny how easily that came out. I snapped the compact shut and dropped it back into my purse.

"If I were you, I'd work on making him *your* friend. Or better yet, boyfriend. He's yummy. Can you imagine standing at the altar with him next to you?"

That was a leap. "I think you're getting ahead of yourself," I said. "We're just going out to dinner."

"That's how these things start," she said, a bit too smugly for my taste. I was glad when I was able to slip my purse strap over my shoulder and head out the door. The basement was starting to feel a bit confining.

* * *

Ryan's car, as promised, was right outside the front door. I stood inside the glassed-in entryway and had a sudden thought:

What if he was a rapist or a murderer? The fact that he had money and good looks didn't guarantee he wasn't a psychopath.

If anything happened to me, Mrs. Kinkaid would be a witness to the fact that I'd left with him. But would she remember his name? I doubted it, caught as she was on his good looks. Piper, on the other hand, knew his name. If indeed he'd given her his real name.

I looked at the car idling at the curb. Such a nice little car, all midnight blue and sporty-like. Didn't killers drive four-doors with tinted windows? This car didn't even have a trunk big enough to hold a body.

Finally I went to his window and told him I would take my own car and meet him at the agreed upon restaurant. After he pulled away, I called my house and left a message on my answering machine listing his license plate number along with a description of the vehicle. A little something the police could use if I turned up dead. A girl couldn't be too careful.

* * *

Half an hour later, we were looking at menus in a place called Sardino's. Our table was covered with a red-checked table-cloth; our waiter, Antonio, lit the candle in the Chianti bottle.

"I'm glad you like Italian," Ryan said. "This is one of my favorite places."

I looked around the dimly lit restaurant, the strains of recorded violin music playing in the background, a few tables occupied by couples leaning forward to speak to each other in whispers. The only thing missing was a round table with Lady and the Tramp slurping one shared strand of spaghetti. "I love

Italian food," I said. "I pass this place all the time, but I've never eaten here."

"I don't come very often," he said. "Each meal here means an extra two hours at the gym. But sometimes you've just got to live a little, you know?"

We ordered, and Ryan requested a bottle of a wine called Primivito. I'd never heard of it, but Antonio approved. "Very good, sir," he said before whisking away the menus.

There was a lull that made me uncomfortable. I wasn't ready to broach the subject of Piper's plan just yet, so I fell back on something my mother once told me regarding talking to men: cars and sports are usually safe subjects. I was at a distinct disadvantage due to profound ignorance of both topics (during a baseball game I once asked when it would be halftime), but I thought I'd wing it. "So," I said, "I couldn't help but notice your car. It's beautiful."

"Yes, it is nice. I've only had it about six months, and I still get a kick out of driving it."

"What is it, a Mustang?"

"Pardon me?" he asked, looking entertained. I noticed the creases at the corner of his eyes when he smiled.

"Your car—what kind is it?"

"It's a Jaguar."

"Oh." I'd heard of them, of course. I knew they were out of my league, but after that my knowledge base was pretty much depleted. "That dark blue color is really striking."

"It's indigo, actually."

Indigo I knew. It was the *I* in the color spectrum. I remembered from my school days that Newton divided the spectrum into seven named colors: red, orange, yellow, green, blue, indigo, and violet. Easy to remember because the first letters spelled out the name Roy G. Biv. I was about to blurt out this fact when thankfully Antonio arrived with the bottle of wine, saving me from my own geekiness. If only the waiter would pull up a chair and join us so I'd be saved from making future idiotic comments.

Luckily, Ryan seemed oblivious to my social awkwardness. He leaned over as if to tell me something in confidence and said, "You wouldn't believe how long it took to get the car from the dealer. They tried to get me to buy one off the lot, but I insisted on custom ordering everything. I figured if I was going to spend that kind of money, I should get what I wanted." For the next five minutes I let Ryan talk about his car, while I nodded and did my best to look attentive. But after the wine was poured, I decided to just come out and ask the question that was on my mind. "Piper says you live in my neighborhood?"

"Yes. Isn't it a small world?" He smiled again, displaying those beautiful teeth. "I'm over on King Street."

"Me too!" I felt my eyes widen in delight.

"Really?" He smiled. "That is a coincidence."

"What's your address?"

"Four-twenty-seven King Street."

My address was 424. I did some calculating. "Why, you must live right across the street from me. Next to Brother Jasper?"

"I don't know any of the neighbors," he said apologetically. "I travel more often than not, so I'm not there much."

A laser pointer went on inside my head. "I know you," I said, waving a finger in his direction. "I've heard the neighbors talk about you. You're the guy everyone wonders about. The buzz is that you're CIA or in the witness protection program or something."

Ryan gave me a startled look. "What?"

"Oh yes, I heard this from several of them. You're the talk of King Street. They call you the mystery man."

"Get out." He tilted his head like he was trying to decide if I was serious. "Really?"

I held up three fingers. "I swear—Girl Scout's honor." It had been awhile since I was a Girl Scout, and I wasn't sure if it was two fingers or three. For all I knew, I was swearing Boy Scout's honor.

He chuckled. "CIA? The witness protection program?"

I nodded, and he started to laugh unabashedly. A couple at an adjacent table stopped talking to look in our direction. Finally, after a few awkward moments, he picked up his linen napkin to dab his eyes. "They really say all that?" he said. "But I've only talked to the neighbors in passing, and I'm almost never home. I don't know what they'd base this on."

"Ah, but it's your absence that makes you mysterious. That and all the UPS packages and the fact that you never put out garbage. Very suspicious."

"I like to order things," he said. "Because I hate shopping. And I don't generate much trash since I'm not home much. I'll have one Hefty bag at most, so I just set it next to the bags at the curb of the blue house so the garbage men don't have to make an extra stop."

"No one sees you out and about much."

"I'm not invisible," he said. "Honestly, I do come and go, but like I said, I travel a lot. If I were home more, I'd probably see the neighbors when I shovel the driveway or mow the lawn, but I hire out for all that. It's easier."

I took a sip of my wine and gave Ryan a long look. Belinda, the dog woman, had told me the mystery man was movie-star handsome. She wasn't kidding.

Antonio delivered our chopped salads, and I proceeded to fill Ryan in on the neighbors. He knew about the college students on the corner and was familiar with Belinda's dogs. Crazy Myra's house he knew because of the garden gnomes, and he'd seen Brother Jasper having late-night smokes on his porch. Coincidentally, he'd taken tae kwon do lessons with Ben Cho's dad, but he wasn't aware they lived in the same neighborhood.

"I think it's great you know everyone," he said, stabbing a piece of feta cheese with his fork. "I've always found it difficult getting to know neighbors."

And I've always found if difficult warding them off. "Well, it's not like I have a choice," I said. "They loved my aunt—she's the one I inherited the house from—and that seems to have transferred over to me. I'm like their pet project. They're always checking up on me."

"You don't see that level of caring too much nowadays." He looked thoughtful. "So often people just come and go and don't interact with those around them. Having people look out for you, that's a gift."

"I guess."

"And you have such a wonderful friend. Piper just couldn't say enough nice things about you."

"Really?" Now the conversation was taking a better turn.

"Oh yes. She said you were smart and funny and a great friend. And that you were a great writer."

My jaw dropped; I was momentarily speechless.

He continued. "When she said you had a great personality, I thought maybe that was a nice way of saying you weren't good looking." He took a sip of wine before continuing. "But you're really pretty, so I guess she honestly meant you have a great personality."

"She actually said all those nice things?"

"Absolutely. We had quite the talk."

He said I was really pretty. I wondered if he meant exceptionally pretty, or just pretty considering he thought I might possibly have been ugly.

Antonio came to pour more wine, and then he took my salad plate away.

It was a shame to move from the topic of me being really pretty to the subject of the wedding, but it had to happen sometime. "I know Piper told you all about my sister's wedding."

"Yes, she did. I've already checked my schedule, and I'll be in town that weekend. I'm willing and able to be your fiancé." He gave me a two-fingered salute. "At your service, m'lady."

"See, that's the thing." I exhaled slowly. "When I had the original discussion with Piper, I was just venting. My sister Mindy had me so upset that Piper came up with this grand plan for revenge. At the time I went along with it because, frankly, I was in a bad place emotionally, if you want the truth of it." I shook my head at the thought. "And besides, I half thought Piper was joking. But now…" I drummed my fingers on the table and looked toward the back of the restaurant where the kitchen doors swung open like saloon shutters. Antonio came out carrying a large tray. Not our meal, though. Too many plates.

"Are you saying you don't want to go through with it?"

"I'm not so sure it's a good idea after all." I glanced at Ryan, who looked dismayed. "I'm sorry you went to all this trouble, coming to my office and now dinner and everything." He frowned slightly. I was shocked he was taking this so hard. "I'll pay for dinner, if that's the issue."

He leaned forward to move the candle to one side, and then he placed his hand over mine. His fingers were warm. "Could you do me an enormous favor?" He spoke through clenched teeth, his eyes darting to one side. "Just go along with whatever I say, OK?"

"What?" I started to turn to see what he was looking at.

"Don't look." He squeezed my fingers so hard I felt the bones meet. "Just play along. I'll explain later."

14

I looked up to see a tall blond standing over our table. "Hello there, Ryan." She said his name with a sneer, and her mouth held the shape. What she wore reminded me of a jogger in a Nike commercial: cropped aqua-colored athletic pants and a matching zippered jacket. Her hair was pulled back in a thick ponytail. Despite the fact that she wore no jewelry or makeup, she looked better than I ever had in my entire life.

"Tanya." He lifted his chin and smiled. "Imagine meeting you here."

"Imagine, my ass," she said. "I saw your car outside, you bastard. You haven't wasted any time finding a new one, have you? Whatever happened to not wanting a relationship because your job is so demanding?"

He let go of my hand, and I massaged my tender knuckles.

Tanya turned to me. "Did he order the Primivito and then tell you how beautiful your name is? Does he act like you're the center of the universe? That's how it starts, sister, but trust me, that's not how it ends."

I opened my mouth to speak, but then I thought better of it.

Ryan held up his hands. "Tanya, please." The tables surrounding us quieted in a ripple effect. "This isn't a good time or place. We can talk later. I'll call you."

"Sure, we can talk." She opened and closed her hand, like a puppet mouthing words. "You're good at talking, but not much else." She had the wild-eyed look of a woman who hadn't renewed her prescription.

"Tanya." Now Ryan looked serious. "That is really hurtful."

"He's a liar, too." She stuck her finger so close to his face I thought she might puncture his eyeball. I caught a whiff of her musk perfume when she turned her head in my direction. A heavy, serious scent. "He says he's an international consultant. Ha! I checked with the companies he supposedly works for and none of them have even heard of him. And his stories about his family? They don't check out at all. The Jag doesn't even belong to him—it's leased. He's all lies and promises and nothing else."

I touched Ryan's sleeve. "You know, I can just go home. We can get together another time."

Ryan shook his head and stood up abruptly, his chair scraping against the tile flooring. "That's enough, Tanya," he said evenly, and then he put an arm around her shoulder. I thought she might shake him off, but instead his touch seemed to relax her. As he guided her toward the front of the restaurant, I saw him speaking to her in hushed tones, and she responded with a limp nod. The transformation was amazing. It was like he was the Jilted-Girlfriend Whisperer.

While he was gone, I ruminated on the trend of seemingly intelligent men entering into relationships with women from hell. I'd spotted Kelly's shortcomings right from the start, but Hubert fell hard for her glib talk and cosmetically enhanced beauty. And now Ryan, suave and educated, was somehow connected with this Tanya, whose mental health history was practically written across her forehead. It would be interesting to hear his side of the story.

By the time he returned, I'd devoured a breadstick and polished off another glass of wine. The alcohol was working its magic—now I saw the dining room through the rosy haze of semi-tipsiness. The sound of Dean Martin singing "That's Amore" was a perfect accompaniment to the smell of tomato sauce and garlic.

"I apologize," Ryan said, sliding into his chair. "I know that didn't look good. I hope you don't hold it against me."

"She seemed a little unstable," I said.

"You could say that." I watched his face as he spoke and thought about the expression "easy on the eyes." Watching a good-looking person is such a pleasure. Shallow, I know, but there's a reason gorgeous models and actors get the big bucks while the rest of us schlubs struggle every day with face creams and control-top pantyhose and ultra-whitening Crest—always hoping small measures will make a difference. Right on cue, Ryan smiled; I could have sworn I saw a glint off his dazzling teeth. "I met Tanya at my health club, and we only went out a few times. I could tell it wasn't going to work out, and she seemed agreeable when I explained. I thought we were good." He took a sip of his wine. "I'm sorry you had to see that. And I'm *really* sorry to have kept you waiting."

I brushed the breadcrumbs off the table onto my hand and then held them indecisively for a moment before dropping them under the table onto the floor. "Not a problem. I've been fine here."

"Tanya's a really good person," he said. "But kind of needy. She never understood how demanding my job is. When you travel three weeks out of four, there's not time for much of a relationship."

"Ahh," I said in sympathy. Gone three weeks out of four? No wonder the neighbors never saw him. "So where do you go on your business trips?"

"Anywhere and everywhere." He looked upward for a moment as if recalling. "It varies—Bangkok, Sri Lanka, Bangalore. Recently I've been to Eastern Europe and South America. The companies that hire me are international, so I go wherever they need me. And most of what I do is troubleshooting, so all my work is confidential." Reading between the lines, he was addressing Tanya's accusation. "Most companies don't like to admit when they have to call in my kind of help."

I wasn't sure what he was talking about, but he was easy on the corneas and a joy to listen to. He had the smooth voice of an anchorman or radio announcer, and I was willing to bet he could really sing. A beautiful baritone voice, if I had to guess. I looked at his mouth and tried to imagine him singing "Happy Birthday" to me during a private celebration.

Luckily for me, Antonio delivered our dinner before I could start drooling. We'd both ordered the same thing: angel hair pasta tossed in butter and topped with shrimp and vegetables. It was delicious. I'd only had an apple and yogurt for lunch. This meal filled a void I hadn't even realized existed.

Ryan was an attentive listener. He asked question after question about my childhood, my parents, my sister. We were on our second bottle of wine, so I was more of a blabbermouth than usual. Mindy in particular seemed to fascinate him, maybe because he saw similarities with his older brother.

"She really pretended to be you at the gynecologist?" he asked, fascinated. "How did she pull that off?"

I felt my cheeks redden. Up until now I'd only shared that story with Piper. I hadn't even told Hubert.

"I mean," Ryan said quickly, "she must be good at pretense. Most people can't lie convincingly."

"Mindy doesn't think of it as lying. Once she says something, it becomes the truth for her. She'd probably even pass a lie detector test." I speared a piece of shrimp and popped it in my mouth.

"Hmm." He tapped his index finger on the table and looked thoughtful. "Has she always been this way?"

"Always. When she wants something, she goes after it. And she never gives up, no matter what it takes." I shook my head. Why was life a competition for her? I'd always wanted to have a sister who was a friend. I grew up watching *Little House on the Prairie* reruns and envisioned Mindy as Laura and myself as Mary, her older sister. Before Mary went blind, of course. The two of us would weather all kinds of calamities, from natural disasters to sisterly quarrels, and only become closer in the end. I'd watched the shows where Pa played the fiddle and the girls danced in their little house, and I was jealous of their closeness. Our father had a harmonica, but the only song he knew was "Michael, Row Your Boat Ashore." Listening to him play was a special kind of torture. Nope, we weren't the Ingalls. Or the Waltons either, but maybe *that* was a blessing in disguise—all those people in one house and only one bathroom. I don't care how much love there is in your family, if you can't pee when you want to, your quality of life is pretty poor.

Ryan broke into my thoughts. "And what does Mindy do for a living?"

"Her degree is in business." I twisted some pasta around my fork. "Like the world really needed another business major. She speaks French and Spanish fluently, so she was talking about doing translations for the UN or something, but her fiancé Chad would never leave Wisconsin. For now, she's processing mortgage applications." I made a face to indicate what I thought of that, and Ryan grinned. "Someone's got to do it, I guess."

"I guess," he agreed.

When we were done with dinner, Ryan suggested coffee and dessert. He said the tiramisu was to die for, and after a few delicious bites, I agreed. Of course, in my slightly inebriated state I might have agreed to anything.

We finished our dessert and lingered over coffee. Ryan told me about the best coffee he'd had recently—in Panama, of course. "I brought home the type they don't even export," he said. "They usually keep the best for themselves." That led to a discussion of restaurant customs around the world. When he spoke he looked right into my eyes, and when I talked he seemed to find my opinions enthralling. Not that I had much to contribute to a discussion of global cuisine.

Antonio had refilled my decaf for the fourth time when I noticed we were the last table in the restaurant. "Oh my, what time do you close?" I glanced at my watch.

"We closed at *nine*, but the bar is open until eleven." He motioned in the direction of the lounge. I got the distinct impression he wouldn't mind if we vacated the table.

"Would you like an after-dinner drink?" Ryan asked.

"Oh no, I have work tomorrow. I really should get home."

Antonio presented us with the check. I went for my wallet to pay my own way, but Ryan waved away my offer. He pulled out a thick wad of fresh bills, peeled off a few, and left them on the table.

When we walked out to the parking lot, I felt the wine I'd

consumed go straight to my head. "I think I had a little too much to drink," I said, trying to keep my eyes focused. Ryan regarded me with concern. "I don't normally have more than one or two."

"Why don't you let me drive you home?" He put a brotherly hand on my shoulder. "It's not too far out of my way." A joke, I thought.

"Well." I looked at my car and hesitated.

"I can tell the restaurant we're leaving your car overnight, and I'll drive you here in the morning to pick it up."

"Oh no," I said, my mind clearing. "I have a friend staying with me. He can drop me off tomorrow." And that's when it hit me: *I'd never told Hubert I was going out after work.* I was so used to living alone, so used to never accounting to anyone, that it had never even occurred to me to give him a call. My cell phone, the only way he could have reached me, had been off all evening. I thought guiltily of his cheery send-off that morning— "See you at dinner!"—and hoped he hadn't gone to the trouble of cooking. I would have called him right then, except it would have been a little like getting out the fire extinguisher after the shed had already burned to the ground.

No, it would be better to wait twenty minutes and explain in person. Even if I was a teeny bit wasted.

15

The inside of Ryan's car smelled like leather and something else—a pleasing scent. It wasn't like what you get from having a cardboard pine tree hanging off your rearview mirror—more like cinnamon potpourri. I didn't see the source of the smell, which made me wonder if luxury cars came with their own air-freshening system.

Despite the ease of our dinnertime chatter, I found myself silent during the ride home, content to look out the window at the office buildings and strip malls on the way to our neighborhood. I hadn't been a passenger in a car for a long time, and it felt good to sit back and let someone else navigate lane changes and watch for merging traffic.

Ryan had the radio set to Milwaukee's cool jazz station. Out of the corner of my eye, I noticed the fingers on his right hand tapping the beat on the steering wheel. The saxophone riff put me in mind of Lisa Simpson. I almost said as much, but then I decided against it. It's one thing to be a rube, another entirely to advertise it.

When we pulled up to the curb in front of my house, I was surprised to see that the lights were on and there was movement behind the closed drapes. It looked like the scene the burglars saw in *Home Alone*, when the kid rigged up mannequins and cardboard cutouts to give the house a party look. Who the hell was in my house? Would Hubert have invited his poker buddies over without checking with me first?

"Looks like your friend has guests," Ryan said. I made a move to open my door, but he squeezed my arm to stop me. "I'll get it," he said and exited the car, only to appear on my side. Such an odd, old-fashioned courtesy, but one I could get used to. He slammed my door shut and motioned toward my front door. "Is everything OK?"

"I think it's fine, thanks." I squinted at the house. My first impression was correct—there were flickers of movement inside, like moths inside a lampshade. It wasn't just Hubert in there, by the looks of it. A window must have been slightly open, because I could hear the hum of conversation and what sounded like a dog whining.

"All right then. This was fun. I'll give you a call, and we can work out some details before the wedding."

The wedding? Oh shoot, hadn't I made it clear I'd chickened out on the fake engagement? I couldn't really remember how I worded it, but I knew the issue had come up at dinner. I cleared my throat and stood, fuzzy-headed, for a second. I was torn between wanting to clear things up right away and needing to head inside and find out what was going on with Hubert.

"Maybe we could do dinner and a movie later in the week?" His tone was so sweet, so tentative, like he wasn't sure I'd want to go out with him. I found that so appealing.

"I'd love to," I said.

"Great." The corners of his eyes crinkled when he smiled. He leaned over and gave me a quick embrace, and then he pulled away to look at me and leaned in for another hug. A European good-bye without the cheek kissing. "I'll just see you safely to the door, and then I'll be on my way."

I thought of Hubert and company possibly seeing Ryan and me from the front window and felt as self-conscious as a teenager on her first date. I motioned to the house. "That's sweet of you, but I can take it from here."

"OK then." He nodded approvingly. "Goodnight, Lola."

I liked the way he said my name—drawing out the two syllables—Lo-la. If life were a Barry Manilow CD, he would have burst into song just then. *Her name was Lola, she was a showgirl...*

I headed up the walkway and heard Ryan whistling as he got back inside the Jag. I paused on the porch to wave. He waved back before pulling away from the curb. Oh, I did hope I'd see him again, and not just around the neighborhood. I thought back over the last several hours. Conversationally I'd held my own pretty well, and he *had* laughed at my jokes. Always a good sign. If only I hadn't had too much to drink. But maybe he found my low tolerance for alcohol to be a charming quirk rather than a character flaw? I could only hope.

As I approached my front door and turned the knob, I could hear a murmur of voices, which only got more distinct when I entered the small foyer. I dropped my purse inside the front closet and walked into the living room. The group didn't notice me at first, but I saw them clearly enough. Hubert stood with his back to me. Seated on my couch were Crazy Myra, Brother Jasper, and Ben Cho. Belinda, with her husky dog at her side, stood in front of my wing chair. I had a sudden sick feeling that the neighborhood watch committee now met at my house.

The dog spotted me at the exact moment I saw him. He got up and scrambled past Hubert to assault my crotch with his nose.

"Lola's here," Brother Jasper said, rising to his feet. "Oh thank the Lord. What a relief."

I pushed the dog away just as Hubert turned around. His face had a troubled look that melted into joy when he realized it was me. "Lola, thank God," he said, giving me a hug that nearly lifted me off my feet. He had such a tight hold on me that my nose and mouth pressed into his chest, making it hard to breathe. He pulled away to look at my face. "Where were you? I've been so worried."

The others gathered around him, asking the same question and nodding in agreement. Belinda patted the big dog's head and murmured, "Good boy, Roger. Good boy."

He was worried about me?

"Oh no," I said. "I'm sorry. I just went out after work. Something came up at the last minute." I looked at their faces and realized my words weren't working. "I got so caught up in what I was doing, I completely forgot to call."

Hubert dropped his hands to his side. "You forgot to call?" He turned to the group. "She says she forgot to call." I'd never seen him so aggravated. The way he clenched his fists made him look downright angry. I tried to think of the right way to apologize, but I was distracted by the pulsating of his Adam's apple.

"I know I should have, but honestly I forgot you were staying here. I know that sounds terrible, but I'm used to coming and going on my own."

"But you did call, Lola. You left me a message."

He looked so sure, but I knew it wasn't true. "I should have called," I repeated. "I'm really sorry. I just—"

Hubert held up a hand to stop me, and then he leaned over the end table and hit the button on the answering machine. I heard my own voice. "Hi, this is Lola. He's driving a dark blue car, two doors, I think it's a Mustang. License plate number MOR-007." Then there was a long pause. "He's about six foot two, with dark hair and brown eyes. He said his name was Ryan." Even to my ears it sounded like I was reporting a crime.

When the machine shut off, there was a silence a person could slice with a knife. Hubert spoke up. "What does that mean, Lola?"

"I was just..." I pressed my hands to my cheeks for a moment, trying to fend off the embarrassment of a red face. My neighbors stood looking for an explanation; Ben Cho cleared his throat and shifted his weight. I blurted out the story. "I went out to dinner with someone Piper knows, but since I didn't know him I thought it might be a good idea to take down his license plate and description. Just in case." It sounded lame. The dog cocked his head as if weighing my logic.

"But I called Piper, and she had no idea where you were," Hubert said. "All she could tell me was that you hung up rather abruptly when she was talking to you at work, which I found really troubling. And then I called your parents, and they didn't know anything, but they weren't worried at all. 'She'll turn up eventually,' your mom said." He looked disgusted. "After that, I drove back and forth between here and your office six times looking for you. I knocked on doors in the neighborhood to see if anyone had any idea where you might be. No one had a clue, but at least they cared enough to drop everything and come help me out. I thought you were kidnapped, or in some kind of accident. And the police wouldn't do anything because not enough time had gone by."

"You called the *police*?" Talk about overreacting. Next he would have had my photo on a milk carton. "Why would you do that?"

"I thought something terrible happened. I thought you were *dead*." His voice reminded me of my mother at her most irrational.

"Don't be ridiculous! Of course I wasn't dead. I was just out on a date." I knew as soon as I said it that it was the wrong response. I saw the look on Hubert's face and knew I'd been too flippant, but there was no turning back. He threw up his hands and walked out of the room. Stormed out, actually, his shoes making more noise than necessary on the hardwood floor. I didn't miss his point.

"Well," Brother Jasper said, addressing the others, "since Lola is safe and sound, I guess we can all return home." He smiled in my direction. "I'm very glad you're back and it was just a false alarm." Then he leaned forward and whispered in my ear, "Hubert was sick with worry. He really cares about you."

I nodded. Like a flight attendant, I stood by the doorway while the group shuffled out. "Thanks for your concern," I said to Myra, who just grunted. Brother Jasper and Ben Cho each gave me a smile as they passed. "I'm sorry for the mix-up," I said as Belinda passed over the threshold. She stopped to hand me a sock, one of my own. From the dirty laundry hamper, judging by the smell of it.

"We were going to have Roger try to track you if you weren't back by midnight. I really think he could have done it, too. Did you see how he shot right over to you as soon as you came in the door? I was so impressed. He's got some blood-hound in him, I'm sure of it."

I smiled weakly. "Thanks for coming, Belinda." I didn't really mean it, but it came out automatically, like putting a napkin on my lap at dinnertime.

"Oh," she said, "my pleasure. I wouldn't have missed it for the world."

I closed the door and locked it, and then I clicked the dead-bolt for extra protection. I pulled the curtain back and found the open window, and then I closed that as well. What was Hubert thinking, letting them all in? And why had he gone so berserk? I knew my message on the answering machine sounded odd, but really—the police? And even if he was worried, I didn't under-stand the advantage of having the neighbors over. Their butts sitting on my couch didn't speed up my homecoming. If anyone should be irritated, it was me.

I'd heard him go upstairs, and even now I could hear him walking around in his room. Later, after he'd cooled down, I'd apologize and we could sort it out. I suspected he was still reel-ing from his breakup with Kelly and this was just a symptom.

I went to straighten up the newspapers and magazines on my coffee table and came across two photos from my distant past. Hubert's—they had to be. One was my senior picture from high school; the other was a four-by-six of Piper, Hubert, and me taken the year we all graduated from college. Well, actu-ally Piper had graduated a semester early, but it was the sum-mer after our graduations, anyway. Piper and I were on either side of a Hubert sandwich—he had an arm around each of our shoulders. All three of us were grinning. My hair was really shiny that day, I noticed. I looked on the back side of the pic-tures; neither one was dated. The group shot had our names printed neatly on the other side. On the back of my senior photo

I'd written, "To Hubert, the best friend anyone could ever have. Love, Lola." My handwriting hadn't improved since then.

I glanced down at the coffee table again and spotted an index card on top of the magazine pile. I picked it up and turned it over to see this: "Lola Jane Watson, Height 5'5", Weight 118 pounds, brown hair, hazel eyes," in Hubert's handwriting. Oh. He'd really thought I was missing and cared enough to write down my description.

I was touched by his concern. I was also touched by the fact that he gave me an extra inch and lopped off twelve pounds.

But mostly I was moved that Hubert had gone to so much trouble. He'd really been worried that I'd been abducted or killed. My own parents hadn't been alarmed, but Hubert, old buddy Hubert, had knocked on doors and driven the streets searching for me. I thought back to what Ryan had said in the restaurant: *Having people look out for you, that's a gift.* He was right—it *was* a gift, especially when I thought of the alternative, which was having no one care at all.

I went upstairs to apologize, but Hubert's door was closed and all was quiet. I whispered, "Hubert?" but there was no response. I stood outside his door for a few minutes, giving him a chance to answer, before I gave up.

Later, after taking a shower and climbing into bed, I regarded the whole situation in a better light. Hubert was just being Hubert, looking out for me like he always used to. That's how we met, in fact, when we were in seventh grade. Three older girls had been harassing me every day on the way home from school. They taunted me, threw pebbles at my back, and just generally made my life miserable. Why me? I never knew. Maybe it was simply because I was a grade younger, or smaller, or walked home in their direction. Who knows what sets off bullies? I tried taking different routes, hanging out at school a little longer, or dashing out the moment the bell rang. It didn't seem to matter—they always found me. And by trying to avoid them, I made it a game.

One day they moved in for the kill, cornering me in the back of the school by the dumpsters. They didn't seem to want anything—just to see me squirm.

"You think you're so great," the leader of the group said, pushing me so hard that my head slammed against the brick wall. Christina Olson was her name. All the girls in seventh grade knew to avoid her.

One of her friends said, "We saw you giving us the bird, you little bitch. We're gonna teach you a lesson. Your ass will be grass."

I did not, in fact, know exactly what they meant by the bird. I also wasn't sure how my ass could actually become grass, but I thought it was safest to say nothing. They had me blocked in now. The three of them pressed against me while I had my back against the school building. I looked around, hoping the janitor might bring out some trash and I'd be saved. Near my feet was a small pile of refuse that had missed the dumpster, a rotting banana and some wadded-up wax paper.

The third girl noticed the way my eyes darted toward the school door and said, "Don't bother looking for help." She dug her fingernails into my shoulder, and I cried out in pain. "No one is going to come."

She was wrong, though, because suddenly the new kid in school was standing behind them saying, "Stop it," in a clear, loud voice. He was in one of my classes, but all I knew about him was that his name was Hubert. The three girls turned their attention away from me to look at him.

Christina sized him up and decided he wasn't a threat. "Just go away, you," she said, making a shooing motion. "This is none of your business." The one who'd squeezed my shoulder made a derisive snort.

"No," he said, standing like he wasn't going anywhere. "Just leave her alone."

"Look," Christina said impatiently, "this is between us girls. It has nothing to do with you. Just go away and let us settle this."

"No, *you're* the ones who need to go. Leave her alone."

Christina drew herself up to her full height and took a step toward him. She was older, but Hubert was a good six inches taller. Even from my spot in the lion's mouth I thought her brave. "And who's going to make us? There's three of us and only one of you."

I heard the click before I saw the glint of metal. Christina took a step back—she was as shocked as I was by the switch-blade in Hubert's hand. He held it up like it was a sword. All wrong, I knew. I'd seen *West Side Story* and knew switchblades were supposed to be aimed directly at a person like you're going to carve your initials on their gut. Christina and her friends didn't seem to notice his handling faux pas, though. One of the girls let out a gasp.

Christina recovered quickly. She shrugged and said, "Come on, girls, let's go." She pointed at me like aiming a gun. "She's not worth our time." Once they rounded the corner of the build-ing, I exhaled in relief. Hubert snapped his switchblade shut and offered to walk me home. On the way to my house, he told me the story of the switchblade. Over the summer he'd mowed a neighbor's lawn just to be nice, and in return the old man gave him an old toolbox filled with odds and ends. The switchblade had been among the wrenches and needle-nose pliers. Hubert liked carrying it with him. "But I never thought I'd use it to save someone's life," he said. "That's way cool!" He sounded so tickled I resisted the urge to remind him they were only a group of girls. And he hadn't actually used it.

After that, Hubert walked me home every day. Christina and company eventually found another target, a boy with a lisp. His nightmare ended only when his mother started driving him home from school. I'm not sure who they picked on after that, but I know it wasn't me.

For a long time the smell of rotting bananas reminded me of a switchblade and Hubert standing tall, but I hadn't thought about that day for a long time now. I could clearly remember the determined look on his face when he said, "Leave her alone." Seventeen years had passed, and we'd had a few disagreements since then, but I'd never seen Hubert really angry with anyone, let alone me. I'd be lying if I said it didn't bother me.

Thinking about this now, I shifted beneath my comforter, waiting for the pull of sleep to move me to unconsciousness, but it was no use. I was wide awake.

I got up and padded down the dark hallway to Hubert's room. The door was still closed. I rapped on it lightly. "Hubert?" Again, this time louder. "Hubert?" No answer. I debated going back to bed and talking to him in the morning, but we both had work, and there was the pesky matter of my car still parked at Sardino's. And more importantly, I couldn't sleep knowing he was still angry with me.

I opened the door and peered into the room. The venetian blinds on the opposite window let in slits of light from the street lamp below. Once my eyes adjusted, I could see his form on the bed, a blanket covering his body. He was face up, like a mummy in a sarcophagus. I tried again. "Hubert?"

"Yes, Lola." He let out an exasperated sigh.

He *was* awake—and still upset with me. I sat on the edge of the bed like a parent about to tell a bedtime story. He'd been at my house for three days, and his bedding still smelled like fabric softener. "I couldn't sleep. I hate that you're mad at me."

He didn't say anything, just sighed again and pulled his hands out from under the covers. I thought he might touch me, but instead he folded his hands as if in prayer. "You have no idea how worried I was," he said. "I was out of my mind thinking something terrible happened to you."

"I know. I'm sorry."

"It didn't help that you came waltzing in from your date with a buzz on, not even caring how I felt."

"I do care. I just—"

"I couldn't bear it if anything happened to you, Lola."

"You mean, because of Kelly."

He lifted his head to look at me. "What would Kelly have to do with it?"

"I just thought…" I knew I had to phrase this carefully. "Since you two aren't together anymore, maybe your friends are more important now."

"How can you say that? You've always been important to me. That didn't change when I moved in with Kelly." He rested his head back against the pillow.

"No offense, Hubert, but until recently I hadn't even seen you for months. I kind of wondered if we were even still friends."

"Well, of course we're still friends," he said indignantly. "We'll always be friends. I just didn't see you much because, well frankly, Kelly had something against you. I'm not sure what. She hated when we talked on the phone and she heard me laughing. She hated all our joking around—she said you were trying to make her feel like an outsider. Kelly didn't really understand how it is with old friends, so I tried to keep things separate. It didn't help that my mom was always asking about you."

"Really? How's your mom doing?" I'd always liked her. She was the type of mom who put a hand on your forehead when you looked peaked. When we hung out at Hubert's house during our high school years, she always kept the rec room fridge stocked with Dr. Pepper and brought us homemade cookies on a silver tray. Mrs. Holmes was friendly to both Piper and me, but I always felt like I was her favorite. She still sent cards on my birthday.

"She's good. Real good. Last time I saw her, she said to say hello."

"Tell her I said hi back."

"You could stop in and see my folks sometime, you know. They'd like that."

"Maybe I will." A nice thought, but I knew I wouldn't do it. My place in the Holmes' house was a thing of the past. I used to ride there on my bike and knew I was always welcome for dinner. But that was then. Visiting at this point in my life, without Hubert, would just be weird. "Anyway, Hubert, it's late and we should probably both get some sleep. I just wanted to tell you how sorry I am."

He looked up at the ceiling. "So what's the story with the guy you were out with? Anyone I know?"

"No, he's someone Piper met at Mike's work. A client. His name is Ryan Moriarty."

He propped himself up on one elbow. "He's a *client* of Mike's firm? What are they having, some kind of deal—invest with us and get a date?"

It sounded like a joke, but there was *something* underneath the kidding. I just couldn't put my finger on it. "No, he's just a nice guy. Piper organized the whole thing. She thought he could be my date at Mindy's wedding, so I wouldn't have to show up alone and pathetic. I wasn't so sure about the whole thing, but she practically begged me to go out with him. You know how she can be."

"She's persuasive, all right. But you know, Lola," and here he stretched out my name like taffy, "I'd be glad to be your escort at the wedding. There's no reason you'd have to go alone."

"That's good to know. I'll keep it in mind."

We were both silent for a minute, and he patted me absent-mindedly on the leg. Self-consciously I shifted on the bed. "So are you still mad at me?" I asked.

"Well, a little," he said. "For God's sake, Lola, I was insane not being able to find you. Then all the neighbors came over, which was very nice of them. Monday is Myra's favorite TV night, you know. She looks forward to it, but she gave it up when she thought you were in trouble. Then in you come, all loopy-doopy from your date and acting like I was making a big deal out of nothing." He exhaled. "Yes, I am a little angry."

Well, when he put it that way...

"I understand," I said. "How about we make a deal? You forgive me for tonight, and I'll forgive you for ignoring me during your Kelly period. Then we'll be even and we can put it all behind us and start fresh tomorrow. No grudges."

He considered it. "I can live with that. OK, it's a deal. I forgive you."

Relieved, I leaned over and kissed his forehead. "I forgive you too. And I promise to let you know where I am from now on." I stood up and looked down on him.

"That would be good."

I made my way to the door and was about to leave when I had another thought. "Hubert, my car is still at the restaurant. Sardino's, right off of the highway on Cedar Road. Do you think you could drop me off on your way to work tomorrow?"

"No problem. Good night, Lola. Sweet dreams."

"Good night, Hubert."

16

As the week went on, Hubert and I fell into a morning routine. I was never sure what time he woke up, but by the time I came downstairs, coffee was made, breakfast was underway, and the daily newspaper was next to my place at the table. For my part, I gratefully ate whatever he prepared and took care of the dishes afterwards. A small price to pay.

The first time he did this, I marveled at all the trouble he'd gone to, making an omelet with sautéed onions and mushrooms, topped with a sprinkling of shredded cheese and chunky salsa. He'd toasted whole wheat bread and cut it into little triangles, artfully arranging them around the edges of the plate.

"Can't run an engine without fuel," he said, pouring my coffee with a flourish. "Breakfast is the most important meal of the day."

I'd always heard that but never quite believed it. Previously, my engine had run just fine on cereal and milk. Still, I couldn't deny his way seemed better. Especially since he was the one doing all the work.

At the office Mrs. Kinkaid asked me for details about Ryan on a daily basis, but I'd learned my lesson and wasn't giving up much. Poor Drew had to hear the story of the vending machine more than once, how Ryan hit it with the side of his fist, disengaging the candy bar. Her version of the story made Ryan sound downright heroic. He was the man of the hour, a liberator of snack food. "And boy, was he easy on the eyes," she exclaimed every time. Drew looked less than interested. He'd shown up for work on Tuesday, entirely forgetting he'd called in sick the day before. When Mrs. K. asked if he was feeling better, the question puzzled him. Later he let it slip that he'd been up north hiking with his girlfriend. After he realized his error, he changed the hiking story to a different day and dove into a fit of coughing to illustrate he wasn't completely recovered. I gave him a cough drop.

On Thursday morning Piper called at her usual time—another new routine. She'd phoned me at the office every day since my outing with Ryan, always midmorning, when Brandon took what she called his mini-nap. It only lasted twenty to thirty minutes, but it was amazing, she said, how much a person could accomplish in that time. "I just hung a butt-load of laundry," she said on one occasion. All this and she managed to talk to me too. I imagined her working with the phone wedged between her head and shoulder. Babies are the reason women are experts at multitasking. I'm sure of it.

This morning she asked again, "Have you heard from Ryan?"

I glanced over to the other side of the room where Mrs. Kinkaid and Drew were debating the outcome of some reality show involving an island or maybe a boardroom. Someplace where people got cast out, anyway. "No, he hasn't called. I told you I'd let you know first thing."

"But he said for sure he'd call, right?"

"We've been over this, Piper. He said later in the week, but I'm not holding my breath. If he calls, he calls." As much as I hoped I'd hear from him, I also dreaded hearing from him. If he didn't call, the whole Mindy's wedding plan could be laid to rest. I was OK with letting it go; I knew the drill. She'd humiliate me, I'd pretend to let it roll off my back, and eventually the whole thing would fade to black. Until the next time. I was used to it, almost. If she had to be top dog, I could be a big enough person to let her— "big enough person" being the key phrase here, seeing as how Mindy prided herself on her petite size.

"I think he will call," Piper said, as if reaching a decision. "I just have this feeling. A guy doesn't spend hours talking in a restaurant if he's not interested. If you bored the hell out of him, he could have cut it short instead of ordering dessert and coffee. And after all that, he offered to drive you home. That was really gentlemanly."

Ahem. Well, it may have been that he didn't want the liability of a drunk driver on his hands, but her take on it sounded better.

She continued enthusiastically. "And that double hug thing sounded cool. Hey, I have a thought. Why don't you make up some kind of excuse and go over to his house?"

It was just the sort of thing Piper would have done in her single days, and she'd have been able to pull it off perfectly. For me, though, it was not a good idea. "I'm not going to be doing that." I shuffled through some paperwork to give my coworkers the illusion of workplace busyness.

"You could say," she went on, as if I hadn't voiced an objection, "that you thought you left something in his car. Your sunglasses! That would be perfect. I'm always losing my sunglasses. Just go ask. What could it hurt? At best it will give him a chance to ask you out again. At worst he'll say no he hasn't seen them, and then you say thanks and go back home. No harm, no foul."

"I can tell you right now—not going to happen."

"Oh, Lola, live a little. Just promise me you'll think about it, OK?"

Classic Piper. In an effort to persuade, she always tried going in the front and then the back. And if that didn't work, she'd come at you from the side. "I'll think about it, but it goes against my nature, Piper. If he wants to call, he will. You gave him my number, and he knows where I live. And where I work. It's not like he can't reach me."

"Oh pooh, you're no fun. Hey, I hear Brandon over the intercom. I have to go. Call me as soon as you hear from Mr. Smoking-Hot, OK?"

"Will do." I hung up the phone and was startled to see Drew standing over my desk. "Yes?"

"There's some dude wants to talk to you on line two."

"OK. Thank you." I started to reach for the phone and then stopped to return Drew's stare. He got the hint and shuffled back to his desk. Honestly. I cleared my throat and put the receiver up to my ear. "Lola Watson speaking."

"Hey, Lola."

Oh drat, I'd hoped it might be Ryan. What a letdown. "Hi, Hubert."

"Is this a good time?"

"It's fine." I glanced across the room, where Mrs. Kinkaid and Drew were both uncharacteristically silent. I knew they were hanging on my every word.

"Because if it's not good, I can call back."

"No, this is fine."

"OK, as long as I'm not interrupting anything."

"What's up, Hubert?"

"I was wondering if you'd go to this thing with me on Saturday night?" I heard him gulp. "It's a show I want to go to. I've heard good things about it. We could go out to dinner before or after, if you want."

I knew without looking that my social calendar was wide open. And I hadn't been out to hear a band in eons. If Ryan called in the meantime, I just wouldn't be available. That's what you get when you wait too long to call a popular girl like me. "OK, sounds good."

"So you can make it? That's great! It's kind of a dress-up thing, just so you know. They're serving wine and cheese."

Wine and cheese? Wait a minute. I switched the phone to my other ear and leaned over to fake looking through my lower desk drawer. "Hubert. Is this by any chance a show at an *art* gallery?"

He hesitated and then said, "The Michaels Gallery, downtown."

"Let me guess. Kelly is having an exhibit."

"Not just Kelly," he said defensively. "A lot of artists, and I know most of them, too."

"Hubert, I'm telling you as a friend, this is a very bad idea."

The silence on his end was heartbreaking.

"She hasn't answered your messages. If she wanted to talk to you, you'd have heard from her. You need to just let it go."

"I can't let it go," he said quietly. "I have to see her. I can't rest until I understand what happened."

I paused to think of a good way to put this. "You know, Hubert," I said, "you might never fully understand what happened. It seems like Kelly just wants a clean break."

"Please, Lola, just come with me on Saturday night. I don't want to have to do this alone."

I looked up to see both Drew and Mrs. Kinkaid staring straight at me. I guess it didn't take much to figure things out from my end of the conversation. Mrs. K. had her head tipped to one side in sympathy. She'd never met Hubert, but even through the phone she appeared to sense his sadness and desperation.

I sighed. "OK, I'll go with you. But I can't see any way this will turn out to be a good thing."

"Oh thank you, Lola, you're the best. And just think, if this leads to Kelly and me getting back together, I'll be moving out and you'll get your privacy back."

"Oh, Hubert, don't even worry about that. You're welcome to stay as long as you want."

He made a strange sound in his throat. "Well, thanks. I have to go now, Lola. My kids are coming back in from recess. I hear them out in the hall. I'll see you tonight, OK?"

I hung up the phone and saw Mrs. Kinkaid and Drew were still gazing in my direction. "What?" I said, a little more sharply than I'd intended.

They exchanged a look, and then Drew spoke. "That was your friend, Hube?"

"Hubert," I corrected.

"He's the one who got booted out by his girlfriend?"

I never should have told them. Me and my big mouth. "Yes, that's the one."

"Man, he sounded all down," Drew said.

"He's going through a rough time right now." Their faces were so serious; Hubert's mood had somehow infected the whole office. We needed something to bring us back up, and I had just the ticket. "Why don't we go over the entries for the contest?" I said brightly. *Parenting Today* was running a "cutest baby" photo contest. I'd been putting off going through the submissions—it was time consuming, not to mention hard to do. Babies are cute, all of them, even the ones with sticky-out ears and weird, patchy hair. Choosing *the* cutest was difficult, but I knew from last year that going through the photos was a joyful experience, which was just what we needed right now.

My suggestion had the desired effect. "I'll get the folding table," Drew said, hopping up to go to the janitor's closet out in the hall.

Mrs. Kinkaid scooted her chair to the middle of the room to where she anticipated Drew would set up the table. "You know," she said to me, "a good way to get over a heartbreak is to start dating again. I have the perfect girl for your friend Hubert: my niece Lindsey. She's twenty-six and teaches grade school just like he does. Lovely, lovely girl. So pretty and talented and smart. We're all amazed she hasn't been snatched up already. If you like, I can set up the whole thing."

I shook my head. Hubert and Lindsey? The two names didn't even sound right together. Lindsey was a fussy-sounding name. She was probably one of those girls who wore high heels with everything, even blue jeans. "I don't think Hubert would be interested in a blind date," I said.

"You never know," Mrs. K. said smugly. "Just ask him. You might be surprised."

Thankfully the conversation was cut short by Drew, who came in the door with the collapsed table under his left arm. "Time for Babypalooza," he said. "Bring on the pictures!"

17

The next day, a particularly warm and sunny one, Mrs. Kinkaid called in sick. In true *Parenting Today* fashion, she'd called early enough to avoid actually talking to me. Her voice mail message had just the right mixture of regret and sick-tonal quality. If it weren't for Drew remembering that Mrs. K.'s younger daughter was flying in that morning from California, I wouldn't have given it another thought. Considering the level of dedication in the office, it was a lucky thing putting the magazine together was only a two-person job.

Drew and I worked well together, and by that I mean he didn't interfere much with what *I* was doing. He kept busy that morning writing a piece about head lice for our annual back-to-school issue. We'd recently scored two lucrative ads with shampoo companies that specialized in treating infestations, and we needed an article to showcase the advertisements. I gave the job to Drew because just thinking about it made my head itchy.

It was eleven o'clock when someone rapped on the office door and then pushed it open. The knocking had all the hallmarks of my boss from the newspaper upstairs, so I assumed it was him, checking up on us. He always had some kind of lame-o excuse for stopping in, but the real reason, I suspected, was to make sure we hadn't turned *Parenting Today* into a party palace, complete with disco ball and spiked punch bowl. I looked up expecting to see Mr. Warner's bald head popping through the doorway, but instead I saw Ryan Moriarty in all his dark-haired glory. The contrast between the two was as vast as the Grand Canyon.

"Hi." He grinned in my direction and stepped inside the room. "Am I interrupting anything?"

"Can I help you, sir?" Drew asked. He straightened up in his chair and regarded Ryan the way one would a lice shampoo salesman.

"Hello!" I rose up out of my seat to meet him. He held out his arms, and I walked right into them for a quick hug. So out of character for me, but maybe my character needed some updating. We pulled apart, and I said, "How wonderful to see you." I felt my face widen in a huge smile.

"I'm Ryan Moriarty, a friend of Lola's," he said to Drew, who nodded and pretended to turn back to his work.

So now Ryan and I were friends. *That* happened quickly. Oh happy day.

"I'm sorry to drop in unannounced," he said, "but I lost your phone number, and I was in the neighborhood anyway."

"Oh, don't worry about it. This is a nice surprise." Out of the corner of my eye, I thought I saw Drew smirk.

"I know this is last minute," Ryan said, "but I was wondering if you were available for dinner and a movie tonight? I would have asked sooner, but I was called out of town on business and haven't been home."

"I'd love to," I said. The words flew out of my mouth without thought. A lip-jerk reaction.

"Great. Why don't I pick you up at your house at six thirty? We can go to an early movie and then do dinner. If that's fine with you." He raised his eyebrows questioningly, in a way that made him look like a young James Garner, before his *Rockford Files* days. A resemblance that would win points with my grandmother.

"Sounds perfect." I did a quick calculation. If I left the office a little early, I'd have time to change clothes and do something with my hair and makeup. But fitting in a shower and shaving my legs was iffy. Not that I was planning to do anything that required clean-shaven legs, but I did like the idea of having every inch of me the best it could be. Good practice.

"I'm glad," he said, and I believed it. He sounded glad and looked it, too. I couldn't remember the last time anyone looked that happy to be going to a movie with me. Maybe never.

He gave me one last hug before he headed out the door. Watching his backside as he left, I realized I probably wouldn't get much work done the rest of the day. Floating on a cloud is very distracting.

After Ryan left, Drew broke the silence. "So that's the guy?" He jerked a thumb in the direction of the door. "The one who got the candy out of the machine?"

I grinned and nodded. "That's the one." My voice was uncharacteristically chipper. I couldn't help it.

"I don't think he's all that great shakes. He looks kind of shifty to me."

"What do you mean?"

Drew shrugged. "He just seems all shifty-like."

That helped. "Can you expand on that statement? Give an example of what you mean, maybe?"

"I don't know. Just the way he came in here looking around. It was hugely suspicious. Like he was casing the joint. And why was he wearing that jacket? It's like sixty-five degrees outside. I'd be wearing shorts if I wasn't at work."

It *was* pretty warm out, but it had been cooler earlier that morning. I myself had worn a sweater, which I'd left in the car. "Well, everyone's different. Maybe he gets chilled."

"Plus," Drew said, "what's the deal with him supposedly losing your phone number? You're in the book, and so is *Parenting Today*. Why would he park his car in the lot, walk through the building, and come down a flight of stairs to talk to you for all of three minutes? It doesn't make sense."

"Because he wanted to see me?" I hated that Drew was chipping away at my rainbow. Oh, where was Mrs. Kinkaid when I needed her?

"Do you have *his* phone number?"

"No, he never gave it to me." I had tried to look it up earlier in the week, but he wasn't listed.

"There you go. He's shifty."

"Well, I don't think he's shifty at all," I said defensively. "I like him." What did Drew know, and why would I listen to a guy who couldn't even remember calling in sick on the *previous day*?

"Have it your way." He rifled through some papers and jotted down some notes on one of the pages, but under his breath I heard him mutter, "But he still seems shifty to me."

18

I left the office an hour early, passing my boss, Mr. Warner, on the way out. When he raised his eyebrows, I smiled, gestured toward my mouth, and said, "Dentist appointment."

"Have fun," he said with the sort of forced jocularity he's known for. He's the kind of administrator who thinks he's tough, and if you didn't know any better, you'd believe it. I was, in fact, intimidated when I first started. It took three weeks and a heads-up from Mrs. Kinkaid to learn the secret of Mr. Warner—he accepts everything he's told. If I said the magazine was running right on schedule, he assumed we were on schedule. If I told him we needed more supplies, he signed the order without checking. In dealing with him, I had the power of a Jedi warrior. I half suspected I could say, "You never saw me leave," and he'd nod mutely in agreement and echo my words.

When I got home, Hubert was already there. It was still a shock to have someone else's car in my driveway. Each time I saw it I had to self-correct the notion that I had a visitor and remember that Hubert lived with me now. In high school I thought that the coolest thing ever would be for Piper, Hubert, and me to share a house and a trio of cars—no parents in sight. What could be better than living with friends? As it turned out, our individual college choices ruled out anything like that. After graduation, real life got in the way, but having Hubert with me now was a small taste of the dream. I didn't suppose Piper's husband would let her come for a week or two without Brandon in order for me to get the full effect, so what I had now was as close as it would come.

I walked into the house and dropped my soft-sided briefcase next to the couch. I heard a clattering in the kitchen, like the rattling of cookware lids, and I could smell roast chicken. And potatoes. Or at least I thought it was potatoes. Did they have a smell, or was I just guessing?

"Hubert, I'm home," I said, doing my best Ricky Ricardo impression.

"Hey." He stood in the doorway, oven mitts on both hands. "You're early. That's perfect. I have dinner going already. I hope you have an appetite."

Oops. "Oh no, Hubert. I'm sorry, but I already have dinner plans."

He frowned. "Since when? I asked you this morning, and you were wide open. You even said we should rent movies tonight."

"I know, but Ryan stopped in at the office, and we made plans for tonight."

"Ryan?"

"The guy I met through Piper."

"Sort of last minute to be asking someone out, don't you think? I'm surprised you agreed." His voice was kind of mopey.

"He was out of town until today." I didn't actually know when Ryan had returned, but it sounded right. "I thought you wouldn't mind. I didn't know you were cooking. If you keep it for tomorrow night, I'm sure it will be delicious reheated. Or if you want to invite someone else over, that's OK too."

"I know I could invite someone else over. I wanted you." He held up his arms like a doctor who'd just scrubbed for surgery.

"Well, I'm sorry. I won't be here."

He clapped the two mitts together, like he'd had a thought. "Well, how late will you be out? Because I still have an idea for later."

"I don't know. It might be a late night." I *hoped* it would be a late night. "We better not plan on anything. I can't really say for sure when I'll get back."

"OK then." He sighed. "I'll have to rethink my plans. Now I don't know what to do."

"We can watch a movie another night." I glanced at my watch—the shower awaited, as well as an appointment with my tweezers. I needed to bushwhack my brows before I'd even allow myself to think about going on a date.

"It's not the movie," he said. "What I was really hoping was that—" Behind him the oven timer went off with a continuous *beep, beep, beep, beep*...

"You better get that," I said, pointing. "And I really have to get ready. We can hang out all day tomorrow, OK?"

"OK."

I left him looking like a kid who'd been abandoned at a bus station. Such an odd turn of events. A week ago I hadn't seen Hubert in months. Now, just when I finally had a potential boyfriend in the works, Hubert assumed I'd spend every available moment with him. Well, he'd just have to wait.

Getting ready, I made a mental note to visit Sephora online to buy some new cosmetics. And as long as I had the computer fired up and the credit card out, it wouldn't hurt to order some new shoes. Piper had some sandals with a metallic-y bronze look that I just loved. They went with everything and were so cute.

I'd have to ask where she got them. A trip to the mall wasn't the worst idea, either. I tended to shop for pieces—a new top here, some jeans there. Piper had been telling me for years that I needed to purchase whole outfits, accessories and all. That always seemed like a lot of work and money, but I was starting to see the advantages.

Even with my own incomplete wardrobe, I was able to put together a fairly cute ensemble. I'd made friends with Mr. Round Brush when I was blow-drying my hair, and it turned out sleek and full of body. With some effort and makeup, I actually looked presentable. No heads would turn, but when I smiled I was passably attractive. I practiced expressions in the bathroom mirror and was horrified to realize that my interested-listener face actually looked like a frown, complete with an ugly vertical forehead wrinkle. I'd have to remember to use an alternate expression. Keeping my face neutral made me look simple-minded. My half smile and head-tipped-back pose was good, but it would look odd if used too much. Oh well, I'd just have to wing it.

When I got downstairs, I was stunned to find Ryan and Hubert sitting in the living room talking. I hadn't heard the bell ring, and it wasn't six thirty yet—I'd been watching the time.

Ryan sat up straight in the wing chair, looking like an interviewer's guest on a PBS show, complete with button-down shirt and pleated pants. Hubert sat slouched over the coffee table, wearing jeans and a T-shirt splattered with something—gravy? Ryan was talking about the history of King Street. Something about how he'd researched the records at city hall. When I entered the room, both men stood.

"Look who's here," Ryan said, grinning. "Lola, looking lovely."

Nice alliteration. "I didn't know you were waiting," I said. "I'm sorry."

"Oh, no trouble at all," Ryan said, smiling broadly. "Hugh and I were having a great time talking, weren't we?" He turned to Hubert, who looked pained. Over the years people had tried various abbreviations—Hugh, Bert, Big H. Our physics teacher in high school once even called him Hube. But she only did it once. Misusing Hubert's name was like waving a red cape at a bull. He might not charge, but he's not going to like it.

"He goes by Hubert," I said, attempting a bit of damage control.

"Hmm?" Ryan didn't catch the conversational shift.

"His name. He prefers Hubert."

Ryan's face softened. "What did *I* say?"

Hubert coughed into his fist. "You called me Hugh."

"I'm sorry. I can't believe I did that." He smiled, but Hubert was clearly not placated, so Ryan tried again. "But it's sort of the same thing, isn't it? Just a shortened version?"

"Sure, Ry. Exactly the same thing." Hubert's sarcasm startled me. I'd never heard that tone coming from him. In fact, it sounded more like something I might say. Hubert smiled then. If I didn't know better, I'd think the moment had passed. He stuck his hands in his pockets and said, "So, where you kids going tonight?"

I could tell Hubert was annoyed that I wasn't going to be staying for roast chicken and DVDs, but too bad. How often did I have a date? Couldn't he see that this was an opportunity for me? I opened my mouth to answer the question, but Ryan was ahead of me. "We're going to an early movie and then out to eat." He turned to me and said, "I made reservations at Singha Thai Restaurant. I hope that's fine with you."

"Singha Thai? Perfect," I assured him. Hubert gave me a surprised look. I knew he was remembering a previous conversation in which I'd said I didn't like Thai food, and that had once been the case, but with Ryan I was determined to be more open-minded. I really needed to learn to be adaptable. "Well, I guess we should go," I said, gesturing toward the door. "Goodbye, Hubert. See you tomorrow." Ryan said good-bye too and followed me out.

His Jag was parked curbside in front of my walkway. When I was putting on my seat belt, I glanced over at my house and saw Hubert watching us from a gap in the drapes at the front window. I lifted my hand and waved, but I guess he didn't see me because the drapes dropped shut and then he was gone.

19

While we stood in line to get our tickets for the movie, I had time to admire Ryan properly. It wasn't just his good looks, which were considerable; it was the whole package. He had the look of a man who was comfortable in his own skin. And what great skin it was—covering all six-feet-plus of lean physique. I could tell from the fit of his suit that he was muscular, but not vein-bulgingly, freakishly so.

His face was handsome, though not in a Ralph Lauren model way. You wouldn't see him and automatically think he's full of himself, or if you did, his smile would negate that notion. He had a killer smile, one I could get lost in. It made his whole face light up and caused these cute little wrinkles at the outer corners of his eyes.

We made small talk about our choice of movies, finally settling on a romantic comedy. I noticed that when he spoke he leaned over to give me his undivided attention and made full, shiver-inducing eye contact.

The theater was only a few miles from my childhood home, and there was a pretty good crowd, but sadly I didn't see one person I knew from high school.

"Popcorn?" Ryan asked after he'd bought the tickets and we entered the lobby. Behind the refreshment counter, teenagers in striped vests flitted around like hummingbirds, squirting golden liquid onto tubs of popcorn and filling cups with crushed ice and soda. The popcorn smelled wonderful. I could almost taste the salty goodness of it, but I turned it down, telling him I didn't like to eat during movies. I ixnayed a beverage, also. I couldn't imagine maintaining a good impression with greasy fingers and a pressing need for the bathroom.

Ryan ordered a soft drink for himself: half regular Pepsi and half diet. As soon as he told the girl what he wanted, a shudder went through my body. Half and half was exactly the way *Mindy* took her cola. And here she thought she'd invented the fifty-fifty combination. Ha! Coke was her cola of choice, but she'd reluctantly accept Pepsi in a pinch. She was very particular about the drink being exactly half and half—I'd seen her send back drinks she thought were too sweet. Besides her, I'd never met anyone who specified a combination when ordering a soft drink.

"Interesting choice of beverage," I said as the girl handed him his change.

He stuck a straw into the X on the lid. "I always order it this way. Regular soda is just too sweet. I really prefer Coke, but I'll take Pepsi if that's all they have." He saw me give him a look. "What?"

"Nothing, it's just that my sister orders it the same way. I never met anyone else who drank it like that."

"Your sister—the one who's getting married?"

"That's the one."

His eyebrows furrowed. "Interesting." He stepped away from the counter. "Should we go sit down?"

Inside the theater we discovered that we liked sitting in the exact same spot: the middle of the middle. He let me go first, and I found the exact center of the row. I liked that he was sitting on my right. Piper always said it was my best side. "The sound is perfect when you're right in the center," I said.

"I've always thought that too," he said, taking a pull on his drink and setting the cup in his holder. "This is nice. I haven't been to a movie in a long time. Nothing against your friend, but I just wasn't up for staying in and having roast chicken tonight, although it did smell good."

I had to have heard wrong. "What was that about roast chicken?"

"Your friend—what's his name?"

"Hubert."

He smiled apologetically. "I'm sorry, I just can't get that name to stick in my head. It's so odd. Anyway, Hubert suggested we eat dinner with him and then all of us go out and do something downtown. He really made a case for it. I felt sorry for the guy, but I wanted to spend the evening with just you."

I was stunned.

"I hope you don't mind?" Ryan leaned in toward me.

"No, of course not. I already told him I wasn't staying for his dinner. I can't believe he asked you after we'd already discussed it." What was the deal with Hubert trying to horn in on my date?

"I told him maybe another time. He seems like a nice enough guy. How long ago were you two a couple?"

"Hubert and me? We were *never* a couple." I wanted to make this very clear. "We're just friends. I've known him since junior high. Until recently I hadn't seen him in a long time. His girlfriend kicked him out of their apartment, so I said he could stay with me."

"That's strange. For some reason I got the impression he

was a former boyfriend. Something about the way he talked about you."

"No, just friends. That's all."

"Well maybe it came off that way because you've known each other for so long," he said.

"That's probably it."

"Because he was reading me the riot act about treating you right."

I felt my stomach drop. "Please tell me you're kidding."

"No, I'm completely serious."

"The riot act?" I tightened my grip on my armrest. Was Hubert losing his mind? And if so, why couldn't he do it elsewhere? Ryan must think I was a complete freak.

Ryan set his hand over mine, and I felt myself relax. "Maybe 'riot act' isn't the right way to put it. More like he's your dad, or something. He told me what a terrific girl you are and listed off all your good qualities. Nothing I didn't already know, though." His fingers curved underneath my palm. Our hands fit together perfectly. "Then he said he hoped I realized what a special person you were."

Oh good Lord. "What did you say to that?" I felt my heart quicken.

He gave my hand a little squeeze. "I said sure, of course I could tell you were special from the moment I met you, but he didn't seem very convinced." He looked distractedly around the theater. I got the impression he didn't find Hubert to be a very interesting topic of discussion.

When the lights dimmed, there was a scuffling of activity as people turned off their cell phones and settled back in anticipation of the movie. The teenaged girls in front of us slouched down in their seats and rested their feet on the chairs in front of them.

I'd always liked the previews, and this time they were particularly good, even the obnoxiously loud Mountain Dew commercials. Ryan continued to hold my hand as if it were the most natural thing in the world. To anyone else, we might have looked like two people who'd been dating for years, or a married couple with a newborn back home with the babysitter. I wondered what it would feel like to be married to Ryan. He seemed so mellow; I couldn't imagine anything getting him down. Not like Piper's husband, Mike. Piper had told me he'd been worthless when she was in labor with Brandon. Mike had alternated between being impatient that it was taking so long and acting agitated that she was in pain. At one point he'd even left the room, saying he couldn't stand seeing her face during contractions. Piper thought it was funny—the whole "men are such babies" thing—but I was appalled. He left the room? What a jerk. I wouldn't even *want* a baby with a guy who wasn't going to be there for me.

I wasn't sure what kind of father Ryan would be, but I was willing to bet he'd make beautiful babies. For some lucky woman. Probably not me, but still, here we were in a dark movie theater, his thumb stroking my knuckles in a way that would have made my knees buckle if I weren't sitting down. And who would have thought this particular scenario was even a possibility a week ago? Certainly not me. So maybe there was hope after all.

I watched the movie from two different places emotionally. Part of me viewed the story on the screen in the usual way. I saw beautiful people involved in humorous, implausible situations. I laughed along with the rest of the audience when the couple was trapped in the elevator. She was adorable, all Southern accent and petite build, and he was tall and good looking and serious. I wanted them to end up together even though she was flaky and he was unsure.

But another part of me was acutely aware of Ryan sitting next to me, the length of his arm alongside mine, our hands touching. At one point he repositioned his hold on me so that our fingers interlocked. I glanced down then; in the dim light our hands folded together reminded me of prayer.

I'd written an article for the magazine once about the value of physical touch for babies and toddlers. The doctor I'd interviewed was adamant that touch deprivation was detrimental to a young child's health and development. He went on to talk about its importance for adults and how many people, especially elderly people living in nursing home environments, often lack the physical touch needed for their emotional health. None of the adult stuff was relevant to my article, of course, but I listened politely. Touch deprivation, he'd said, was an epidemic in America. At the time I'd agreed that yes, never being hugged or caressed, or having sex for that matter, was a sad thing indeed. It was only later that I realized *I* fit into that category. Me and eighty-year-old ladies with names like Mabel and Cora had more in common than I'd like to admit. But maybe now my personal drought was over.

The movie was over much too quickly. I could have sat in the comfort of my padded seat indefinitely, smelling the popcorn and alternating my gaze at the screen with sneaky peeks at the handsome man next to me. All my senses satisfied in one sitting.

When the credits ran, half the audience got up to leave,

including the teenage girls in front of us. The murmur of voices in the theater sounded generally pleased with the movie. I could always tell by the collective tone whether or not people felt they got their money's worth. Ryan sipped from his Pepsi and made no effort to move, so I remained motionless as well. I was glad he was a stay-for-the-credits kind of guy. I myself liked to see things through to the end.

"So what did you think?" Ryan said when the house lights went on. He had leaned over to ask, his lips just inches from my ear. "Did you like it?"

I was startled for a moment, until I realized he was talking about the movie. "Oh yes, it was great," I assured him. "Really funny."

"I thought so too." He took a thoughtful sip from his cup. The last of the soda, judging by the sucking noise. "I always go for something funny, rather than serious or depressing, if I have a choice."

"Me too." Another thing we had in common. Too bad he was seriously out of my league.

We rose out of our seats and followed the few remaining stragglers out to the brightness of the lobby.

"Our timing is a little off," Ryan said, glancing at his watch. "We have an hour to kill. We can either go for a leisurely drive before heading for dinner, or go straight to the restaurant and have a drink at the bar while we wait." He looked at me questioningly. "Whatever the lady decides."

Quick—call the Associated Press! Chivalry was alive and well, after all. "Either way," I said, and then I realized I sounded wishy-washy. "Or we could do both—go for a drive and then if we have time, stop in the bar?"

Ryan made a slight bow. "As you wish."

We were grinning at each other like overjoyed third grad-ers when I felt a tap on my shoulder. I turned to see Mindy and Chad standing behind me.

"I thought it was you!" she said.

20

"I *told* Chad it was you." As she spoke, Mindy grinned and bounced on the balls of her feet. Such a little bundle of energy. "He just couldn't believe you'd be out on a Friday night. Aren't you usually in your jammies watching Netflix right about now?" She spoke as smugly as if she'd caught me joining Weight Watchers.

I had a few strategies for dealing with Mindy, the most effective of which was to ignore her barbs. I touched Ryan's elbow to indicate we were together. "Ryan, this is my sister Mindy and her fiancé Chad." I gave my sister a threatening look, even though that never worked.

Ryan extended his hand to Chad. "Ryan Moriarty. I've heard so much about you both. It's a pleasure to finally meet you." In return, Chad pumped his hand vigorously and grinned.

"But I've heard *nothing* about you." Mindy dramatically pushed her hair behind her ear with a broad sweep of her hand. A childhood habit designed, I always believed, to draw attention to her crowning glory. She always complained about her hair, but her protests didn't fool me—she was just fishing for compliments. Her hair was thick and gleaming and gorgeous. And she knew it. "Lola, you sneaky thing, you. I had no idea. How long

have you two been going out? You are going out, aren't you?"
She directed the question at Ryan.

I swallowed and looked up at Ryan, who gave her his most
radiant smile. "I first laid eyes on Lola the day she moved in
across the street from me. We hit it off immediately, didn't we,
hon?"

I nodded, relieved that he knew to play along. To further
illustrate his point, he put his arm around my shoulder.

"Really?" My sister looked like she wondered what the catch
was.

"Really," Ryan said. "I've heard so much about the two of
you. It's great running into you like this. I was really hoping
we'd meet before the wedding."

"You're getting married?" Mindy was stunned.

"He's talking about *your* wedding," I said. She didn't have to
sound so shocked. Honestly.

"Oh."

"You're coming to our wedding?" Chad said. "Cool. It's
going to be a hell of a party, man." He put his hands in his jeans
pocket and then stuck his fingers through his belt loops like he
was the lead dancer at a hoedown. I'd never *dis*liked Chad—he
was a pleasant enough guy—but conversation-wise he hadn't
evolved much since high school. He had a few key phrases.
Things were "cool" and "wicked" and "sweet." Occasionally he'd
even say "bummer" like he was a character in a 1980s teen movie.
He'd called me "man" only once before I'd asked him not to, but
I heard him use it often when talking to other people. I think it
saved him from having to remember names.

Ryan gave my shoulder a squeeze. "Yes, Lola asked if I'd go
to the wedding with her, and I'm really looking forward to it."

Mindy looked from me to Ryan like she couldn't quite figure us out.

Ryan continued. "That's OK with you, isn't it? If I attend the wedding?"

"Sure, that would be great," Chad said. "We've got plenty of everything."

"Of course it's fine," Mindy said. "I told Lola she could bring a guest. I'm just surprised because she hadn't mentioned it." She looked thoughtful. "It does throw things off a bit though. She'll be standing up with Chad's cousin. He's not bringing a date, so I was kind of thinking they'd be together."

Inwardly I groaned. Chad's cousin was a forty-year-old, never-married geek whose idea of scintillating conversation was debating which *Star Trek* captain was the best. During a previous social gathering, I'd made the mistake of saying Captain Kirk was my favorite, which set off a lengthy monologue of all the captains' strengths and weaknesses. Who knew there was so many of them? And really, who cared? I couldn't believe Mindy was pushing the guy on me. Again.

"Oh, I understand she'll have her bridesmaid duties," Ryan said, pulling me close to his side and smiling at me. "But we just couldn't stand the thought of being apart on her birthday." The look of love he gave me was unmistakable. If he was going for the Oscar, he definitely got my vote.

For once Mindy didn't have a quick response. Her silence gave me a chance to work in an exit.

"I don't want to be rude," I said, "but we have dinner plans and you have a movie to go to. We'll talk later, Mindy." I made the phone gesture and held it up to my ear. "I'll call you."

"We just got out of our movie," Chad said, pointing. "And we were just gonna get something to eat. You should come with us."

"Oh, I don't think so," I said. "We have reservations at a Thai restaurant." I was sure Chad and Mindy were going to a fish fry, or even worse, to get a butter burger at the local custard stand. They were one of those couples that started out in high school and held onto their favorite haunts. She talked about me and Netflix—ha! She had her own rut; she just didn't see it.

"I *love* Thai food," Mindy said, a little too loudly. A passing couple turned to look as they walked by. "Chad really likes it too. We were just saying we should go out for Thai one of these days, weren't we Chad?" He looked confused but nodded in agreement.

Ryan looked thoughtful. "If you want to join us, I'm sure we could ask for a table for four when we get there. Is that OK with you, hon?"

Damn, she'd done it again. I was emotionally cornered. I looked up into Ryan's dark eyes. His eyebrows were raised questioningly. Finally I exhaled and nodded. "That would be fine."

Mindy lifted her head and shot me a triumphant look. Score one for Mindy.

"It's settled then," Ryan said. "Dinner for four."

"Should we drive together?" Mindy asked.

I had the answer for that. "His car only has two seats. It's a *Jaguar*." Score one for Lola.

"We could go in my car," Chad said. "The backseat is kind of messy, though. I'd have to move some stuff." I thought of the floor of his car layered with empty Big Gulp cups and fast-food wrappers. My fingers felt sticky just thinking about it.

"You can follow us," Ryan said decisively. "It's not far."

21

In the car I let Ryan know I was less than thrilled that Mindy and Chad were joining us. "I know she seems nice, but she can be so annoying," I said. "And Chad isn't all that interesting, frankly. If it were up to me, we'd have said good-bye at the theater and called it a day. I'd rather have gone out to dinner with just the two of us."

"I sensed that," he said, tapping on the steering wheel in time to the music. "And I'm really sorry, but she came on so strong, I would have felt rude not inviting them." He sounded contrite. I could tell he'd be a hard guy to stay mad at. "And it also occurred to me that this is the perfect opportunity to lay the groundwork for our announcement at the wedding. I know your friend Piper wanted it to be a complete surprise, but I think this is better. Not too many people become engaged to someone their family hasn't even met. This will make it more convincing."

Oh, *that* again. I needed to clear this up once and for all. "Speaking of the wedding, Ryan, I'm not so sure I want to go through with this fake engagement. It sounded good in theory, but I hate the thought of lying to all my relatives. I don't know that I even *can* lie to my relatives. My mother could always tell if I was lying when I was a kid, and I haven't gotten much better at it as an adult." I turned my head to see Mindy and Chad following behind us. I wondered if Chad knew one of his headlights was burned out.

"It's completely up to you. I love the idea, but we'll go with whatever you decide." Ryan's forehead furrowed. "Would you still want me to be your date?"

"Of course, that would be great. I'd really appreciate it."

"My pleasure," he said and smiled as he turned into the parking lot of the Singha Thai Restaurant.

Despite our early arrival, they had a table ready. Switching from two to four diners wasn't a problem, the dark-haired hostess assured us. How nice. She seated us in a half-moon-shaped, red leather booth. Mindy scooted into the center and patted the seat next to her. "Ryan, why don't you sit here and let Lola have the outside? She always has to get up to go to the bathroom."

"I think I can get through a whole dinner, Mindy, thank you very much," I said, but Ryan was already sliding in beside her, leaving Chad and me to sit facing each other on the ends.

Each menu was like a book, pages and pages of dishes and descriptions. The cover was a shiny black laminate. We sat quietly for a few minutes reading. "It'll be hard to decide," I said. "It all sounds so good."

Across from me Chad flipped through the pages and sighed. "I was just thinking *none* of it sounds good." He wrinkled his nose. "Prawns in yellow curry. Ginger trout. Pork eggplant. Yuck. Don't they have any regular food?"

"In Thailand this *is* regular food," Mindy said, as if making a profound statement. "Please excuse him, Ryan. Chad's taste in food is pretty low class. If it weren't for me, he'd eat nothing but corndogs and burgers."

"Hey, I like Mexican too," Chad said. "Have you guys tried Taco Amigo over on Strand Street?"

Ryan and I shook our heads at the same time and then realized we were both doing it and smiled at each other. An inside joke.

"You should go there sometime. The food is great."

"It's a hole-in-the-wall." Mindy rolled her eyes. "Fast food."

Chad looked bewildered. "You always said you liked it." To me he said, "They deliver, too, Lola, if you're ever just home watching TV and you get a taste for Mexican. They bring it right to your door."

"We'll keep that in mind," Ryan said, giving me a sideways glance.

When the waitress asked about drinks, Mindy copied Ryan by ordering the same cocktail he did—an apple martini. Chad had his usual beer, and I, having learned my lesson previously, stuck with diet soda.

"A martini?" I said after the waitress walked away. "That's a new one for you, isn't it, Mindy? I always thought you were a wine cooler kind of girl."

She sat up straight and turned to Ryan. "That's the trouble with family. They think they know everything about you, but it's just not true."

Oh yes, Mindy was such an enigma. Not. Despite what she thought, she was as transparent as cling wrap.

She continued. "There's a lot about me you don't know, Lola."

"I think I've got the main idea," I said. "I've known you your whole life."

Mindy looked at Ryan. "It's tough being the younger one. Always with the comparisons. Why can't you be more like your sister? Lola always got straight As. Lola always came home on time. Why can't you do your chores without us having to ask? We never had to nag Lola."

"I'm a second child too," Ryan said. "I heard the same kinds of things. I think it's pretty typical."

I didn't like the way the tide of sympathy was turning in her direction. "Wait a minute," I said. "You always got good grades. You were on the honor roll most of the time."

She shook her head sadly. "As and Bs. I never had a four-point-oh." Her mouth made the "oh" and froze in a pout.

Her pout killed me—it was so obviously manipulative. "I never heard Mom and Dad complain about you. In fact, all I heard was how proud they were when you got the lead in the school play. And how great your senior photos turned out." I touched Ryan's sleeve. "They have a framed eleven-by-thirteen of Mindy sitting on the fireplace mantel—front and center. It's the first thing you notice when you walk into the room. My picture is a five-by-seven sitting on the bookcase in my dad's den." I craned my neck to meet Mindy's eyes. "And I also had to hear how nice it was to have Chad mowing the lawn and shoveling the snow." I pointed at Chad, who looked pleased to be part of the conversation. "She got points for her boyfriend's work."

Ryan turned to Chad, amused. "Are they always like this?"

Chad shrugged. "Sometimes. They like to give each other the business. You know how sisters are."

Mindy directed her remarks toward Ryan. "So my grades weren't as good as hers, but you know what? I really don't care. Because while Miss Bookworm spent most of her high school years in her room studying, I was out doing things—going to movies and dances and bonfires."

"And we were always at the football games," Chad said.

"Yeah, under the bleachers." The sentence popped into my head, and I couldn't resist saying it. Across the table, Chad's cheeks flushed bright red. Without knowing it, I'd apparently hit on a truth.

Mindy waved her hand like slapping a face. It was a playful gesture, but I knew her well enough to know I'd pissed her off. And nobody pissed off Mindy without some sort of repercussion. There were times I'd thought she'd forgotten about disagreements we'd had or comments I'd made, but that was only because she wanted me to *think* she'd forgotten. The girl had a long memory. I said, "Only kidding," and returned her expression of half-joking irritation, but we both knew where we stood. The arrival of the waitress with our drinks saved us from the situation deteriorating into a bitchfest. For now.

The apple martinis were so pretty, making Chad's beer and my soft drink look like homely cousins by comparison. The stems of the martini glasses were crazy zigzags, and the liquid inside was a beautiful luminous green. Ryan's came with a lime wedge on the side; Mindy had asked for a cherry, which was now skewered and resting on the bottom. Disregarding proper table manners, she fished it out with her fingers and popped it into her mouth. "I think all fruit would taste better if it were marinated in vodka first," she said, setting the pick on her napkin.

"I've always thought that too," Ryan said, ever agreeable.

Thankfully, the focus of the conversation shifted to the menu. Ryan patiently explained what various entrées were, breaking them down by flavors and spiciness in an effort to find something that sounded agreeable to Chad. I was impressed with Ryan's knowledge of the ingredients and the way the food was prepared, and I said so.

"I've always had an interest in ethnic cuisine," he said. "I've even taken some classes. It's a good thing I have diverse tastes since most of my meals lately are eaten in other countries."

"You travel a lot?" Mindy's eyes widened. She was impressed.

"All over the world. For work."

"Which countries?" she asked.

But before Ryan could answer, Chad broke in. "Man, if they have something that tastes like chicken nuggets, I'd go with that."

Ryan scanned the menu. "What about something similar to barbecued chicken?"

"That would be OK, as long as it's not too hot. You know how sometimes it feels like your lips are burning?" For some reason, he was asking *me* this question. As if I'd know anything about burning lips. "I hate that feeling."

"It's not hot," Ryan said, closing the menu. "It has more of a sweet and sour flavor."

After we ordered and the waitress took the menus away, Mindy leaned in toward Ryan and asked question after question about his travels and then hung on every word he said. Poor guy—she had him boxed in, and it would have been rude of him not to answer. I could tell he saw through her game, but he was a gentleman and behaved admirably. Meanwhile, Chad sat nodding attentively. Once the meal was served, he stopped pretending to be interested in the discussion and concentrated on munching the carrot shreds that were part of his garnish. I could tell he wasn't so sure about the chicken itself; he rearranged it with his fork, but not much made it to his mouth.

"Mindy and Chad have been going out since they were juniors in high school," I said when the air cleared of Mindy's chatter for a moment. "They met at the pool the month before school started. Why don't you tell Ryan that story, Mindy? It's so sweet. I never get tired of hearing it."

Her mouth set in a firm line. I knew I'd hit a bull's-eye by derailing the conversation. "Oh that," she said dismissively. "There's not much to tell. Typical high school romance—we met at the pool and started dating. That's all."

Chad set down his fork. "But baby, you forgot the part about how you were talking to Jessica and not looking where you were going and bumped right into me." He grinned at the memory. "She knocked me right into the deep end, and then she felt just awful about the whole thing. I was sopping wet, and I'd already put on my T-shirt and had a towel around my neck. I was messed up, my hair all slicked down weird, and I was out of breath. I think she only agreed to go out with me because she felt so bad about the whole thing. But once we went out, that was it. There was no other girl for me."

"Even then you could tell they'd wind up getting married. They were inseparable." I clapped my hands together for emphasis. The sound startled Mindy. "When they weren't together, they were on the phone. They *had* to be connected. Constantly. At the time I thought it was a little sickening, but you know, a lot of people go their whole lives and never find that special someone, and here Mindy and Chad found each other when they were only sixteen. I've always seen them as sort of an ideal couple."

"What a remarkable story," Ryan said. "So you went to the same college then, too?"

"We did the first year," Chad said, "before I dropped out to work for my dad." He reached over to touch Mindy's hair and then smoothed a curl on her shoulder. She jerked her head to one side.

"*Chad*," she said, stretching his name out into one long whine. "You're going to get my hair all tangled. You know I hate that."

"Sorry."

She narrowed her eyes at me. "Anyway, I don't know why we have to talk about my boring ancient history when Ryan has had so many fascinating experiences, traveling all over the world. I'm sure I'd much rather hear what he has to say than talk about the pool at Walter Park."

"I don't think you realize how exceptional you two are," I said. "High school sweethearts almost never make it."

Mindy gave a self-satisfied smile. "Well, that's true enough." She took a sip of her martini.

"I knew the minute I saw her she was the one for me," Chad said.

I said, "I've often thought they should put a sign up at Walter Park, commemorating your relationship. Maybe near the turnstile where you go into the pool? Right where they check your feet. It could say something like, 'Romantic meeting place of Mr. and Mrs. Chad Fellows,' and underneath it they could have the date you met."

"Do they put up signs like that?" Chad wondered.

"I bet they would if you donated money to the park system. Hey! You could put it on your bridal registry as a gift option." I was having fun now. And the more I talked, the more Mindy wanted to poke her fork in my eye, I could tell. "If they got enough money, they'd probably name one of the concession stands after you too." I did an impression of a teenaged swimmer at the pool. "Hey, dude, let's stop over at the *Fellows Stand* for some nachos, how about it?"

"I'd rather they name it after Mindy," Chad said.

"Oh, that's so sweet. *The Mindy*—I like it," I said, tapping my lower lip with one finger. "I can hear it now: 'Let's go over to *The Mindy* to get an ice cream sandwich.' All the cool kids will go there. *The Mindy* will be *the* place to be." I gave a little laugh to show I was joking.

Mindy rolled her eyes. "Lola's quite the kidder. Always has been. My father says she's easily amused," she said to Ryan. "I've always thought her humor was rather juvenile, but some people enjoy it."

"*The Mindy*," Chad said, chuckling. Ryan had a big smile on his face too. I sat back in satisfaction, knowing that despite my sister's best efforts I'd wrested control. It was no longer *The Mindy Show*, and we wouldn't be returning to that channel if I could help it.

"So, what movie did you guys see tonight?" I asked.

Chad lit up—finally something he could answer. "It was that new horror film, *Demon Keepers*. Slick computer graphics and great suspense. Really jumpy in parts too."

"It was stupid and predictable." Mindy feigned a yawn.

Chad pointed a fork in her direction. "Sure, she says that now, but you should have seen her hanging on my arm and covering her eyes. You can't fool me, Mindy, you were terrified."

"Tell us about the computer graphics," I said, knowing full well what would follow. And it did. Chad rambled on and on about the special effects, an interest of his. He'd read up on this movie way back when it was still in production, and he had followed the blog of one of the visual effects guys, so he was up on this. The whole thing was close enough to a video game to hold his attention.

When he stopped to catch his breath, I fed him a question. "Weren't you telling me once about a method where they film a few people and then make it look like a crowd? How is that done?" I gave Mindy a friendly smile to show her I was pulling her fiancé into our discussion just because I was so very nice.

The three of us were able to eat our meals while Chad regaled us with descriptions of how motion picture magic was achieved. I was quite pleased with myself, frankly, and Chad was the happiest I'd seen him since the day he passed his driver's test.

By the time our dinner plates were cleared away, the balance had successfully shifted from Mindy, and we'd achieved table equilibrium. Ryan and I talked about the movie we'd seen, and I smiled, thinking about the feel of his hand over mine in the theater. Such a simple thing for most people. Mothers hold their children's hands when they cross the street, and teenagers at the mall hold hands and think nothing of it. But for me, the significance was enormous. It was a beginning.

"*That's* the movie I wanted to go to," Mindy said. "I love Kate Hudson. But Chad had to see *Demon Keepers.*" Again she pouted. I caught Ryan's eye, and we exchanged a glance—*there she goes again.*

"We can go to your movie next time. How about tomorrow night?" Chad was sweet in his puppy-dog-wanting-to-please sort of way.

"Go to the movies two nights in a row? Please. I don't think so." She folded her arms like a spoiled child.

"Would anyone like dessert or coffee?" Ryan asked.

I matched his brilliant smile with my own, thinking that he missed his calling. If his consulting work ever fizzled, he'd be an excellent diplomat. "I'd love some coffee, thank you," I said, knowing that neither Mindy nor Chad drank coffee—they weren't that grown-up yet. I hoped Ryan and I could do a repeat of the other night by lingering over steaming cups, while my sister and her fiancé paid their part of the bill and took their bickering act elsewhere. That's what I was hoping for anyway, but I should have known Mindy would screw it up for me somehow.

"I'd love some dessert," she said. "I could use the calories. I've been trying to gain a few pounds. It's really a struggle." She didn't meet my eyes, but I knew when a jab was intended for me. Keeping my weight down had always been a battle for me. I was the one who had trouble resisting sweets—Mindy, on the other hand, could take them or leave them.

"They have some excellent choices," Ryan said. "Their cheesecake is particularly good."

"Thailand-ish cheesecake?" Chad said. "What is it, like mixed with weird spices, or what?"

"Cheesecake isn't a specialty of Thailand," Ryan explained. "I think the restaurant serves it because it's a popular here. It's actually believed to have originated in ancient Greece. The first recorded mention of cheesecake was when it was served to the athletes during the very first Olympic games."

"Wow, it's been around a long time then," Chad said.

When the waitress came with the dessert tray, Chad and I declined. Ryan chose a raspberry cheesecake, while Mindy picked the amaretto.

"Make sure you bring her the biggest piece you have," I told the waitress. "She says she needs the calories."

The woman raised her eyebrows in surprise but said, "Very good," as she lifted the tray to her shoulder.

After she left, Mindy gave me a steely look. "That wasn't necessary, Lola. I certainly don't need the biggest piece."

"Oh, I'm sorry," I said. "I must have misunderstood. I thought you said you wanted to put on a few pounds."

When the desserts arrived, I was heartened to see that the cheesecake looked as solid as a brick. Mindy's plate held a piece and a half, surrounded by a pool of amaretto sauce. The waitress announced brightly that we were in luck—they had the additional smaller wedge because a regular customer had ordered a partial piece.

"Really," Mindy said, pushing the plate forward, "I couldn't possibly eat this much. You can take it back. A regular-sized piece is plenty."

The woman frowned. "I didn't charge you extra."

"Come on," I urged. "Give it your best try."

"I could help you out," Chad said. For him this was a sacrifice. His taste in extraneous calories veered more toward Doritos and Cheetos and all the other snack foods with the "-tos" suffix. Sugar held no allure for him.

The waitress stood with her arms folded, as if she wasn't giving in. My guess was she'd pulled some strings to get the extra chunk of cheesecake. Taking the piece back to the kitchen would be a failure of sorts. Earlier in the meal, I would have said she seemed meek. Now, with the cheesecake at stake, our server's true personality came through. I had to admire her resolve.

"It's such a nice gesture; it would be a shame to send it back." Ryan's voice was kindly. "You could always take the rest home." The man was a saint.

"Sure, save it for later," I said. "Who knows? Around midnight a hunk of amaretto cheesecake might be just the thing."

Mindy looked at Ryan and then at me. She reluctantly pulled the plate toward her. "It's fine," she told the waitress. "I'll keep it. Thanks."

It was empowering to see Mindy forced to eat her cheese-cake. She took miniscule bites. "Delish," she replied when Ryan asked how she liked it. Meanwhile, I sipped my adult coffee, no sugar, no cream, a beverage devoid of calories. I felt a smidge superior. The situation, I realized, was as much about power as it was about food. Control is what I'd been lacking, that was clear to me now. And not just in food, but in my life in general. But things were going to change. Enough with being passive. There was a new Lola in town. I was going to make an effort to be the kind of person who made things happen instead of being the type who sat at home night after night watching clips on Youtube.com.

I looked at Ryan, and he smiled back, a forkful of raspberry cheesecake halfway to his lips. I decided at that exact moment that I *would* announce our engagement at Mindy and Chad's wedding. I could picture myself standing at the head table calling out for everyone's attention and then motioning for Ryan to come to my side. In my bridesmaid dress with my hair and makeup professionally done, our disparity in looks wouldn't be quite as apparent. Not so much of a stretch after all.

And then I'd lay it on them. To quell my nervousness, I'd think of the crowd as my audience, my adoring fans. And so I wouldn't look egocentric, I'd first thank Chad and Mindy for allowing me to share my news on their special day before introducing Ryan. I could almost hear the collective gasps of surprise and the smattering of applause, which would swell in volume as people realized the magnitude of my revelation. Maybe, to make it fair, I'd even set our wedding date on Mindy's birthday. I wondered what Ryan would think of a winter wedding?

Mentally I rehearsed: *I have an announcement to make. I'm engaged to be married!* Then I'd gesture like Vanna White. *I would like to introduce you to my fiancé, Ryan Moriarty.* I stared into my coffee, so engrossed in thought that when I heard my name and Ryan nudged me with his elbow, I thought for a moment that I'd spoken the words aloud.

"Lola?"

My head rose with a jerk, and I looked at Ryan, who pointed at the source of the voice. Brother Jasper. He stood in front of our table, his hands clasped together. "Miss Lola, I'm so sorry to be interrupting your dinner, but you're needed at home."

22

Seeing Brother Jasper out of context was so jarring I had difficulty processing his words. A feeling came over me—the same mix of disbelief and panic I'd once felt when I spotted my uncle at a bar I frequented as an underage drinker. "Excuse me?"

Brother Jasper cleared his throat. "There's a problem with your friend Hubert. He needs you."

"Hubert? Is he hurt?" A thousand injury possibilities raced through my mind, most of them cooking related. Fire, second-degree burns, smoke inhalation...

"He's not hurt physically." He spoke slowly, considering his words. "But he's had quite a shock, and he's not doing well."

"A shock?"

"I'd rather not say any more right now. He can give you the details himself." Brother Jasper gave the rest of my group an apologetic glance. "Nothing against you folks. I just wouldn't want to violate the boy's privacy. But Lola really is needed at home."

Across the table Chad looked as confused as if Brother Jasper had proclaimed that the survival of the planet depended on me and me alone. "This is Brother Jasper," I announced, suddenly remembering my manners. "He lives across the street from me."

"Oh, then you must have known my great-aunt," Mindy said, pointing to her chest. "I'm Lola's younger sister, Mindy." She cocked her head in a way meant to convey concern. "It was such a shock for me when Aunt May died. She was a dear. Such a loss."

Brother Jasper nodded thoughtfully. "May was a lovely lady and a great friend of mine." He shifted his attention back to me. "I was hoping you'd come back with me?"

"We were just finishing up." I gestured to our full coffee cups and half-finished desserts. I looked at Ryan, hoping he'd offer to drive me home on the spot, but he lifted the coffee cup to his lips as if time wasn't an issue for him.

Brother Jasper shifted his weight. "I think it's best to leave now, if you don't mind. I'd be glad to drive you if your friends want to stay."

Ryan set down his cup. "Lola, I completely understand if you have to go. I'll stay to take care of the bill and call you tomorrow."

Not the response I was hoping for, but Brother Jasper was waiting, so I grabbed my purse and scooted out of the booth. Ryan slid out as well and stood next to me, to say good-bye, I thought—but then he extended a hand to Brother Jasper. "This is so kind of you, sir. I'm Ryan Moriarty, by the way."

Brother Jasper looked amused and gave Ryan's hand a cursory shake. "Oh, I know exactly who you are. You live next door to me." He placed his hand on my back. "I'll fill you in on the drive home, Lola."

I felt myself being guided toward the door and shot a helpless look back at the table, where Mindy was jubilant and Chad puzzled. "Good night," I called out to Ryan. "Thanks for a great evening." He gave a salutary wave before sitting back down.

Damn. No goodnight kiss for Lola, or anything else for that matter. The romance gods had conspired against me. Again.

"We'd better hurry," Brother Jasper said once we were outside. He owned a four-door junker the color of moss, which he'd parked illegally on the street, blocking in two other cars.

"What's this all about? What's wrong with Hubert?" I asked once we were settled inside. The seat belts in his car were like the kind found on airplanes. I had to adjust the clip manually, and there was no shoulder harness. No air bags either. Lucky we were surrounded by two tons of metal.

Brother Jasper started up the car and eased it down the road. When he accelerated, the engine made a loud thrumming noise. "I can tell you what I know," he said, keeping his eyes on the road. "But I don't want to give away anyone's business. You'll have to get the rest from Hubert or Piper."

"Piper?" *Piper?*

"I was sitting on my porch smoking a cigarette," he said. "I know, I know." He held up his hand as if to silence me. "I know I should quit, but it's my last bad habit. Anyway, I was out smoking, and I saw your friend Piper's car pull up in front of your house. She'd given Hubert a ride home from the bar, apparently."

The bar? When did a bar enter the story? When I left, he was basting chicken.

"Piper was having some trouble getting him out of the car and into the house, so I went to help, of course. He'd had a lot to drink. Way too much to drink." He sounded regretful about the whole situation. "Not that I'm judging him. Lord knows I wasn't put on this earth to point fingers at anyone else. I'm as flawed as any man, that's a given." He fell silent and tapped his fingers on the steering wheel. His gaze seemed to go further than the road ahead. I could tell I was losing him.

"So you went to help…" I prompted.

"Oh yes," he said, returning. "Between the two of us, we managed to get him up the steps and into the house. It was a challenge. He's a tall young man, and he was not holding up well. He could barely stand up straight." Brother Jasper shook his head. "And he was so upset."

None of this made sense. It was so unlike Hubert. The more I heard, the more questions I had. "I'm confused. Did he and Piper go out together? And why is he upset? Did someone *die?*"

"No one died." Brother Jasper turned the corner by palming the wheel, a technique that would have horrified my high school driver's ed teacher. "Hubert has woman trouble. Someone named Kelly?" We paused at a stop sign, and he turned to look at me.

I nodded to acknowledge Kelly's name. "But she broke up with him a week ago. I thought he was over that by now. Or at least getting over it."

"The heart takes a long time to heal." He sighed. "Apparently he was out somewhere and saw Kelly with someone else. After that, he went out and got drunk. Sometime later he called Piper for a ride home. And that's all I know. You'll hear more from your friends, I'm sure."

"How did you know where to find me?"

"Hubert knew the name of the restaurant. Said you were going to a movie first, so I thought there was a chance you'd still be there."

"Oh." I did some quick addition—the movie was two hours at the most, and we hadn't been at the restaurant more than an hour or so. Even throwing in some driving time, I'd been out of the house no more than a few hours. "I wasn't gone very long. That's awfully quick to get falling-down drunk."

Brother Jasper shrugged. "What can I say? The boy applied himself."

For the next few miles, I didn't say a word. Brother Jasper maneuvered the big car as deftly as a city bus driver. Despite the fact that he was a smoker, the car didn't smell of cigarettes, and the ashtray was filled with change. I'd heard from the neighbors that he often used this car to give people from the homeless shelter rides to and from the free clinic. I myself had watched him load it full of canned goods to take to the food pantry. And Belinda had once told me that Brother Jasper *always* headed up the search party when her little dog got loose. I got the impression it happened fairly often and that she thought I'd offer to help, but that would be the day. I couldn't imagine I'd ever be one of those neighbors who would drop what I was doing to beat the bushes for a mutt in need obedience training. I wasn't that good a person.

But Brother Jasper was.

Tonight, at the end of a long day, instead of slumping in front of the TV like most people, Brother Jasper had helped Hubert and Piper, near strangers, and then retrieved me from a restaurant across town. An extremely nice thing to do. And instead of acting grateful, I'd been resistant and questioning.

It struck me that I was in the presence of an extraordinarily good man. Every day he probably did more good deeds than I did in a year. "I really appreciate you doing this," I said, breaking the silence. I wanted to say more, but I couldn't quite figure out a way to say it that wouldn't sound like apple-polishing.

"The pleasure's mine," he said, turning onto our street. It was dark, but the houses were lit from within and the street-lights illuminated the leafy canopy of trees that lined either side of the road.

As we pulled up in front of my house, I was surprised to see Piper's minivan in my driveway. I'd assumed she'd left once Hubert was in the house. "Piper's still here?"

"She was waiting until you got home. She didn't want to leave him alone."

Oh. "Well thanks," I said. "If you ever need anything, let me know. I owe you big time."

"You don't owe me anything. That's what friends are for."

The word "friends" startled me. I never would have included Brother Jasper on my list of friends. He was older than my father, maybe older than my grandfather even—it was hard to say. But now that he'd said the word, I was proud he considered me friend material. He'd be a good one to have. I felt a sudden warm surge of emotion, not unlike what the Grinch experienced when his heart grew three sizes that day.

"If you need anything, day or night, just call or come knocking," he said. "The world can be a big, cold place. No reason we can't give each other a hand and ease the way a bit."

"OK." I lifted the lever to open the car door. "I'll remember that. Thanks."

It was a short trip home for him, seeing as our driveways were across from each other. I stood for a moment watching. After he pulled into his driveway and the brake lights glowed just short of his garage, I turned and went up my walkway.

The front door was unlocked. When I went into the living room, there was no sign of Piper, but I saw Hubert's long form stretched out on the couch, his feet dangling over the end. Someone had covered him with one of Aunt May's crocheted afghans and placed a bucket on the floor near his head. He was awake, or conscious at least. His eyes were closed, but he moaned very softly, like an old man with a toothache.

I crouched down next to him and rested a hand on his shoulder. "Hubert?"

He turned his head toward me and opened his eyes partway. The movement seemed to take an enormous effort. "Lola?"

As soon as he opened his mouth, I was assaulted by the smell of whiskey and recycled food. Yuck.

His lips moved, not quite a smile. "Oh good, Lola, you're here."

"Yes, I'm back. I heard you had a rough time."

"God yes." He groaned. "You wouldn't believe it. Kelly—" And here he lifted up his head, to talk to me I thought at first— but when his mouth changed shape like he was about to expel a ping-pong ball, I knew what would follow.

"In the bucket!" I said, picking it up and holding it close.

He made it 99 percent of the way, but it was the other 1 percent that grossed me out. "Piper!" I yelled. "A little help here."

Piper came out of the kitchen trailed by Crazy Myra, who was wearing a quilted housecoat and holding a coffee mug. My coffee mug.

"Oh, Lola, we didn't hear you come in." Piper's tone was incredibly calm considering I had a man on my couch dying of an overdose of alcohol and the evidence was splattered on my arm.

Hubert wiped his mouth with the back of his hand and sank back onto the couch. I released my grip on the bucket and set it down on the floor. "He was just sick," I pointed out, in case they didn't catch what happened. Or notice the smell.

"Again?" Piper said.

Myra shook her head. "Can't hold his liquor, I'm telling you. Not that it's a bad thing. The ones who can aren't worth having."

"I can hear you," Hubert said softly. "I'm not dead."

I said, "Could you keep an eye on him, Myra? I need to wash up and get some towels. Piper, why don't you come with me and help?"

Myra settled herself into the wing chair with the coffee cup resting on her knee. Piper followed me into the kitchen.

"I'm glad you're back," she said as I turned on the tap. "I didn't want to leave him alone, and Mike's called three times. Brandon's getting some teeth—he's been wailing at the top of his lungs the whole time I've been gone."

"Piper, what happened to Hubert?" Like a surgeon, I immersed both arms under the running water.

She gave me a blank look. "Didn't Brother Jasper tell you?"

"Not really."

Piper looked at her watch. "There's not much to tell. Apparently Hubert went up to the Michaels Gallery because he knew Kelly would be setting up for tomorrow night's opening. He gets there and lo and behold, she's in a clinch with another guy, someone he knows. Turns out they've been sneaking around behind his back for months and he never knew." Behind us a cell phone rang—the theme song from *Goldfinger*. We both turned to look. It came from Piper's purse, which was sitting on my kitchen table.

"Don't get that," I said.

"I have to." Piper pulled the phone out of a front compartment and snapped it open. "Yes?" She mouthed the word "Mike," like I wouldn't know. "Lola just got back. I'm leaving in a few minutes. OK. Love you too. See you soon."

I wiped my arms with a dishcloth. "So after Hubert left the gallery, he went out drinking?"

She tucked the phone back into her purse. "Over to Bender's."

Ah, the aptly named Bender's, a favorite stop in our younger days.

"And then," she said, "he ran into another guy he knows, a friend of Kelly's, and it turns out that everyone in that circle knows about Kelly cheating on him. This guy even brought it up, if you can believe it. I mean, really, why would anyone do that?" She shook her head. "So bizarre. Then I guess Hubert started doing shots. When Kelly's friend saw him getting sick in the bathroom, he got hold of Hubert's cell phone and called me using speed dial. By the way, you really need to start keeping your phone on. You were number one, but they couldn't reach you."

"OK." I'd try to remember.

"By the time I got there, he was barely upright. He was clutching his stomach and saying he was in pain. If it weren't for Brother Jasper, I never would have gotten him from the car to the house."

"Do you think he's going to be OK? Should we call a doctor or something?"

"I think he's going to have one hell of a hangover tomorrow. But physically, he'll survive. Emotionally, that's another story. He was a mess in the car, saying how could Kelly do this to him. I tried to talk to him, but it was pretty pointless. Once we got him inside, your other neighbor showed up, and the three of us got him on the couch. We made some coffee, but he didn't want any."

"I'm sorry you were inflicted with Myra." I lowered my voice in case it could be heard from the living room. "She's really an odd duck."

Piper raised an eyebrow in surprise. "Oh no, she was a big help. First off, she knows where everything is in this house. And then we got started talking, and she's really interesting. I was telling her about Brandon, and she told me about her little girl who died. So sad. And how horrible is it that just a few years later her husband and parents died within months of each other? That's so tragic. I can't even imagine how someone would cope with something like that. How could you keep going?"

Maybe by tending a garden for hours and muttering to ceramic garden gnomes? I felt a pang of guilt. I'd been so quick to label, but I'd never stopped to think *why* Myra might be the way she was.

"I have to get going," Piper said, looping her purse over her elbow. "Call me tomorrow and let me know how he is."

"I will."

"Tell him if it makes him feel any better, I'm willing to go to the gallery tomorrow and take a flamethrower to Kelly's sculptures."

"It might not make him feel better, but I'd love to see it." I could picture her stupid paper sculptures consumed by fire. There would be a certain justice.

Piper grinned. "You can come with me. We'll make it a girls' night out." She gave me a hug. "Seriously, now I really have to go."

23

Myra, still carrying my coffee mug, left just after Piper drove away. I let the mug go without voicing an objection. I had liked that coffee mug a lot, actually, but I remembered the saying about letting the things you love be free. If it really belonged to me, it would be back. If not, it was never really mine to begin with. Or something like that. In any case, I had more important things to think about.

I traded Hubert's bucket for a different, better bucket. Better because it was empty. I took care of the icky one—emptied and rinsed it—and then put it away. I got a bottle of water from the fridge, went into the living room, and sat cross-legged on the floor next to the couch. Hubert's arm dangled over the side; his fingertips rested on the floor. I lifted his arm with the intent of reuniting it with the rest of his body, and I jumped when it moved of its own accord and patted me on the shoulder.

"Oh, you're awake," I said.

"I've been awake the whole time." His words didn't come out as clearly as usual, but I could understand him easily enough. "I'm not in a coma. I'm sick."

"Sick being the new word for drunk?"

He grimaced. "I'm drunk too, but mostly sick. Food poisoning. I had a bad seafood sub from Sub America at lunchtime."

"Food poisoning?"

"Yep." His eyes were closed now, and I could clearly see the rise and fall of his chest as he breathed.

"And you've narrowed it down to a seafood sub? Are you sure that was it?"

"I wasn't sure it was the seafood going down, but coming back up—I definitely knew." He talked as if he had marbles in his mouth, like Marlon Brando in *The Godfather.* "I tried telling Piper it was the sandwich, but she wouldn't listen."

So he was drunk, had food poisoning, *and* was heartbroken? Talk about a bad day. I unscrewed the cap from the Aquafina. "Do you want some water?"

He propped himself up on one elbow, grabbed hold of the bottle, and took a few careful sips before lying back down.

"Do you think you're done throwing up?" I asked.

"For now."

I capped the bottle and set it on the floor next to the bucket. Outside I heard a car drive past and the barking of dogs in the distance. All was right in the neighborhood.

"I'm really sorry about Kelly," I said after a few minutes of quiet.

"Yeah, me too."

"But you know, Hubert, you'll get through this. I never thought of you and Kelly as an ideal match anyway." This was completely true seeing as Kelly, to my mind, was more of a bride-of-Satan type. "You'll find someone new, someone more worthy of you. There are lots of women who would give their eyeteeth to date a great guy like you." Dozens probably, within easy driving distance.

"I don't want a date." He sounded aggravated. "I'm tired of dating. I'm through with all that. I want someone for life. To get married, have children. The whole thing."

"You'll have all that. Really. We both will." My words hung comfortably in the air. Just saying it made it all seem attainable. Maybe there *was* something to positive affirmations after all. I felt myself getting pumped with possibility. If someone like Ryan would ask me out, it seemed obvious I was date-worthy. Even if Ryan and I didn't wind up together, there had to be someone out there for me.

And if Ryan and I did wind up together, well, I hated to even think about it for fear of jinxing it, but wouldn't that be a great ending to my story? It sure would make going to high school reunions more fun.

I thought about my life, and it was like looking past fog that had lifted. Suddenly my future seemed clear. I had the house, the job, friends, my health. Why wouldn't a husband and kids follow? Why not?

And hadn't someone recently said I was smart, pretty, and kind with a great sense of humor? Not to mention what a good friend I was. Surely someone like me wouldn't die alone. I'd been selling myself short.

And Hubert deserved the same. He wanted to get married more than any other thirty-year-old guy I knew. Probably because his parents were such a perfect match. The curse of having happily married parents: they're a hard act to follow.

I stroked his head, brushing his hair back off his forehead. "You mark my words, Hubert. Sometime in the very near future, we *will* be married."

I saw him swallow—his Adam's apple ducked, and his forehead relaxed under my fingertips. "Are you proposing to me, Lola?"

"What?" My hand froze in midair.

"Because if you're asking, yes, I will marry you."

I heard myself laugh, but it was one of those nervous, forced laughs. *Heh heh heh.* "I was talking in general. I didn't mean we should get married to *each other.*"

He raised himself up on one elbow and looked at me through half-lidded eyes. "Why not, Lola?"

I laughed again, this time sounding like Nelson on *The Simpsons.* "*Ha* ha!" I waited for him to join in, but he just gave me a questioning look. "Really, Hubert, you can't be serious."

He struggled to a sitting position. "Hypothetically speaking, it could work, don't you think?"

He was obviously still influenced by the alcohol and the shock of seeing Kelly with another man. "Hubert," I said, trying to think of the best way to put this. Hubert and me together? How weird would that be? "I can't marry you. You're one of my best friends. I've known you since seventh grade. We used to ride our bikes together." I'm not sure why I added the part about the bikes, but it seemed to give my point some added weight.

"Would that be the worst thing in the world—to be married to one of your best friends?"

Why did that sound familiar?

"Really, Lola, think about it. We're completely compatible. And just think, if we got married, neither one of us would have to be alone."

Neither of us would have to be alone? How pathetic was that? The poor man was speaking out of desperation. Of course we were compatible, and yes, I loved him to pieces. Who wouldn't? But didn't he realize there had to be some kind of physical attraction? And clearly there wasn't, but I couldn't say that. How do you tell someone that you can spend hours with them and never wonder what they look like naked? Or watch them talk and not even try to envision what it would be like to kiss their lips? He was the only man on the planet I could belch in front of without blushing, but that didn't mean we should get married.

I gave his arm a squeeze. "I'll tell you what, Hubert. If you still feel this way tomorrow, we'll talk. But once the alcohol wears off and your stomach settles down, I'm betting you'll feel as mortified by this idea as I am right now."

24

Hubert spent the rest of the night on the couch, with me at his side for most of it. Thankfully, he didn't need the bucket again, although he did make a few urgent trips to the bathroom. I didn't ask for details.

The next morning I waited for him to bring up our conversation from the night before, but he never did, which gave credence to my theory that drink and desperation initiate ideas that fall apart in the light of day.

Most of Saturday was taken up with recovery. I wasn't hungover or suffering from food poisoning, but I was tired and had dirty laundry up the yin-yang. I shuffled through the house with baskets of clothing and paid a few bills online. Hubert and I took turns napping on and off, reminding me of the day after final exams in college.

Late afternoon, when Hubert finally made it into the shower, I took the cordless phone into my bedroom, shut the door, and settled back on my bed.

When Mike answered, we went through out usual exchange. Like Mr. Rogers, all was wonderful in his neighborhood. I told him I was glad and could I please speak to his wife? If it wasn't too much trouble?

For the first time in ages, Piper came to the phone with something resembling enthusiasm. "Hey, Lola," she said. "I was just thinking about you! Honest to God, I was on the verge of picking up the phone when it rang and was you."

Flattering, but it left me wondering why Mike answered it if she was on the verge of picking it up. How did that work? Did he race over and grab it away from her outstretched hand? I couldn't picture it, but whatever. It was the thought that counted.

She continued. "So, how's Hubert doing today? He must have one hell of a headache."

"He's much better, actually. Turns out he only had a few drinks—he was mostly sick from something he ate at lunch." I explained further, but I could tell she was dubious about the food poisoning angle. I suppose I couldn't blame her. If I went to a bar to pick up a friend who reeked of whiskey and could barely walk, I'd have opinions on the subject myself.

"Well, I'm glad to hear he's much improved. Mike and I were really worried about him. So," she said brightly, "tell me about your date. Hubert said you went out with Ryan?"

She always did get right down to business. "Overall it went *very* well," I said, "until Mindy showed up."

Piper listened, fascinated, while I recounted the events of the evening. She stopped me frequently to ask questions and to insert the appropriate outraged comment at Mindy's behavior. "She's such a piece of work," she said when I paused to take a breath.

"Always has been," I said. "But at least she's consistent. With Mindy you always know what to expect—it's just the same crap, different pile. But the good news is," and here I paused for dramatic effect, "and you'll like this, that I decided to go ahead and announce my engagement to Ryan at Mindy's wedding. He's totally on board with it, so I thought, what the hell." I grinned and clutched the phone to my ear.

She squealed. "Oh my God, I'm so happy for you. I wish I was going to be there to see it. But you can show me the video footage, right?" From her tone you'd think I was actually getting engaged. "Now we just have to go shopping for rings. I was just reading in *Cosmo* about these simulated diamonds that are so close to the real thing only a jeweler can tell the difference. You can buy one at a fraction of the cost of a regular engagement ring. What kind of cut do you like?"

"It really doesn't matter." I wasn't a superficial person. Any large, sparkly rock would do.

"Hey, can I be your maid of honor?"

"But of course." I was hers, so it was only fair.

"And Hubert can stand up too, don't you think? He did at mine."

Her mention of Hubert reminded me of the real reason for my call. "Speaking of Hubert, I had the weirdest conversation with him last night. Wait till you hear." I filled her in on the exchange, ending with, "And then Hubert said we should get married. *To each other.* At first I thought he was yanking my chain, but he sounded serious. Can you believe it?" I waited for her reaction, expecting a wow, or a gasp, or more questions. Instead, I got a silence that could be dissected by a Ginsu knife. It occurred to me that maybe we'd been disconnected and I'd been rambling to myself. "Piper, are you still there?"

"I'm still here."

"Isn't that unbelievable? Here we've been friends since seventh grade, and out of the blue he says we should get married?"

"Hmmm." I got the sense she'd pulled Brandon onto her lap. I could hear his babbling close to the phone.

I tried again. "I'm thinking that the combination of bad seafood and whiskey shots has this effect on men. And if that's true, I could make a fortune selling the information to other women. Hey! Maybe the one who holds the bucket becomes the love interest. Like those geese that migrate following an ultralight because they think it's their mother." I chuckled, but Piper didn't join in. Distracted by the baby, no doubt. "And the most ironic thing is that until recently nobody was interested in me, and suddenly I have two men who want to marry me." OK, technically Ryan's offer wasn't genuine, but still, we were dating and that was no small thing. Who knew where it might lead? "By next week I'll have men following me in droves." I laughed again, but there was still no response on the other end.

When she finally spoke, her words were measured. "What did you say when Hubert talked about getting married?"

"Of course I said no way. The whole thing was ridiculous."

"And his reaction?"

"He looked a little disappointed, frankly. He was obviously still drunk and upset, because marriage proposals don't come out of nowhere."

"Well, I wouldn't call it nowhere," she muttered, almost as if to herself.

"What does that mean?"

Now Brandon was making a vibrating noise—*brum, brum, brum, brum*—like she was bouncing him on her lap. "I always thought Hubert had a thing for you in high school."

"He did not."

"He did too. Remember junior year when he asked you to prom?"

"He did that to be nice. He knew I really wanted to go with Luke Sorenson, but Luke never asked me." Luke had, in fact, asked a girl in my grade named Allison, who coincidentally was the older sister of Mindy's friend Jessica. After that I didn't like Luke anymore. His taste in girls sucked.

"No, there was more to it than being nice. I picked up definite crush vibes. He had a thing for you."

"If that's so, why is this the first time you've mentioned it?"

"I *did* try to tell you back then. Remember me saying I thought Hubert wanted to be more than friends?"

That phrase resonated. Funny how memory works. As soon as she said it, I could recall hearing it the first time and even remembered where we were: in Piper's bedroom listening to her stereo and flipping through a stack of *People* magazines. She'd looked at me sideways and said, "I have a feeling Hubert wants to be more than friends with you." She told me she could tell by the way he looked at me. I thought she was joking, or worse yet, throwing me, the undesirable one, a bone.

She continued. "I tried to tell you, but you just kept brushing it off, saying he was just being nice and you didn't want a pity date to the prom."

So instead of going to the prom, Hubert and I had gone to see a movie and gotten something to eat, and then we drove around afterwards singing along to the car radio. I thought back to that evening and tried to examine it through a different lens. He had liked me? Like that? No way. I would have known. Wouldn't I?

"You were so insecure," Piper said. "And you always liked the guys who weren't interested in you. I always wondered if you did that on purpose subconsciously. You know what I mean—

picked an impossibility so you wouldn't have to deal with the reality of a relationship."

She'd been psychoanalyzing me? WTF? Please. "Stop already, that was a long time ago." I hated talking about high school. I hated even thinking about high school. "Even if Hubert had a little crush on me, and I'm only saying *if*, I'm sure he hasn't carried it all this time."

"Maybe. Maybe not," she said. "But I'm pretty certain he isn't randomly asking women to marry him. There's got to be something there. And just for the record, I always thought you two would make a good couple."

"What?" A good couple, Hubert and me? A better fit than Hubert and Kelly maybe, but that wasn't saying much. "Why would you say that?"

"I don't know." I pictured her shrugging on the other end of the line. She exhaled loudly. "OK, I do know. You get along well. You like the same music and movies. Your parents like him, his parents like you. You both laugh at the same stupid stuff."

That last part was true. Like a movie montage playing in my head, I pictured the hundreds of times Hubert and I had cracked up while Piper looked on straight-faced and perplexed. One time, when we were just out of college, the three of us had eaten at an outdoor café. When a young couple was seated next to us, we watched as they discovered their table was uneven. Without skipping a beat, Hubert leaned forward and whispered, "Watch. In one second they'll both look underneath it."

Just as he predicted, both the guy and girl, without discussing it, stuck their heads under the table, searching for the cause of the wobble. It was a perfectly logical sequence of events, but something about Hubert calling it before it happened made it funny to both of us. We both burst out laughing. Piper had looked at us as if we were insane, and then she got up and offered the couple some sugar packets to prop up the short leg. Even now the memory made me smile. "We do have things in common, and he really makes me laugh," I agreed, "but marriage requires a lot more than that."

Piper sounded unconvinced, but she didn't argue with me. "Yes, marriage requires more than that," she said, "but it's a really good start."

25

The only good thing about Hubert's sickness was that we got out of eating kimchi over at the Chos' house. I, quite honestly, had forgotten all about the invitation Hubert had accepted on our behalf, so when I hung up after talking to Piper and heard the doorbell ring, for one excited moment I thought it might be Ryan. When I opened the door to see Ben Cho standing there, all I could think was that he was *so* not Ryan.

"Hello," Ben said. "Here's something for you." He held a large Bath & Body Works bag, which he thrust forward for me to take. If he weren't my neighbor, I would have thought he was a door-to-door salesman. "My mother said to tell you she's sorry you can't join us for dinner. We all hope Hubert feels better soon." News traveled fast on King Street. It reminded me of an ancient joke that I mentally modified to fit the situation. What are the three best ways to spread news quickly? Telegraph, telephone, and tell-a-neighbor. Ha! I smiled at my own cleverness, and Ben smiled back thinking it was for him.

I took the bag and peered in to see the shiny tops of what looked like canning jars. "What have we here?"

"My mother says since you can't come to dinner, she's sending the dinner to you."

"How nice," I said. "Tell her thank you." We stood for a moment, and I gestured backward. "Would you like to come in?" I hoped not.

"No thanks, I still have a few more deliveries to make. Just tell Hubert to give me a call when he's up and about."

"Will do." I closed the door and went into the kitchen, where I unloaded the four glass jars. Apparently the Chos hadn't heard of Ziploc bags or GladWare. Now I'd have to return the emp- ties, which involved more personal contact with the neighbors. I could feel myself getting sucked into their little vortex. Bit by bit, I was losing ground.

Aunt May had kept a radio on the kitchen counter, the old type with the circular dial. She'd been partial to an oldies sta- tion, mostly music from the forties and fifties, and I'd gotten in the habit of listening to it when I was emptying the dishwasher or putting away groceries. I turned it on now and smiled when I heard Frank Sinatra singing "New York, New York." After adjusting the dial to get rid of the static, I turned back to the jars on the kitchen table. They weren't labeled. I held one up to the light of the window and wondered about the contents. I lined them up in a row on the table as if that would help, but I came up with nothing. One I knew was kimchi, but the rest were a mystery. Unidentifiable chunks were as close as I could come to labeling them.

"What's that?" Fresh from the shower, Hubert stood in the doorway of the kitchen in his bathrobe. Even though we were heading into the summer months, the robe was a heav- ier terrycloth type, with a knotted tie that looked substantial enough to be used for a mountain climbing rescue. I had a fleet- ing unwelcome thought that right behind that flap of fabric hung an example of what separated the men from the boys. My mind flashed back to my former roommate, the Celtic music fan, comparing the private parts of every guy she ever slept with. Andrea could be disgusting. She'd say things like, "Most women complain about the smaller ones, but the cocks I really hate are the ones that are long and skinny, like Dodger dogs." I had huge problems with hot dogs for about three years after hearing that. Even Italian sausages and brats bothered me if I thought about it too much. And forget about condiments—that was a whole other area. Remembering Andrea's assessments made me wonder what category Hubert's would fit under.

Had he asked me a question? "Excuse me?"

"What's in the jars? It looks like a science experiment."

Did he notice my face was turning red? "Ben Cho dropped off dinner because you were too sick to come over." When I noticed the confused look on his face, I prompted him with, "Kimchi night?"

His face flooded with recognition upon hearing the word. "Oh, of course. You were smart to cancel for us. I'm not up for that today."

"It wasn't me," I said. "I mean, I didn't call. Ben just dropped by a minute ago. They must have heard from Brother Jasper or Myra. Or else they saw you come home." I regretted my words as soon as I saw his wince of embarrassment. Nothing like the day after to make a person fully understand the meaning of regret.

Hubert absentmindedly tugged on the end of his bathrobe tie, then let it go slack. "I guess I owe everybody for taking care of me yesterday. Talk about doing someone a favor. I'm really indebted to you and Piper and Brother Jasper and Myra."

"You don't owe us anything," I said. "That's what friends are for. And when you feel up to picking up your car, just say the word." I ran my index finger around the lid of the closest jar. The metal was cold to the touch. Hubert nodded but stood silent, so I turned to put the jars away in the refrigerator. I wasn't sure what any of this stuff was or how it was supposed to be eaten, but keeping it cool was a safe bet. No need to keep the food poisoning cycle going. When I looked back, Hubert was still standing in the doorway as motionless as a palace guard. "Can I get you anything? Pepto Bismol? Water?" I held my hands out questioningly.

"No, I don't need anything," he said slowly. "Thank you. But I did want to say…I mean, I wanted to tell you—" He stopped and smiled wanly.

"Yes?"

He cleared his throat. "You know last night when I talked about us getting married?"

"I remember." Who could forget?

"I know it made you really uncomfortable." He fidgeted now with the robe belt as if *he* were the one who was really uncomfortable. "It was just, I was pretty upset and I'd been drinking, so my filters weren't on. I'm not even sure why I said what I did, but I don't want it to get in the way of our friendship." He looked at me to gauge my reaction. "Just forget that I ever brought it up."

"I pretty much have," I said, to make him feel better. I waved a hand over my head to simulate a thought flying out of my brain. "Zoop. It's completely gone."

"Good, because I'd hate to have it come between us."

"*What* would you hate to come between us?" I joked. "I don't even remember what you're talking about. What conversation?"

He exhaled in relief. "I'm glad that's resolved. We're OK then?"

"We're more than OK—we're best friends, and we always will be." OK, I might have been laying it on a little thick, but the guy was trying so hard to smooth things over. To emphasize the OK-edness of the situation, I made the A-OK sign—thumb and pointer together, the remaining fingers splayed like a peacock's feathers. It was the kind of thing my grandpa did—my dad was partial to the thumbs-up. Every generation comes up with variations of the same thing.

"Forgive me?" he said, reaching out with his arms.

"There's nothing to forgive." I walked into his embrace, and he wrapped his arms tightly around me. My face was chest level, so I had to turn my head to one side with my nose toward his armpit. The terrycloth fabric was softer than I would have thought, and he smelled like Ivory soap. I glanced up and noticed we were positioned under the doorframe, the safest place to be in the event of an earthquake. Not that Wisconsin had earthquakes.

After about ten seconds, the meter for a casual hug had expired, but Hubert hadn't let go. In fact, he'd shuffled even closer, moving his feet on either side of mine so that I was pressed up against him. It wasn't uncomfortable, but it was a little weird, especially with him being in his bathrobe and all. "Uh, Hubert?"

"Yes, Lola?" His voice was above my head and out of my line of vision, like God speaking from a cloud.

"We're still hugging."

"I know that. Do you mind? It's nice." I could hear his breathing right above my ear—he sounded relaxed.

I held on and patted his back a little bit, wondering how much longer this would go on. Hubert and I had hugged before, many times in fact, but this was a new one. After a minute passed, I found that I didn't mind so much. I didn't have plans for the day, and since he'd brushed his teeth and taken a shower, there was nothing objectionable aroma-wise. And he was a comfortable man.

I found myself relaxing into him, like we were partners in a dance marathon and I needed him to hold me up. I thought back to the article I'd written about the importance of human touch, and I wondered how long it had been since I'd had my share.

Hubert was definitely a good hugger. Much better than Danny, the guy I'd dated for two years in college. Danny insisted on resting his chin on the top of my head, leaving me with the sensation of a railroad spike being driven into my skull. Who could believe a chin could feel so sharp? To avoid it, I'd lower my head, causing my neck to compress in an uncomfortable way. He'd respond by shifting his head downward so that his chin was back on my head. Thinking about it even now gave me a headache.

"We fit well together," Hubert said, stroking my hair.

His fingers running through my hair set off my inner alarm system. Was he having a momentary lapse and thinking I was Kelly? Or just being extra friendly? Either way, it was awkward and suggestive. I tried to think of a way to break the seal and get things back on the right track. I looked up at him. "Hubert, I have to—" But before I could finish my statement about the necessity of emptying the dishwasher, he took the hand that had been caressing my hair and moved it under my chin to tilt my head back. It was a pretty slick move, and if I were being completely honest, I'd have to admit that the suddenness of it made me a little breathless. He lowered his face toward mine, and I saw it coming. I knew he was going to kiss me. It occurred to me to pull back, but part of me was curious to see how it all turned out. I felt like I was watching a play that had taken an unexpected turn during act two.

At first his lips just brushed against mine, and I thought he might be giving me the kind of quick hello kiss my Uncle Stu used to give me and Mindy—smack dab on the lips—until my mother asked him to stop doing it. But this kiss lasted longer than a hello kiss. When I didn't pull back, he pressed harder. All I could think was, *Oh my God, Hubert's kissing me.* He was so smooth—who knew? I considered stopping it before we went any further, but the hedonistic, just-one-more-drink side of my brain wanted to see it through.

I lifted my hands to cradle the back of his head. *Oh my God, I'm kissing Hubert.* My mouth parted to let him in. *Hubert.* What an unbelievably good feeling.

"Oh, Lola," he murmured, pulling me close.

We stood there making out for a few minutes, the radio playing Nat King Cole's "For All We Know" like a soundtrack to our own personal movie. It crossed my mind to insist we quit, but that would have required stopping, and I wasn't ready to do that yet. *Just one more minute, just one more minute.*

My brain raced with alternating viewpoints. My internal sensible advisor was all, *You shouldn't be kissing Hubert. Once that line is crossed, you can't be just friends anymore.* My free-spirited hippie side, whom I almost never heard from, said, *Don't over-analyze it. Live a little. If it feels good, do it.* And then Piper's voice chimed in: *I always thought you two would make a good couple.*

The inner conference was interrupted by a rapping noise coming from behind me. A noise like a bird hitting the window. I tried to pull away, but Hubert didn't see the need. "Ignore it," he whispered, holding me tight. "They'll go away."

He had me in such a firm squeeze I couldn't have made a complete turn even if I wanted to. But I didn't particularly want to. If it were a neighbor kid or the meter man at the window, let them see. We weren't doing anything illegal. I did wonder though. "Who is it?"

He whispered, "Just Mindy and that Ryan guy."

"What?!" I pushed Hubert back with a force that caused him to rock back on his heels. I caught the look of shock on his face right before I whirled around and saw Mindy and Ryan's faces peering through my kitchen window. Ryan had a hand held up to his forehead like a visor. Mindy gave me her trademark wave—her fingers fluttering one by one. She had a smug look on her cute little face.

Score one for Mindy.

26

"Go get dressed," I hissed at Hubert. "I'll think of some explanation."

"What's to explain?" He glanced over at the window. "It's not their business, is it?" He waited for me to agree, but instead I gave him a pleading look. For a second I thought he might stand his ground, but he must have realized the enormity of the situation, because he left the room with a sigh.

I motioned for Ryan and Mindy to go to the back door and went to let them in. "What a surprise," I said, leading them into the kitchen.

"We could tell." Mindy smirked. "Did we interrupt something special, or is this how things always are around here?" She tossed her head, and her curls glistened, reminding me of the posters hanging on the wall of my hair salon. Further proof that life was unfair. "You and Hubert—who would have thought?"

I ignored her questions and smacked back a few of my own. "So what are you two doing together? And why did you go around to the back? Most people use the front door."

"We tried the front," Ryan said apologetically. I noticed for the first time that he held a carafe of what looked like fresh blood.

"No one answered. And then your sister thought you might be sitting out in the backyard since it's such a lovely day." He flashed me that soul-melting smile. Today he wore a dark blue polo shirt. My father had one just like it, but on Ryan it looked anything but paternal.

"And you came together?" It was half question, half statement.

Mindy was grinning deviously. Catching me in a compromising position with Hubert was like something she'd have orchestrated in her dreams.

"I was going to come over anyway." Ryan held out the carafe. "I overheard some ladies chatting on the sidewalk in front of my house. They were talking about Hubert's adventures at the bar last night, and I thought this might help him feel better."

I took it from him and gave it the once-over. "Is he supposed to drink this?"

"It's my own hangover cure," he explained. "Tomato juice and Tabasco sauce and a few other ingredients I can't reveal. Some things just have to remain secret."

"Well, thank you." I went and put the carafe in the fridge alongside all of the other indescribable neighborhood offerings. Food, food everywhere, but nothing much to eat. "That's very thoughtful of you." I turned back to face both of them, pleased with myself for being so cool.

"Mindy pulled up as I was crossing the street to your house," he said, as if anticipating my next question. "We just ran into each other."

"You were coming to see me?" I asked her. That would be a first. Mindy dropping by to visit and doing it *alone*. My sister never went places by herself if she could help it. In high school, she was one of those girls who traveled in packs. As she got older, the number of hangers-on dwindled, but she was rarely seen without either Jessica or Chad at her side.

"No, I didn't come to see *you*," she said, kind of meanly I thought. "I was going to Ryan's. I thought I might have left my sunglasses in his car. I haven't been able to find them since last night, and I've been squinting all day. I don't want to wind up being one of those thirty-year-olds with the little wrinkles next to their eyes."

She left her sunglasses in his car? What? Something definitely smelled bad, and I was picking up an uncomfortable vibe from Ryan. It was subtle, just a shifting of posture while he studied my face for a reaction, but it was unmistakable. I kept my tone steady, less accusatory than curious. To Ryan, I said, "Why would her sunglasses be in your car?"

Ryan waved a hand—*oh that.* "Lola, I didn't get a chance to tell you how last night turned out after you left us. We had a very nice time talking over dessert. You were greatly missed, of course, but Mindy told me some stories from your growing up years, so you were with us in spirit."

Oh God, I could only imagine which stories she chose. No doubt the one about the time I was in my grandparents' bathroom and couldn't get out, no matter how many times I jiggled the temperamental door lock. My dad had to get a ladder and come in through the second-story window to free me. He himself had a heck of a time getting the lock to unlatch, so it was hardly my fault. Still, Mindy loved that story, especially since she'd been in the bathroom five minutes earlier and had no problem with the lock. And she was five years old at the time, compared to my ten, as she liked to remind me.

"And then," Ryan continued, "Brad had to leave."

"Chad," Mindy corrected.

"Right, *Chad.*" Ryan nodded. "Chad had to leave. Something about a TV show he had to see. We had just gotten our after-dinner drinks, so instead of rushing, Mindy suggested I just drive her home."

There were so many holes in this story I didn't know where to begin. First off, what was Mindy, *my engaged-to-be-married sister,* doing out with my pseudo-fiancé? What nerve—had she no sense of decency? OK, she didn't know Ryan and I were engaged yet, but she thought we'd been dating since I first moved to King Street, which was going on five months. Five months I had in this relationship, and she felt entitled to mack on my guy?

Not to mention the old sunglasses trick. If she was going to make up a lie, it should at least make sense. "So you thought you left your sunglasses in his car. And you were wearing them at night, why? To cut the glare of the pitch black?"

My questions caught her off guard, but she recovered quickly. "Of course I wasn't wearing them. I thought they might have fallen out of my purse."

"They weren't in my car." Ryan held his hands up—*search me.* "I don't remember seeing them at all."

I had one more inquiry. "What TV show did Chad want to see?" Nothing was on Friday nights. Everyone knew that.

"Aren't you just full of questions today?" Mindy said. She tucked an errant curl behind her ear and tilted her head to one side. She probably thought it was a cute look, but it just made her head look lopsided.

Ryan's gaze ping-ponged between us. "I really have to get going," he said, looking uneasy. "I just wanted to drop off my cure for your friend."

"You're leaving so soon?" Mindy said. "I was just thinking we should round up Hubert and the four of us could do something."

Ryan smiled in my direction, and I felt my irritation drift away. "I have some contracts and work e-mails to get through, but I should be free by tomorrow, Lola, if that works for you. I'll give you a call." He gave Mindy a cursory nod. "Nice meeting you again. I'll see you at your wedding."

I took his arm and guided him toward the living room. "You can use the front door like a real guest. Mindy can go out the back." I gave her a glare that I hoped conveyed, "Stay here," but she followed us through the house. After twenty-five years of avoiding me, suddenly she craved sisterly closeness. "Mindy," I said, "if you'll just wait here, I want to talk to Ryan." She didn't say anything, just made her famous Mindy pout. If she didn't watch it, she was going to need Botox for those little lines around her mouth. Any day now she was going to wake up and find them permanently etched.

I pulled my front door shut. "I'll walk you home, if you don't mind."

Ryan looked amused. "But what if the neighbors see?"

"Trust me, they'll see," I said. "There are eyes everywhere on this street. Nothing gets past them." I pointed to Myra's house next door. "Those garden gnomes are actually secret agents in disguise." I waved to the end of the block. "And Belinda's dogs are equipped with special smelling capabilities."

"Aren't most dogs?"

"Not like these dogs. They can smell farther, faster, and more accurately than any canines on the planet."

Ryan leaned over so his face was close to mine. "This is fascinating. I've lived here for years and thought it was just a nice neighborhood on a quiet street. In only a few months, you've figured out what it's really all about." He rested his hand against my back. "Please tell me more."

"Over at the Chos'," I said, with a gesture to my left, "every member of their large clan is capable of doing tae kwon do with such ferocity—"

"Is ferocity a word?"

"I do believe so, yes, but I can say fierceness if that works better for you."

"Either way."

"Anyway, every man, woman, and child Cho can bring a healthy man to his knees in a matter of seconds, so we never have to worry about criminals on this street."

"Even the Cho children?"

"Even little Cindy Lou, who is not more than two."

"You're making this up."

"No, it's all true."

"We shall proceed very carefully then." He slid his hand around my waist. I thought guiltily of the last time I experienced the same feeling—ten minutes before with Hubert. I put the thought out of my mind. That was a fluke. A girl would have to be completely incompetent to spend ten years looking for her soul mate only to wind up with her best friend from seventh grade. "Better hold tight. I'll protect you in case of a speeding ice cream truck or sudden tornado." As we crossed, Ryan looked up and down the length of the block like a preschooler following directions. "I think we're safe."

"That's what they want you to think."

When we reached his front steps, he said, "Now are we out of harm's way?"

"I think so." Oddly enough, none of the neighbors were out-doors at the moment, and there wasn't a car in sight. But that didn't mean we weren't being watched. For once I hoped we were. I leaned against the railing of his covered porch. Crazy Myra's house was directly opposite, and my place was to the right. My house looked stately and impressive. The lawn needed mowing, but that was a minor point. "This is kind of interest-ing, seeing my house from this angle."

"Welcome to my view of the world." Ryan half sat on the railing next to me. "The two of us, alone at last."

"I really wanted to talk to you without Mindy around," I said. "First off, I have to apologize for her. She's always been a flirt, but considering she's getting married in three weeks, she was way out of bounds."

"Actually, considering I'm dating her sister, she was way out of bounds."

His words made my heart soar with relief. I looked at his beautiful face, so calm and concerned, and wondered, *What would it be like to kiss this man?* Which led to the second thing I needed to mention. "I'm glad you understand about Mindy. I also wanted to bring up Hubert. I know you saw us kissing, and—"

"You don't owe me an explanation. We've only gone out a few times."

Actually it was two times, but I liked that he said a few—it felt like he'd given me a promotion. I flexed my fingers nerv-ously, preparing for what to say. "I still would like to get this out in the open. Yes, we were kissing, but I still consider Hubert to be just a friend." A really good friend, who just happened to be a great kisser. "He's gone through a lot lately, and one thing led to another. We were having a moment. I know how it looked, and I can't really explain it myself, but I know it won't happen again." I looked up to see him grinning broadly.

"You're so cute when you're worried," he said. "Everything's fine, Lola. Don't sweat it."

"Really?"

"Absolutely. Nothing is a problem. Not your flaky sister or your needy friend. Everybody has people baggage in their life. Trust me, yours is not a big deal. I've seen far worse."

"Whew. I'm so relieved."

"I understand how it goes. I have my share too."

"There's another thing," I said. I'd gone this far—I might as well take it all the way home. "I've been thinking about my sister's wedding and your generous offer to be my stand-in fiancé."

"Yes?" His eyes crinkled at the corners in an adorable way.

"I know I said I didn't want to go through with it, but I've changed my mind. Are you still willing to come to the wedding and play along?"

"Lola, are you asking me to marry you?"

I grinned. "Yes, I am."

He pressed his hands to his cheeks in mock surprise and spoke in a high-pitched voice like a Southern belle. "Oh, this is so unexpected. I mean, I hoped you'd ask, but I never dreamed you actually would." He fanned a hand over his face. "I just can't believe I'm going to be Mr. Lola Watson. Wait until I tell my friends."

"OK already." I laughed. "Will you do it?"

"It would be my pleasure."

"You'll have to talk to my relatives. And some of them are annoying. Really annoying."

"That won't be a problem. Relatives love me."

At that moment, *I* loved him. What a good sport and all-around great guy. "This makes me so happy, I can't even tell you. I'm glad it's all set and everything's fine."

He stood up straight and pulled me away from the railing so I was facing him. "Of course everything's fine. *We're* fine. We're more than fine."

"Good. I'm glad you feel that way."

"You know, Lola." I loved the way he said my name—so melodic. "I've been thinking a lot about how we met. I was lying in bed last night wondering—what are the chances I'd be in that financial advisor's office at the same time as your friend? And what are the chances Piper would approach me, of all people, with your dilemma? And then, even more unbelievable, what are the odds we'd hit it off so well *and* wind up living on the same street? It's all so incredible. I'm thinking it's more than coincidence." He ran his finger along the edge of my cheek. "I'm thinking it's fate."

My heart sped up as he smiled down on me. I was vaguely aware of the yapping of a dog across the street and the roar of a weed whacker down the block, but the sounds were way outside my circle of interest. The only people in the world who mattered were standing on Ryan's porch.

He leaned over and whispered in my ear, "Lola, destiny has brought us together," and then he kissed my neck right below my ear.

I felt a shiver of pleasure until it registered that he'd used the word "destiny." The reference always reminded me of George McFly's botched line in *Back to the Future*: "Lorraine, my density has brought you to me." It was one of the movie lines Hubert and I sometimes quoted to each other. Between that and the fact that his lips tickled my throat, I found myself wanting to laugh. I tried to hold it in, but despite my efforts I began to make a sound that could only be described as a stifled chortle. Not good.

He pulled away and gave me a puzzled look. "That wasn't the reaction I usually get."

"I'm sorry," I said, gasping for breath. "It's not you, it's me. I'm really very ticklish. It felt nice, really, it was just that spot."

"Oh." He smiled and waited for me to regain control.

I took a deep breath. "Honestly, I'm so sorry." I made a concerted effort to breathe in and out and not laugh. Once I regained my composure, he leaned in again with his mouth still in a smile, like a vampire in a movie. I braced myself, hoping he'd pick a less sensitive area this time, and I was happy to see he was aiming for my mouth, prime real estate for kissing. The man had a quick learning curve.

Ryan was a little taller than Hubert and had to lean over more, making me wish I was less height-deprived or that we were sitting down, but I wasn't in a position to negotiate. He matched his mouth to mine, and I'd just closed my eyes when—

"Evening, folks."

The unmistakable voice of Brother Jasper. Yesterday a savior, today an irritant.

Ryan and I stopped the kiss-in-progress and turned to look at Brother Jasper standing on the sidewalk across from us.

"Good evening," Ryan said, pulling out the social graces so smoothly you'd never know such an important moment had just been completely ruined. "Lovely weather today."

"It certainly is. I was just heading over to the Chos' for dinner and was wondering if I'd see you there, Lola?"

"No, Hubert's not up for it." It was awkward holding a conversation from twelve feet away. I wasn't about to move any closer, though. "Ben Cho dropped off kimchi and some other dishes for us, though. We're really looking forward to it."

"Hubert's better, I hope?" Classic Brother Jasper, always concerned for others. If only he'd do it somewhere else.

"Oh, much better, thank you. I'll tell him you asked."

Ryan said, "I'm sorry I didn't recognize you last night. I wasn't expecting to see you, obviously."

"That's fine," Brother Jasper reassured him. "I was surprised to see you, as well, if we're being completely honest." He wagged his finger back and forth. "I had no idea you two knew each other."

"Oh, we know each other all right." Ryan ran his hand up and down my back. "And we're getting to know each other better all the time."

Could we wrap this thing up? "Thanks for stopping by," I said. "Give the Chos my regards."

"I will." Brother Jasper raised a hand as if to wave good-bye, but then he seemed to think better of it. "You know, Lola, when you get a chance, do you think you could stop over some time? I'd like to talk to you about a few things."

Please not the block party again. Or even worse, the neighborhood watch committee. "Is something wrong?"

"It's just—" He paused and gave me a half smile. "I've lived here for a very long time, and I have a few cautionary tales."

"OK," I said, still not clear, but wanting to be rid of him. "Tomorrow maybe?"

"That would be fine."

On the sidewalk across the street, Belinda was being led by one of her dogs—the one named Roger, if I remembered correctly. Hubert would have known for sure. The dog strained at the leash and pulled with such force she could barely keep up.

"Hello, neighbors!" she called out as she approached. "See you at the Chos'?"

"I'll be there," Brother Jasper yelled back. "But not Lola or Mr. Moriarty."

Belinda waved broadly, like she was on a lifeboat trying to flag down a big ship. "See you there." Her voice trailed off as she sped down the walk.

"Well, Lola," Brother Jasper said, "I'd be glad to escort you home, if you're headed that way."

Did I suddenly look eighty-six? Why would he think I needed help crossing the street? "I'm not going back just yet," I said. "But thanks."

"OK then." He gave us one last look and headed reluctantly for the Chos' house. I realized then that he'd gone out of his way to talk to us.

Ryan leaned over me. "Cautionary tales? What's that all about? Maybe a warning about me?"

I laughed. "I doubt it. I think it has to do with the fact I don't have any deadbolts on my doors. That, and half the neighborhood has keys to my house."

"I'm in the neighborhood, and *I* don't have the keys to your house."

Good lord, the man's very voice oozed with sexuality. "Maybe something like that could be arranged," I said, bolder by the minute. So this was what it felt like.

"Now, where were we?" he asked. Again with that voice. If he ever wanted to give up the consultant business, he'd be a natural at—well, anything really.

"I think," I said, "you were just about to kiss me."

27

Ryan pulled me close. I tilted my head back and closed my eyes, waiting for the payoff. My grandmother always said, "Good things come to those who wait," and I'd been waiting a long time for love. I'm sure Grandma didn't have this particular scenario in mind when she said it, but whatever. I felt like a new Lola, one who was willing to take a few chances.

I felt his lips brush against mine—not a kiss really, more of a tease. Nice initially, but it went on a little longer than I expected. I opened my eyes and was surprised to see him staring back at me. "Do you always kiss with your eyes open?" I asked.

"The better to see you with, my dear."

I stood on tiptoe and placed my hands on either side of his face to take control of the situation. This was definitely not the old Lola. Score one for me.

He looked surprised, but acquiesced as I planted one on him. His mouth opened slightly, and I could feel him pressing back. When we broke apart, he had an amused sort of Elvis lip curl going on. "You're more feisty than I would have thought."

"You don't mind, do you?"

"God no. I love an assertive woman in bed."

Bed? Who'd said anything about bed? Last I looked we were on a porch, which on this street was equivalent to being in a public square. Just to make things clear, I said, "I think you're getting a little ahead of yourself. We're not to that point yet."

He raised his eyebrows. "Well, not yet. But I think we should be to that point soon if we're engaged, don't you? Most couples about to get married are burning up the sheets. If we aren't, it might not look authentic to your relatives when we make our announcement."

I cocked my head to one side, trying to decide if he was kidding. "My relatives won't know the difference."

"Don't be so sure about that. There's something indescribable between a man and a woman when they've been intimate. Anyone who's ever experienced it would pick up on it. And why let them have even a shred of doubt?"

I took a step back to look at his face. He wore the same calm, concerned expression he had when reassuring me that neither Hubert's nor Mindy's behavior was an issue for him. He looked sincere.

"I know what you're thinking," Ryan said. "It sounds like I'm trying to maneuver you into bed for my own evil purposes." He leaned back against the railing, like he was posing for a J. Crew catalog. "I'd be lying if I said the idea of making love to you hasn't crossed my mind many times. You're a sexy, smart woman—what man wouldn't want to be with you? But honestly, and I am being completely honest here, I also do believe it would strengthen our case at the wedding. We'd be completely comfortable together, and it would show." He moved next to me and ran his hand up and down my back. "If we'd been dating awhile, we'd get to that point anyway, don't you think? And I think it's safe to say we're on that path right now. I can definitely see us in a long-term relationship. So really, what's the harm in stepping things up a bit?"

I stood there for a minute feeling his fingers feather lightly between my shoulder blades. For once I understood what it meant to be speechless. I thought of my former roommate Andrea and all her sexcapades. She'd have jumped at the chance to have sex with a man as good looking as Ryan. The fact that she barely knew him wouldn't have been a problem. Most of her stories started with her meeting a hot guy in a bar and ended with, "Then I nailed him." She mentioned it so casually, as if it were in the same category as making a phone call or waving good-bye.

But that wasn't me.

"Well," he said finally, "it's certainly not a deal breaker. Just think about it. I'm up for the wedding either way."

"OK, good." I had to force the words out.

"Because I certainly wouldn't want to pressure anyone to have sex before they're ready. It's completely up to you." He ran one finger down the base of my spine and rested his hand on my backside. "Oh look." He motioned with his free hand, the one that wasn't making me uncomfortable. "There's your sister."

Sure enough, Mindy was crossing the street and headed in our direction. She had a scowl on her face and was moving so quickly that the purse hanging over her shoulder swung as she walked. I got the distinct impression she was not pleased.

"I better go see what she wants," I said.

28

I met Mindy halfway.

"What took you so long?" she said, irritated. "I've been waiting forever." Her nose was scrunched like she smelled something rotten.

"I didn't say I was coming back. I thought you were leaving."

"You did so say you were coming back. Your exact words were, 'Mindy, wait right here.'"

Did I say that? I probably did, come to think of it. I'd lost my mind, and now I was standing in the middle of the road facing Mindy as if we were opponents in a wrestling match. I glanced back at Ryan's house, but he'd gone inside. "Well, I'm here now. What do you want?"

"What do you mean, what do I want? I want to talk to you."

"So talk."

We walked toward her car, a bright red Ford that had always looked sporty to me, up until I'd ridden in a Jaguar. Now, parked directly across from Ryan's house, it had a definite wannabe look to it.

"I was hoping to talk in private," she said, leaning against the driver's side door. "Can't we go inside?"

"It's private here. No one's around. And I have a lot to do, Mindy. I can't be gabbing with you for hours. So whatever you want to tell me, just tell me." I wasn't in the mood for Mindy's drama. She'd been hitting on my fiancé, and she'd taken great glee at intruding on a private moment between Hubert and myself, and that was just in the last twenty-four hours. The past twenty-some *years* she'd caused me enough aggravation that if life were fair I'd be allowed to kill her. Luckily for her, life wasn't fair.

"You don't have to be so crabby," she said. "I came all the way down here to see you. You could at least be nice."

Half an hour ago she said she'd come in search of her sunglasses. Truth could shape-shift when Mindy was involved. I crossed my arms and smiled widely, to show how nice I could be. Hopefully this would speed things up. "I'm just a little upset with you today, Mindy. What's the deal with you having Ryan drive you home last night?"

Her face lit up. "That's what I wanted to talk to you about." She tucked her hair behind her ear. "Ryan is unbelievable. Oh my God, he's funny and smart and really interesting. He's traveled everywhere. I could have talked to him all night."

So my alliance with Ryan was getting the desired effect. Score one for Lola. "He is really great," I said, stating the obvious.

"He's more than great. Almost too good to be true. And he's so incredibly good looking. Like a dream or something."

"That he is." Finally, something we agreed upon.

"So my question is, how serious are you two? Because I was getting a just-friends vibe."

"We're more than just friends," I said indignantly. Hadn't she noticed his arm around my shoulder? The way he addressed me as "hon"? "We're dating. We've been dating for months."

"A few months isn't all that long."

Typical of Mindy to be dismissive of anything concerning me. "Yes, but we've been inseparable the whole time." She still looked dubious. "We're even," I said, moving in closer, "talking about getting married."

She whooped with laughter, as if I'd said something outrageously funny. Her reaction hit me like a smack across the back of the head.

"Well, we are," I said. "What's so funny about that?"

Mindy forced air out her closed lips—*pfffftt*. "Oh please, Lola, be serious. You haven't even slept with him yet. How could you be talking marriage?"

He told her we hadn't had sex yet? No, he wouldn't have. "Why would you say I haven't even slept with him yet?"

"Well, have you?" Her tone was challenging. When I didn't answer, she flipped her hair back and said, "I didn't think so. I can always tell."

She could always tell? No way. Lucky guess, that's what it was.

"See, the thing is," she said, "and this is nothing against you, but he's more my type. Ryan and I are both multilingual and love to travel. We have the exact same tastes in music and movies. Practically everything I mentioned as my favorite was his favorite too. It was absolutely uncanny."

What? What? *What?* "Wait a minute," I said. "Are you saying you want to go out with my boyfriend?" She said nothing, just widened her eyes and tilted her head to one side. It was an expression that never failed to charm my dad or Chad, but it wasn't working on me. "You're insane. He's going out with *me*. Me, me, *me*. It's not always about you, Mindy. Not to mention that you happen to be getting married to Chad, the love of your life, in three weeks. Count 'em—three." I held up the proper number of fingers for illustration. "What are you *thinking?*"

"Lola, chill." She tapped her foot impatiently. "I didn't say I *wasn't* getting married. I just want to see what else is out there before I do. And don't you want me to be one hundred percent sure?"

"You're supposed to be sure already!"

"What's your point?"

A favorite retort of hers, but I wasn't going to stop to think about a specific point. This whole discussion was my point. "Why are you doing this to me?"

"Please, Lola. I just asked. Besides, I didn't set out to do anything. I'm just kind of thinking it's fate I happened to meet Ryan at the same time I was having doubts about me and Chad."

"It wasn't fate. You only met him because I, your sister, am going out with him. Which makes him unavailable. Sorry, Mindy, I got him first. He's off limits."

"Whatever." She looked bored. Another one of her tricks. "I don't know why you're getting so bent out of shape about Ryan anyway. He's not really your type. There's no way a guy like that would ever be serious about *you*. Besides, you've got old backup Hubert right in the same house with you. From what I saw, you two can go at it like minks in heat when the mood's right."

I felt my blood pressure rise and anger grip my throat. I lifted my hand from my side and slapped her across the face. I saw her look of shock right after I felt the sting of my hand against her cheek. She took a step back, and her head trembled from the aftershock.

"You bitch! What was that for?" She pressed her palm against her face.

"Don't talk about Hubert like that," I said. "And leave Ryan alone. Or I'll tell Chad."

"Go ahead." She shrugged. A reddened impression of my hand was forming on her cheek. "Your word against mine." She fished her car keys out of her purse. "I suppose you'll tell Mom then, too. You've always been a squealer. Well, I could tell Mom a few things about you. And don't think I won't." She climbed into the driver's side and slammed the door shut. When she started up the engine, the radio kicked on at full volume. Kelly Clarkson.

"You've got nothing on me," I yelled after the car as she pulled away. I looked up to see Crazy Myra watching me from her front lawn. Today she wore aqua-colored pants and a white button-down shirt. Her head was covered in a bandana wrapped over curlers, and she was drinking from my coffee mug. I pointed down the street. "She has nothing on me," I said, embarrassed.

Myra glanced in the direction of Mindy's car as it screeched around the corner. "Your sister?"

"Yes." I wondered how long she'd been standing there and how much she'd heard.

She took a sip from my mug. "They can be difficult."

"You got that right."

We stood and looked at each other—me from my spot in the road, Myra standing on the grass. She seemed OK with the silence, but I didn't want to walk off too abruptly. "You didn't go to the Chos' for dinner?" I asked.

"No, I'm waiting for my ride. I have other plans." She said it rather proudly, the way someone would announce they'd won a major award.

"Good. Sounds like fun. I guess I should be getting home." I started to gesture toward my house, and then I caught myself and lowered my arm. She knew where I lived.

"Have a safe trip," she said, without a bit of irony.

After I crossed the lawn and was nearly to my porch, Myra called out, "Lola?"

I stopped. "Yes?"

"Don't worry. Things work out."

She sounded pretty confident for someone who knew nothing about anything. "Thanks," I said. "I'll keep that in mind."

I went into my house expecting to see Hubert, yet another person upset with me and wanting answers, but he was nowhere in sight. My mind reeled with everything that had happened—getting caught kissing Hubert, Mindy announcing she intended to make a play for Ryan, Piper saying Hubert had a crush on me in high school, kissing Ryan and then hearing him say he wanted to authenticate our fake engagement with real sex. Did I miss anything? Oh, yes, Myra telling me not to worry, everything would be fine. She hadn't a clue what I was going through, poor misguided soul.

I checked that Hubert wasn't anywhere on the first floor before I picked up the phone to call Piper. Upstairs I heard the soft strains of music. Something classical? He was probably holed up in his room, which was best for now.

I dialed and Mike answered. Thankfully, he didn't give me his normal spiel. "I don't want to be rude, Lola, but I can't really talk. Piper went to pick up the sitter, and I'm trying to get Brandon into his pajamas. I got the bottom and top on no problem, but I can't get the damn snaps to line up no matter what I do." He laughed heartily. "I thought I was pretty smart, but this is beyond me."

"The top's not on backwards, is it?" You learn a few things when you edit a parenting magazine.

"The top? Wait a minute." He set the phone down, and I heard some scuffling noises and Brandon giggling. Boy, what a cute sound.

"Lola?"

"Yes?"

"You were right. It *was* on backwards." Definitely a eureka moment for him. "How did you know that?"

"It happens, Mike. Say, could you let Piper know I called?"

"Sure, but she probably won't get back to you until tomorrow, unless it's an emergency. We have tickets to a game, and it might be late."

"No emergency. She can call back whenever. Have fun." I said good-bye and set the phone down. Now what? I wandered through the house looking for something to do. I settled down with the newspaper, but after I finished with my horoscope and the funnies, nothing really held my interest. From the Chos' next door I heard laughter and the wheeze-slam of the screen door opening and shutting. It sounded like a party. I half regretted turning down their invitation. At least socializing would have forced me to think about something other than my problems. Not that mine were all that large. If I was looking for people with real problems, I was sure Brother Jasper could point me in the right direction. Every day he dealt with people with drug addictions and mental illness, people without homes or much in the way of material things. Comparatively speaking, I was doing pretty well.

Still, when the problems are your own, they always seem enormous. The person who wants to lose ten pounds feels a kinship to those who have to lose a hundred, though it never works the other way around.

Maybe, I thought, it would help to organize things in my head, or better yet, to write it down. My dad always used to have me draw two columns on a sheet of paper when I had a big decision—the pros and cons. When he first introduced me to the concept, I thought it was the hokiest thing ever, but since then I'd used it numerous times and it really helped.

I went into the kitchen and grabbed a pen and pad off the top of the refrigerator, and then I sat at the table to sort out my life.

My three biggest problems all had names: Mindy, Hubert, Ryan. At the top of the page I printed, "What to do about Mindy?" I thought for a second and wrote, "Monitor the situation and/or tell Chad." Telling Chad probably wasn't the best idea, though. Mindy was right. It would be her word against mine, and as far as Chad was concerned, Mindy was the last word on everything. Still, it was an option. My best bet was to be hypervigilant. Most likely Mindy wouldn't pursue Ryan. I'd told her in no uncertain terms to back off. More importantly, Ryan was wise to her. Really, Mindy was more irritation than problem. Chances were she'd only expressed interest in Ryan to needle me.

"What to do about Hubert?" was the next heading on the page. Underneath it I wrote one word: "Apologize." He was upset with me, I could tell, and I needed to get that straightened out. Luckily, he was never one to hold a grudge. The fact that we'd kissed really muddied up the friendship. It was a pretty passionate kiss too, and just thinking about how we must have looked to Mindy and Ryan made me flush with embarrassment. Even so, I thought I could placate Hubert. Once I explained that Ryan and I were now going out, he'd have to respect that.

On the lower half of the page I wrote, "Sex with Ryan," and made two columns, one for pros and one for cons. I stared at the paper and then put down the pen when I realized I couldn't go any further. It was one thing to make this kind of listing when considering a job offer. Sex fell into a whole other category. How could I write "feels great" under pros, and think "possibility of disease/pregnancy" under cons would cancel it out? No, sex couldn't be quantified. It was a decision of the heart. And other parts too, but for my purposes, I'd stick with the heart.

I looked at the page before me and tried to think of something else to write. A few minutes ago I'd been burdened down with problems. Now, looking at them printed on the page, the solutions came down to keeping an eye on Mindy, apologizing to Hubert, and playing it by ear with Ryan. Not so bad. Easy, really. No one had cancer. I hadn't lost my house or my job. And I had two guys interested in me. There was nothing to complain about.

I folded the paper in half and then in half again and threw it in the kitchen garbage. I was heading into the living room when I heard a loud thud from above. One solid *bam*, like a body hitting the floor. My first and only thought was that Hubert had fallen. I raced up the stairs two at a time. "Hubert?" I yelled. I methodically checked each room, starting with his, and called out his name as I went along.

When I got to the end of the hallway, almost to the staircase leading to the walk-up attic, I heard his voice. "Up here."

I bounded up the attic stairs to see Hubert sitting cross-legged in the middle of the room. He was dressed now, wearing jeans and a T-shirt, surrounded by piles of papers and suitcases and boxes. A book was open on his lap. He looked up to greet me. "Hi."

"Are you OK? I heard a big crash."

"Oh yeah." He reached back and patted a steamer trunk behind him. "I was moving it from under the eaves, and it slipped out of my hands."

"So what are you doing up here?" I sat down on the floor across from him. The air had a thick, dusty smell that made me wish I could lift up the roof and let it all out.

"I told you I'd clean out your house, remember?" he said. "I decided to work on the attic before it got too hot. Once summer hits, it'll be unbearable up here."

It was almost unbearable now. I'd been up here ten seconds and already felt like taking a shower. "I thought maybe you were avoiding me."

"I wouldn't avoid you," he said, sounding surprised. "Why would you think that?"

He wasn't going to make this easy. "Because I pushed you away in the kitchen before. You looked really mad. I want to apologize—I just didn't want Mindy and Ryan to get the wrong idea. I'm so sorry."

"You're sorry you pushed me away, or you're sorry you kissed me?"

"Both, really. I'm not sure what happened. Something came over me."

"Not sure what happened. Something came over you."

Was there an echo in the room? "I don't know what else to say, but I'm really sorry and—"

"If you don't mind, Lola," he said, shutting the book, "I really don't want to talk about it anymore. You've made your position abundantly clear."

"OK." I was willing to let it go at that, even though he still seemed upset. From the tone of his voice, you'd think *I* was the one who started this thing. It occurred to me to remind him that until recently he'd been mourning the loss of Kelly. And now he'd moved on to me? He couldn't really think I could be his transition person. I was a good friend, but there were limits. "So how's it going?" I asked, changing the subject. "Have you found anything good?"

He smiled, and in an instant he became the old Hubert, my friend. "Nothing you can take to *Antiques Roadshow*, but there is a lot of interesting stuff here—photo albums and scrapbooks and stuff like that. My biggest find so far was your aunt's diaries. Did you know about them?"

I shook my head. I barely knew she had an *attic*, much less what was in it. The woman was almost a stranger to me. I would have been able to pick her out of an old persons' lineup, but that was about it.

"Oh, and her old record player still works. I tried it a few minutes ago." Hubert became more animated as he talked about his attic project. Unbeknownst to me, he'd been working on the attic every day after school, before I came home from the office. "That pile over there," he said, motioning to the far side of the room, "is junk. Old blankets and moth-eaten clothes, melted Christmas ornaments, rusted tools. You can look through it, but I don't think you'll want any of it."

"I'll take your word for it."

"I'm almost done opening the boxes and suitcases. The diaries look really fascinating. You'll want to read those."

I almost said, "Don't be too sure," but he looked so earnest I just smiled in agreement.

"You know," he said, looking around, "this is a great space. It would be a really cool kids' play area."

"Yeah, if you really didn't like the kids."

"It would have to be converted, of course. Insulated and finished off. But imagine how much fun kids could have in a big open area like this." His eyes shone. "You could put a dormer on one side to give it more light and headroom. It would be awesome."

I looked around but couldn't imagine the attic any other way than its current state. I'd always had trouble visualizing change. "That's a possibility, I guess." The air around me swirled with dust motes. I could only imagine how many of them we were inhaling. "Are you ready to take a break, Hubert? It's awfully hot up here. Maybe get something to eat?"

"No, I'm giving my stomach a rest. I just want to get through a few more piles, and then I'll call it a day. If you want to leave, just go ahead."

I hesitated. How rude would it be for me to flee to the comfort of downstairs, leaving my sick friend to sort through my crap? "I hate to leave you here."

"Nah, I don't mind." He waved a hand toward the stairs. "Get outta here. Just don't forget to take the diaries." He picked up a stack of leather-bound books from near his left foot and held them out as if giving me a gift. "They'll give you some interesting bedtime reading."

I took the pile from his hands. Almost reflexively, I wiped at the dust on the top copy with my hand. Great, now I had a grimy hand and a stack of dusty books.

"You'll probably want to wipe the covers with a damp cloth," he said, amused. "And maybe air out the pages."

"Thanks, good advice." What I probably wanted was to store them in the attic for posterity. But to admit that would be ungrateful. Hubert had gone to a lot of trouble for me. The least I could do was pretend to be interested in his find. "I appreciate you doing this for me, you know. It's a dirty job."

"Ach." He brushed away the compliment. "Glad to do it. Now shoo, so I can get some work done."

29

Hubert left with Ben Cho the next morning to make sandwiches for distribution, whatever that meant. I was invited as well but begged off saying I'd brought work home from the office. In truth, I just wanted some alone time to check my e-mail and mindlessly surf the Net.

The phone rang before I even had a chance to fire up my computer, but when I saw Piper's name on the caller ID, I decided my plans could wait.

"Hey," she said when I answered, "sorry I missed your call last night. Mike and I finally got an evening to ourselves."

I lay down on the couch and dangled my legs over the end. A conversation with Piper deserved comfort. I listened politely while she rambled on about her past problems with babysitters. She'd tried various teenagers, but even the best of them were a disappointment. "Remember when we used to babysit?" she said. "We really worked. We gave the kids baths and picked up their toys. One mom even used to leave laundry for me to fold after the kids went to bed. And I didn't think anything of it—just did it. But nowadays teenagers don't do squat. They talk on the phone the whole time and have their friends over. Mike and I stopped going out because I could never find a decent sitter."

She was ecstatic now, she said, because she finally found some-one she trusted. "And Brandon took to her like you wouldn't believe. I'm telling you, Mrs. Olson is the answer to my prayers."

"That might make a good article for the magazine," I said, thinking aloud. "The difficulty of getting good babysitters. We could tell a few horror stories and profile a few who are outstanding."

"Believe me, I could tell you stories."

I didn't point out that she already had.

"One girl helped herself to some ice cream, which would have been OK, except she didn't put the carton back in the freezer, so when I came home there was this melted mess all over the counter."

"Yuck."

"And even worse, she never put Brandon to bed. He fell asleep on the floor, and she just left him there. When I tried to move him, he woke up all out of sorts, and I couldn't get him back to sleep until four in the morning. He cried for hours."

I'd heard Brandon's out-of-sorts cry. It was nothing you'd want to hear if you could help it. "That's terrible."

"Now that we have Mrs. Olson, we can start going out again. Hey, maybe we can double with you and Ryan sometime."

"And then afterwards," I said, "Ryan and I can go to his house and have sex."

"What?"

By the tone of her voice I surmised that the idea of me hav-ing sex was both surprising and amusing. I told her about my conversation with Ryan and his suggestion that being intimate would make us a more convincing engaged couple.

"He *said* that?"

"He actually expected me to believe that people would be able to tell if we'd had sex or not."

"Well that part's true," Piper said. "I can always tell if a dating couple has had sex."

"You can *not.*"

"Yes, I can. There's just something there. If you're looking for it, you'll see it. In fact, my grandma picked up on it after Mike and I did it. We came to a family picnic when we hadn't seen her in a while. She came up to me all sly and said, 'So I see you and Mike are serious now,' and gave me this wink. I was mortified that Grandma knew."

"Maybe she wasn't referring to sex. Maybe it was just because you were still together."

"No, trust me, she knew. It was like she could smell it on us."

Ewwww. So people really could tell? Were there sex clues that everyone in the world knew about, except me? "So you're saying that if I don't have sex with Ryan, people will know?"

"Not everybody. Some people aren't that perceptive. And other people will think you're a good girl waiting for the wedding night, like Jessica Simpson and Nick Lachey."

Yeah, that worked out well for them. "But don't you think it was kind of…" I searched for the right word, "sleazy of him to bring it up that way? To say, 'You must have sex with me, or no one will believe we're engaged.'"

"He phrased it like that?"

I really had her attention now. "Well, no," I admitted. "It was more of a suggestion. And he did say he didn't want to pressure me and it was completely up to me—he'd be my fiancé regardless. But still, I definitely got the impression he was looking to get me in bed."

"Duh," she said. "He's a guy. They work every angle. That's what they do. At least give him points for coming up with something creative. It's better than most lines I've heard."

"I guess."

"And it's really kind of a win-win situation all around. If you don't sleep with him, you still have a great date to take to your sister's wedding. If you do sleep with him, you have great sex and still have a great date for your sister's wedding."

"Assuming the sex is great." I had my doubts. I hadn't done so well in the kissing department with Ryan. I could only imagine how awkward I'd feel naked in bed with the man.

"Oh, it would be," Piper said assuredly. "He's so sexy, *I* felt a little flushed just talking to him. I can only imagine what it would be like to be right up against that body. He's like a Greek god or something."

"So are you saying that if you were me, you'd absolutely have sex with him?"

"I'm saying I wouldn't fault you if you did. But it's really your call."

"You're no help," I grumbled.

"Just follow your heart."

"My heart doesn't know squat."

"OK then, follow your gut."

"My gut is equally stupid."

Piper laughed. "You'll figure out which part of your anatomy to follow." In the background I heard Mike's voice, his tone serious and low. I knew from past experience this signaled the end of our conversation. I was right. "Lola, I hate to cut you short, but Mike has to take the van to Home Depot, and I need to take the car seat out. I'll call you later in the week."

30

The next few days Hubert worked diligently in the attic during his free time. By the time Wednesday rolled around, we had an impressive number of Hefty bags piled for pickup. Garbage night on King Street was an event. Up and down the block the perfect line of the curb was interrupted by bags and cans and blue recycling bins. As usual, Ryan's house was the only one without trash, but since he'd phoned on Sunday to tell me he was called out of town for a few days, it was less of a mystery than the rest of the neighborhood had suggested.

Hubert and I took down the last load and were arranging the garbage bags in a row when Ben Cho came down his driveway hauling a metal can with a dented cover. "Whoa, you have a mother lode of crap," he said. "You're not moving, are you?"

"Just getting rid of stuff," I said. "Hubert's cleaning out my attic."

Ben nodded. "Good man, Hubert. We still on for Friday night?"

"It's a plan."

"See you then." Ben slammed a fist on the lid to force it into place, and then he gave a quick wave and headed back toward his house.

"What's Friday night?" I asked as we headed up the driveway.

"Racquetball at his club," Hubert said. "He has guest passes."

"I didn't know you played racquetball."

"I do now." His voice was cheerful. He seemed to be in a better mood lately—he hadn't mentioned Kelly since the night he was sick, and our friendship was back on track. He did say once that he really should start apartment hunting, but I told him not to worry about it.

"That's good of you, Lola," he replied, clearing the dinner dishes that night. "But I don't want to get in the way here."

"You're not in the way." I gave him an exuberant hug—he'd cooked shrimp scampi that night. It was to die for. "Stay as long as you like." The grateful look on his face spoke volumes.

* * *

On Friday when Ryan stopped in at my office, I was surprised to see him since I'd been watching his house unsuccessfully for signs of his return. His indoor lights were set on a timer that turned them on promptly at seven in the evening and shut them off twelve hours later. The lamppost in his front yard was dark-activated, switching on at dusk. A lawn service came by on Wednesday and mowed and trimmed his yard. To the casual observer the house looked occupied, but I knew better.

When he came through the office door, I was the only one in the room. Mrs. Kinkaid and Drew were out to lunch, and I'd just finished eating at my desk. He walked in like he belonged there, giving me only a second to scoop up my empty yogurt container and apple core and sweep them overboard to the wastebasket next to my desk. Luckily I'd disregarded tradition and eaten my dessert, Hubert's homemade oatmeal cookies, first.

"Hello there." He smiled as he strode across the room. Everything about him, from his voice to the crisp cut of his tailored shirt, made being in his presence a joy. "All alone today?"

"For now," I said, beaming back at him. "The others are out to lunch." I got up from my desk, and he came and took both my hands, like in a movie. I half wished my coworkers had been there—Mrs. Kinkaid would have approved, even if Drew didn't. "What brings you here?"

"You, of course," he said, giving me a quick kiss on the cheek. "I just got back in town, came straight from the airport, in fact. I was hoping I'd get to you before you'd made plans for the weekend." His aftershave smelled great, like the barbershop my dad went to when I was a child.

"No plans." I detected a flash of an expression on his face, a knowing look, as if he'd been sure I wouldn't have anything else going on, and I regretted being so available. It made me sound a little pitiful. "At least, nothing I can't rearrange." On second thought, I remembered smugly, I did have plans for Saturday. "Except I do need to go shopping with my sister and her maid of honor tomorrow afternoon. Can you believe we're getting the dresses only a week before the wedding? We're buying them off the rack. Well, actually," I amended, "they were already picked out and are being held. I just need to go with them and try mine on and buy it. I told Mindy to just go ahead and pick it up, I'd reimburse her, but she was adamant that we have this little outing. She can be like that." Too much information, I knew, but it all seemed to spill out of me. Ryan didn't seem bored, however. From the look on his face, he found me fascinating.

"You'll have to let me know what color your dress is so we can coordinate colors," he said. "With my tie at least."

Oh, like prom couples. What a cute idea.

"So Saturday during the day won't work," Ryan said. "What about today?"

"I could definitely do something today. In fact, I was planning on cutting the day short and leaving in about an hour anyway." This was absolutely not true, but it was amazing how smoothly the lie rolled off my tongue. I could see how lying could become habit-forming.

"Perfect. I'll just run home and unpack, then jump in the shower." He paused, giving me a chance to think of him sudsing up under a pulsating showerhead. "We can meet at say—" He paused to look at his watch. "One thirty?"

"Works for me." I felt my spirits lift.

"Your place or mine?"

I overlooked the teasing subtext behind the question. "You can pick me up at my house whenever you're ready."

He gave me a quick hug before leaving, a completely appropriate embrace for the workplace.

After he was gone, I jotted down a note explaining about my need to leave due to a sudden splitting headache, and I taped it to Mrs. Kinkaid's monitor. Without me around there was zero chance any work would get done the rest of the afternoon. Probably both of them would decide to follow my example and leave early, but I couldn't be worried about that. Ryan was back. He'd driven straight from the airport to find me. Me, and no one else but me. His touch felt fine, and our conversation was easy. He fit the definition of a perfect gentleman, from his polite behavior to his pressed trousers and polished shoes. All my concerns about his hidden sexual agenda faded away.

At home I got ready quickly, slipping on some capri pants with a tank top and a little jacket. For footwear I chose a new pair of sandals, a slip-on type with a kitten heel. Checking myself out in the mirror, I gave myself a passing grade for smart casual attire. If Ryan showed up more dressed up, I could always switch to pants or a skirt and keep the rest of the outfit intact.

I wrote a note for Hubert: "Went out with Ryan! Have fun playing racquetball. See you later. Love, Lola." I put it in the middle of the kitchen table and anchored it with a vase full of red tulips Hubert had picked up at the grocery store. He'd bought them three days earlier, and they were still holding up well.

With time to spare, I grabbed my purse and sunglasses and headed out the door. I had told Ryan to come to my house, but I was too impatient to wait. When I got to the curb, I saw him leaving his house. We were perfectly in sync.

As usual, he looked overjoyed to see me. When I reached his car, which was parked at the curb, he said, "Oh great, you're ready. I do like a girl who's on time."

And I was that girl. Always on time. Ask anyone.

He went on. "Are you hungry? Because if you are, we can get something to eat. Otherwise, I thought it would be fun to drive to Milwaukee. There's a kite-flying event at the lakefront all weekend, and it starts today. Seeing so many kites in flight is incredible, but I'm not trying to influence you. Whatever you decide is fine with me—I could go either way."

"The kites," I said without hesitating. Hubert's oatmeal cookies had staying power. "Unless you're hungry?"

"God no," he said. "Not at all."

Less than an hour later, we were near the shores of scenic Lake Michigan, a lake so vast that it could pass for the ocean. If you could ignore the stench of the dead alewives, it was a gorgeous sight with sun, sand, and a throng of people out and about. Half the city had called in sick, judging by the number of bicyclists and people rollerblading on the path near the lake.

Ryan pulled into a parking space just recently vacated by an Audi, and we headed toward the beach, where several kites were already aloft. Some of the box kites were the size of my refrigerator; others had a wingspan rivaling a great blue heron. "They're beautiful. I had no idea they'd be so big," I said without thinking. Shoot. I had resolved not to let my ignorance show around Ryan, and here I'd slipped already.

"These folks take their kite flying very seriously," he said, taking my hand as we reached the sandy area. "Hey! We should do this sometime. We could go to the kite store and pick out something special, then make a whole day of it."

A day outdoors didn't really sound like my kind of thing, since outdoors is where the bugs and wind and glare are kept, but I wouldn't turn down a chance to spend a whole day with Ryan. "Sounds great."

He leaned over and said, "We'll bring a picnic lunch. Maybe some champagne and strawberries."

Now the man was talking some sense. "I'd love that." He smiled at me, his teeth stark white in the sunlight, and then he pulled my hand up to his lips and kissed my palm. "What was that for?" I asked.

"Just because."

We watched the kites for a while, admiring the way they swayed and bobbed in the wind. Ryan was right—these people did take their kites very seriously. They worked in teams—yelling directions, concentrating fiercely as they let out more line, and whooping with joy when the kites found their place in the sky. "The kites remind me of Japanese dancers," Ryan said.

Huh? I didn't see it myself. Did he mean the movement or the colors or what? Certainly he couldn't mean it literally—dancers, Japanese or otherwise, were people and grounded, whereas these were geometric structures swaying in the wind. But I didn't want to appear completely clueless, so I said, "Yes, just so graceful."

We watched for what must have been twenty minutes or so, but it seemed like hours. The spike heels of my sandals sank into the sand, forcing me to balance uncomfortably on the pads of my feet. Looking upward was tiresome—the harsh sunlight required me to shade my eyes. Plus my neck hurt. And pretending to be fascinated was exhausting. The kites seemed more like something to do as a drive-by—*Look, kites!*—than something necessitating an excursion. "Too bad there's no place to sit down," I said, hoping Ryan would take the hint.

He gave me a concerned look. "Do you want to walk along the shoreline? It might be interesting seeing the kites from a distance."

Yeah, like from the car as we drove away. I hesitated, not wanting to seem difficult, but wondering how I could maneuver this. "I don't think my shoes are ideal for sand," I said, lifting a leg to show him. "I keep sinking." Already I could feel the straps of my sandals digging into the backs of my heels. The reviews on Zappos.com gave this pair high ratings for comfort. I wasn't feeling it.

Ryan held a hand to his chin in thought. "Why don't you take off your shoes then? I'll take mine off too. That way we can walk in the water." He grinned as if he'd suggested something naughty.

I agreed to his plan because it sounded good in theory. Didn't the classic romance scene of every movie take place on the beach? There was even an expression I'd heard people use in casual conversation— "It was no walk on the beach, I can tell you that much." Meaning, of course, that a walk on the beach was a fabulous thing and whatever they were describing was the complete opposite. So who was I to turn down the opportunity to try something so wonderful?

Ryan had the balancing skills of a flamingo. He stepped out of his shoes and peeled off his socks, making it look effortless. I, on the other hand, had to lean against him while fumbling with my buckles. Bending over made the straps tighten, increasing the difficulty. At home I usually sat on my couch, hoisted my foot up to the opposite knee, and took my sandals off while watching TV. Easy. Here it seemed an impossible feat.

"Having trouble?" Ryan asked.

"A little bit." A little bit of an understatement, that is. "The buckles aren't cooperating."

"Let me do it."

"Oh no, I wouldn't want you to have to—"

"Nonsense." He knelt down on one knee and deftly worked each strap through its opening. His back blocked my view of my feet, but I felt the snap of release when each one came undone. He stood up, looking pleased with himself. "Better?"

"Much better." I slipped my feet out of the sandals and picked them up, letting them dangle from my curved fingers. "Should we leave the shoes here?" Carrying them seemed awkward. Movie couples never carried their footwear.

He looked around and frowned. "I wouldn't want to do that. Some kids might come along and think it's funny to take them." He picked up his shoes and held them out to me—a pair of brown loafers with dark stitching on the seams. "These are Berluti. I'd hate to lose them."

"Good point. I'd hate to lose mine too. I just got them recently. From Zappos." Oh, Lola, why don't you ever learn to shut up?

"I'm not familiar with Zappos." Ryan said it like it was a foreign word. "But they seem very nice. Shall we go?" He reached over, and I slipped my hand into his. I noticed that he cradled his shoes with his outside arm, like carrying a football. "This is a great way to spend an afternoon, huh?" he said as we walked.

"Great," I said. This lying got easier all the time. Could I be the only one bothered by the sharp pebbles on the beach? How could he not feel the constant poke with every step?

As we continued on, he talked, oblivious to my pain. He pointed out seagulls and told me how their flight pattern followed the Great Lakes inward to the Midwest. After that, he compared the lake to every lake, river, and ocean he'd ever encountered in his travels: the blue-green of the Mediterranean, the unbelievably clear water of Costa Rica, and a place in Hawaii where the black sandy beaches were actually made up of lava granules. And as he talked, all I could think with every step was, *Ow, ow, ow, ow, ow.* My fingers cramped from carrying the damn sandals, and the soles of my feet hurt.

"Let's walk in the water," I suggested after he finished telling me about every major body of water in the upper hemisphere. Thankfully, he agreed, and he even went along with my idea to leave the shoes on the sand, as long as they were within sight. I waded in ankle deep. "Ah, this feels good." I wiggled my toes in the sand. The water was cold, and I was picking up a faint scent of rotting fish, but other than that—pure nirvana.

Ryan had rolled up his pants legs and now stood beside me. "This is refreshing. And you can really get a great view of the kites from here."

I looked to where he pointed. Oh yes, they were kites all right. Same as before, only smaller. "Great view."

We walked along the shoreline, me always within reach of the gently lapping waves, Ryan with a constant eye-check toward our shoes. I was relieved when he decided our romantic walk was over and we should head back.

Once I'd wiped the wet sand off my feet with a few tissues from my purse and we were back inside Ryan's car, I felt much better. He started up the Jaguar, and I thrilled to the hum of the engine because it meant putting some distance between me and the kites.

31

As we drove along the lakefront, I felt better with each passing mile. I could have lived in Ryan's car, with its smooth ride and climate-controlled temperatures. The music had a sort of surround-sound effect. And of course, Ryan looked superb, his chiseled features still perfectly chiseled, his wavy hair perfectly in place.

"I have to stop at a client's house not too far from here to pick up a check. You don't mind, do you?" His eyes left the road for a second to meet mine.

"No problem," I assured him. Minutes later we pulled into the circular driveway of a mansion on the lake. The shrubs on either side of the massive front doors resembled grown-up bonsai, and the windows were all leaded glass. I was willing to bet it was gorgeous inside.

Leaving the car running, Ryan asked me to wait. He walked briskly up to the front door and slammed the knocker so hard I heard it from inside the car. The door opened a crack, and he exchanged a few words with someone I couldn't see. Then he stepped off the porch, motioned to me with one finger skyward—*just one minute*—and then disappeared around the side of the house.

I've never been good at waiting. After a few minutes passed, I started playing with the radio, stopping when I got to a station playing George Thorogood's "Bad to the Bone." If Hubert had been anywhere within earshot, he'd have been singing along and playing air guitar. *Bad to the bone—ba-ba-ba-ba bad.*

Now that I'd broken one taboo, I got braver. Glancing up to make sure Ryan was still out of sight, I opened the glove compartment and peeked inside. Hmmm, a bottle of Excedrin, a travel-size pack of tissues, and a road map of southeastern Wisconsin. I moved that stuff aside and found a folded-up chunk of papers at the bottom. I pulled them out and smoothed them across my lap. A lease agreement from a car dealership in Milwaukee. It had Ryan's name on it and another name: Arthur Moriarty. It listed the Jaguar as the leased vehicle. I glanced at the specs to make sure it matched. Yep, two-door, color indigo, leather interior. It was the very car I was sitting in. But this contradicted Ryan's story about buying the car, how it had taken months to get because he'd ordered everything custom, or something like that. I had a sudden memory of the psycho woman at the Italian restaurant who'd confronted Ryan and accused him of being a fraud. Hadn't she said the Jaguar was leased?

I folded the papers and put everything back in the glove box, hoping I'd returned it in the same order. I clicked it shut and glanced up just in time to see Ryan returning, a check in hand. He was followed by an older woman who strode after him with a determined look on her face.

He opened the door and with one swift movement threw himself into the seat and pulled it shut. The woman kept coming toward us even as he started up the car and put it into drive. I guessed her to be in her sixties, with the chic look of a woman with a lot of money and time. As we pulled away, I heard her yell, "This is the last time, Ryan. I mean it. Never again."

I strained my neck to look at her through the rear window. She had her fist raised like Scarlett O'Hara vowing never to go hungry again. "What was that all about?" I asked.

"Just forget about her," he said, folding the check in two and sliding it into his shirt pocket. "She's completely unreasonable. I'd love to drop her account, but I've been managing it for years."

Her account? What kind of account would that be? I thought he did some kind of troubleshooting, quality management type thing. Something wasn't adding up, but before I could question it, he said, "Hey, you changed the radio station."

"Is that OK?"

"Sure. It's fine," Ryan said, but he didn't look too pleased. After the song was over, I noticed he changed it back.

We drove in silence for a few miles. He tapped on the wheel impatiently as he maneuvered through traffic. Once we were on the expressway, it seemed safe to ask, "Do you want to just cut this short and go home? I'm fine with that, really."

"Forgive me." He gave me a sideways look and reached over and gave my hand a squeeze. "I know I seem grouchy. I just hate having to deal with those people. It always puts me in a bad mood. But I won't let it this time because I'm with you, and I don't want anything to spoil this day. Besides, we can't stop now. I have a really special evening planned for us."

"You do?"

"Yes, Miss Lola Watson, I most certainly do. I have a very elegant dinner planned. A celebration."

"And exactly what are we celebrating?"

"We're celebrating that in this big, cold world we somehow managed to find each other. I made reservations at the Palmer House. I hope you approve."

The Palmer House? I couldn't walk past that place, the way I was dressed. "I approve," I said. "But I hope your plan allows me to go home and change clothes first."

"Whatever the lady wants."

32

Hubert was sitting on the couch reading when I walked in the door. I wouldn't want to teach grade school, but I wouldn't mind the schedule. "You're early," he said without looking up. "You got two phone messages. Brother Jasper called to say he wanted to talk to you at your earliest convenience. And then Mindy left one—she won't be at the dress place tomorrow, but you should meet Jessica there."

Oops, I'd completely forgotten to get back to Brother Jasper regarding his cautionary tales. "Did Brother Jasper say what he wanted, exactly?"

"I didn't talk to him. It was on the machine." He turned a page. From the look on his face, he was totally engrossed.

"That must be a really good book."

Hubert looked up. "It's one of your aunt's diaries. You left them on the dining room table—I couldn't resist. You know I have a thing for local history. I hope it's OK."

"Of course it's OK. I've been meaning to get to them, but—" I stopped because I really didn't know why I hadn't looked at them yet. I guess reading about an old lady who'd never been married had no appeal to me.

"She had such an incredible life. And her writing is so vivid,

I feel like I'm there. Did you know she was engaged to be married? Her fiancé was killed in the war. Even reading about it is heartbreaking. She writes about how his sister came to her door with the telegram in her hand. May could tell by the look on her face that he was dead, but she didn't want to believe it."

I sat down in the wing chair to listen.

Hubert looked pensive. "There was one passage she wrote… wait, I'll find it." He flipped through the yellowed pages. "Here it is." He held the book up as if to give the passage significance. "'In one instant I'd lost my best friend, my love, my husband-to-be. And now the future we'd planned was taken away from me. The children not yet born would never be.' And then she goes on to talk about their relationship, how they both loved practical jokes and word play, how no one could make her laugh like him. It's just so sad." He looked up, his eyes brimming with tears.

"Are you crying?" I was shocked. This wasn't like him.

"I guess so," he said, a little embarrassed. He wiped at his eyes. "I have no idea why this is getting to me so much."

"Well, it is pretty awful."

"Yeah, and I guess knowing that she lived in this house her whole life really drives it home. Did I tell you that I found her last diary when I was cleaning out one of the bedrooms upstairs?"

I shook my head.

"She kept these diaries kind of on and off, from what I can tell. Sometimes she let it go for years and then picked it up again. The one upstairs was the most recent, from right up until she died. She kept it in the nightstand drawer. I'd like to read them in order, if that's OK with you."

"Sure. Whatever you want."

He beamed. Such an easily pleased man. "So what are your plans for tonight?" he asked. "I'm playing racquetball with Ben Cho at six, but maybe later—"

"Sorry, but I have plans to go to dinner with Ryan. Didn't you see my note on the table?" I could tell by the look on his face that he hadn't.

"That Ryan guy again?" He set the diary down on the couch next to him and leaned forward with clasped hands. "What are you doing with him, Lola?"

"What? I like him." OK, I sounded a little defensive, but what was with people thinking that a hot guy like Ryan would never be interested in a plain girl like me? In Hubert's case, it was possible he thought he was protecting me from some unsavory character, but really—give me a break. Did any of them stop to think that maybe Ryan was genuinely attracted to me? It wasn't so far-fetched.

Hubert sighed. "He's just so slick. The whole time I was talking to him all I could wonder was, what's his game? You hardly know him. Take it from me—you can think you know a person, and it can turn out that they have a whole other side you know nothing about. I just don't want you to get hurt."

He was comparing Ryan to Kelly? Please. "You only talked to him for a few minutes," I pointed out, "so I hardly think you can cast judgments. Trust me, he has no 'game'—we're just two people dating."

"It's not just me saying it." He rested his chin on his fist. "The whole neighborhood talks about him."

"I know, I've heard. He never puts out garbage, and he's gone a lot, and he has a lot of packages delivered. None of which is a crime, by the way." I looked at my watch. I only had an hour before Ryan and I were leaving for the restaurant.

"Belinda said she looked up his property tax records and they were paid late three years in a row. Not only that, but—"

"I think Belinda should mind her own business," I said, standing up abruptly. "If you'll excuse me, Hubert, I have to get dressed for dinner at the Palmer House."

I went upstairs and got ready for my date, starting from bare skin and working outward. I lathered up and rinsed off in the shower, washing away the sand still encrusted between my toes. I loofahed my elbows and knees, something I knew to be part of Piper's routine but which I never saw the need for prior to this. I reapplied makeup and dried my hair using my round brush, and then I slipped on a deep red halter dress I'd only worn once before, for a wedding. My uncle compared it to the one Marilyn Monroe wore standing over the air vent, and he was close even if the color was different and I was no Marilyn Monroe. Still, it was a great dress—silk, or at least silk-like. It required dry-cleaning, so each use was a seven-dollar investment. The neckline plunged pretty low for me. Luckily, the dress had built-in cups. I wore a gold necklace to take the focus off my breasts and put on the matching bolero jacket, which toned down the look from slutty to sexy.

The ensemble came with a clutch purse, a concept I despised. A regular purse with a strap could be slung over a shoulder or held loosely, but a clutch purse had to be *clutched*, an abnormal position that turned a woman's hand into a claw. Still, the purse matched, so what could I do? I loaded it with my wallet, phone, sunglasses, and lip gloss and then snapped it shut. Men were lucky—they could get by with pockets.

When the time came to leave, I slipped out the back door and yelled, "Bye, Hubert," as I left. I loved Hubert, really I did, but I wasn't up to hearing more penny-ante bad news about Ryan before my date. I was a big girl and a pretty good judge of character. I appreciated his concern, but he'd have to trust me on this.

33

The Palmer House gave Ryan the stamp of approval. Everyone recognized him, from the two young men who did valet parking, to the bartender, to the maître d'. A group of businessmen stopped their conversation to greet Ryan as we were led to our table. ("The corner, just as you requested, Mr. Moriarty.") I felt like I was out with George Clooney. After we sat down, I asked, "How do they all know you?"

"I bring clients here quite often," he said. "And my parents know the owners. We've been coming here for years. You know how that is."

I looked around the elegant dining room with its beautiful chandelier made up of millions of prisms, the thick drapes held back with gold cord, the oil paintings each highlighted with their own little stage light. My family also had a restaurant we'd frequented for years. It was a pizza joint called Barnaby's that featured a little jukebox at each booth. As kids, Mindy and I couldn't wait to finish our meal because then we could pick a prize out of the treasure chest. I always looked for the plastic decayed teeth, while Mindy generally picked toy tiaras or rings.

I let Ryan choose the wine, and after he ordered coq au vin and a spinach salad, I told the waiter I'd have the same. Since he picked the wine to go with the chicken, it seemed a safe choice.

The meal went seamlessly, from wine to bread to salad to the main course. Ryan did most of the talking, telling me about some of his most recent trips and a few minor airport snafus—delayed flights, missed connections. I nodded and drank throughout. At one point, I realized my mind was drifting. Pleasantly drifting. I emptied my glass, and before I could even set it down, our waiter was there to refill it. We never got that kind of service at Barnaby's.

The alcohol was really kicking in now. I felt a surge of affection for everyone in the room, from the dark-haired young man who cleared our salad plates, to the two old ladies at the next table, both of whom looked like the Queen Mother. "Tell me again what you do exactly for your work," I said during a pause.

"Quality control, mostly. I also help companies implement management systems."

"Management systems?"

"Six Sigma, Lean, that type of thing."

"And you like your job?" In my slightly drunken state it seemed important to pin down exactly who this man was.

"I like it well enough," he said, putting his hand over mine. "It pays the bills."

The bills. I thought of his property tax. Late three years in a row. If it weren't for that damn nosy Belinda poking her nose in Ryan's business, I wouldn't even know that little bit of trivia. Big deal, so his taxes were a little late. It happens. He paid them eventually. Maybe Ryan was just one of those people who has trouble keeping track of paperwork. An easy explanation. But there was one more thing on my mind. "Did you say you bought your car six months ago?"

"No, I said I *got* my car six months ago." He took a sip of wine. "It's leased. I find that leasing has tax advantages for me."

Now I was confused. I thought for sure he said he bought it. I remembered him saying he had the Jag ordered. Something about it being customized. My thinking on the subject was fuzzy, and I was having trouble remembering why I'd doubted him in the first place. Or why it even mattered.

"Did I tell you how stunning you look in that dress?" Ryan ran a finger over the sleeve of the jacket. "That's a great color on you. Beautiful."

And suddenly I felt beautiful. I was in a la-di-da restaurant, being pampered and spoiled by the attentive staff. Money was no object this evening. I was with Ryan, a drop-dead gorgeous guy and Palmer House celebrity. We were eating delicious food that had been painstakingly prepared and served on beautiful china. The wine was delicious, light and medium dry. It went down as smoothly as spring rain in a valley.

By the time our dinner plates were cleared, I decided I could have this exact evening played over and over in one continuous loop into eternity, me in my gorgeous red dress across from this beautiful man.

Our wine glasses were full again, and Ryan proposed a toast. "To new beginnings," he said. I held my glass up but didn't try to clink. I had a feeling that was a beer hall move. "Lola," he said, stretching my name beyond the boundaries of its two syllables. "Remember our plan to announce our faux engagement at your sister's wedding?"

"Of course." Man, this wine was good. Was this new bottle different than the previous one?

"If you don't have any objections, I'd like to propose to you tonight. Everyone always asks about the proposal, and I think it would make a great story."

I set down my glass, unsure, while he got up out of his chair and knelt on one knee in front of me. The tables around us hushed with the realization of what was happening. Looking down at him, I noticed for the first time that the carpet had a subtle fleur-de-lis pattern. "Lola," he said, enunciating clearly, "I love you and want to spend my life with you. Will you marry me?" Like a magician, he pulled a box seemingly out of nowhere and flipped it open to reveal a breathtakingly beautiful diamond ring.

"Wow," I said. I realized that was not the right answer when Ryan said, a little more loudly this time, "Will you marry me, Lola?"

"Yes, Ryan," I said, "I will marry you." The other diners applauded loudly, and I heard a few sentimental murmurs. I got an impression of confetti filling the air, flashbulbs going off, and a violinist playing in the distance, but that may have been the wine. I know for certain that a romantic kiss followed, and then Ryan slid the ring onto my finger. It was loose.

"Look," he said, "it's a perfect fit. I think that's a good sign."

34

It was official. I was drunk.

Not falling down drunk, thank goodness, but definitely a little more than tipsy. When the valet brought the car around and Ryan opened the door for me, I had to think hard about the best way to get in. It was dark and the opening looked smaller than before. I managed, somehow, remembering at the last minute the general rule that legs go last.

As Ryan shifted into drive, he said, "That went well, don't you think?"

"Very well." I held my hand out to admire the ring. Ryan had said the center stone was three carats, and the diamonds on either side were a carat each.

"I think my performance was rather convincing."

"Yes, very convincing." I moved my hand, trying to get the diamonds to catch the light from the dashboard.

"Be careful with that," he said, glancing over. "It's on loan from the jeweler."

"A jeweler let you borrow this?" How did that work?

He nodded. "I said I'd need it for a few weeks."

I wasn't sure why I felt disappointed. After all, I *knew* this was a con. Still, there was a small part of me that would have loved to keep the ring. "And they were OK with you taking it? How? I mean, why would they let you do that?"

"They were under the distinct impression," he said, grinning devilishly, "that I might possibly be buying it."

"So what will you say when you return it?"

"I will say that the love of my life turned me down." He wiped away a pretend tear. "And when they see what a heartbroken, pathetic shell of a man I've become, they'll gift me with some cheap cufflinks so I won't have to walk away emptyhanded. A consolation prize to ensure I don't associate the jeweler with rejection."

It sounded like he had experience in this area. I tilted my hand and looked at the ring from every angle. I could see now why newly engaged women kept their nails beautifully manicured.

He said, "I looked at dozens of rings before selecting this one. I know some might consider five carats a little ostentatious, but I thought for our purposes it worked. We want to make a splash." He sounded pleased with himself.

"This will definitely make a splash." A temporary splash. At least he'd end up with cufflinks, unlike, say, me, who would have only the memory of once having gotten a ring.

When we turned onto the interstate, Ryan put in a new CD, one of the Marsalis brothers. I forgot which one immediately after hearing the name. The music was nice though. In my inebriated state, it played like the soundtrack of a movie in which a movie-star handsome man drove his pretend fiancée home after having just made a fake marriage proposal to her at a restaurant. We were enactors, I realized sadly—like Civil War reenactors. No matter how convincingly the soldiers were dressed, with their authentic costumes and mutton chop whiskers, spectators always knew it was pretend. No one ever ran for cover during the fake battles. No one ever called 911 to help the injured. They looked like soldiers, and they acted like soldiers, but it didn't ring true.

Because it wasn't real.

And my relatives would know too, I realized, that Ryan and I weren't real. We could stand in front of all the guests at Mindy and Chad's wedding—Ryan looking dashing, and me a dressed-up version of the Lola they'd known forever—and even with this ring on my finger, the picture wouldn't fit. We'd look like two people who'd just started dating, a couple who didn't even know each other's middle names or toothpaste preference. Frauds. It would be so sad and humiliating not to be able to pull it off. If only there was a way to make it convincing.

If only.

"Ryan," I said, "I've been thinking about the conversation we had on your porch the other day. Do you remember?"

"Sure." He reached over and turned the radio down.

"When we were talking about Mindy's wedding, and you said people can tell if a couple has had sex or not."

"I remember."

"Do you really think that's true?"

"Yes, I do." Ryan exited onto the main thoroughfare that led back to our neighborhood. "Why do you ask?" He sneaked a glance in my direction.

"It's just," I said, "that I think I've come around to your way of thinking."

"I see." And then he said nothing for the longest time. The longest time. The jazz CD played to the end of the song, and then there was a silence before a new song began. His face was completely impassive, impossible to read. I looked out the window and watched the streetlights whiz past and reflected that I'd reached a new low. I'd just offered to have sex with a man and gotten no reaction at all.

We turned onto King Street, and I heard him humming along with the music. I turned my head to see his lips curled in a smile. "Here we are," he said, pulling into his driveway and pushing the button to open his garage door. When the car came to a stop, he shifted into park, turned off the engine, leaned over, and said, "I guess I don't have to ask if you'd like to come in." The garage door closed behind us.

"No, you don't have to ask." Relief flooded over me. I wasn't a complete reject after all. I reached over to open the door, but Ryan told me to wait. He wanted to do the gentlemanly thing, which was good because that consisted of helping me out of the car and across to the side door.

There was a short path between the garage and the house, partially shielded by shrubs. When we stood on the threshold looking toward the house, Ryan whispered, "This is where it gets tricky." He slid his arm around my lower back. "We have to be very quiet because if any of the neighbors are walking by, they'll want to stop and chat and we'll be stuck out here forever."

"I hate that," I said.

"Me too. That one with the dogs is the worst."

Ah, Belinda. He didn't know the half of it.

Inside the house he led me through the dark to the living room. In the dimness I could see the faint outline of a couch and chair on one wall, with the television set in the corner. A pretty sparse setup, not even a coffee table or ottoman. The only light in the room came through the slats of the blinds on the window opposite the couch.

"Come here, you," Ryan said, pulling me up against him. He put his lips on mine and kissed me hard.

I slipped off my bolero jacket and let it drop to the floor. Ryan's face showed approval. "You've been holding out on me," he said. "Wow, you look hot in that dress. I can't wait to see you out of it."

Yes, it was an old line, but it was the first time anyone had ever said it to me.

I slid my arms around his neck, still aware of the ring on my finger. We melted together, kissing so heatedly it was hard for me to tell where my mouth ended and his began. Like it was choreographed, we stopped to kick off shoes. He peeled off his socks. I started to unbutton his shirt, but my fingers fumbled and I couldn't manage it. He took over, and his shirt fell to the floor.

My eyes had adjusted to the lack of light. I ran my hands over his broad chest and felt like I was watching someone else. Lola Watson would never do anything this impulsive. My heart pounded, and my body experienced sensory overload.

"Shouldn't we go to the bedroom?" I asked.

"No, it's better here. My bedroom's a mess." His breathing was heavy in my ear. I thought of one of my former roommate's favorite expressions— "hot and bothered"—and like verbs in French class, I came up with all the conjugations: he was hot and bothered, she was hot and bothered, I was hot and bothered.

He unsnapped the back of my halter dress, and the front fell to my waist. He reached down and tugged impatiently at the waist, but it wasn't going anywhere.

"There's a zipper," I said, reaching back.

But before I could get it, he said, "Oh, the hell with it," and maneuvered me back onto the couch. Once I was down, he lowered his pants. The answer to the age-old question was…briefs. Not tighty whities, thankfully, something darker. His pants and briefs joined the shirt on the floor.

Now he was completely naked on top of me. I was partially unclothed, but all I could think about was the way my dress was bunched up around my middle, making me feel bulky. Like I needed that.

He ran his hand up my thigh-high stocking and between my legs. "Someone has too much clothing on," he whispered in my ear.

You think? I shifted beneath him. "Maybe if I could—" But before I could finish my sentence, he moaned gently.

"What do you think of this?" he asked, taking my hand and guiding it to him. I lifted my head to see my hand up against what could only be described as a Dodger dog. He smiled. "See what you do to me?"

I had a moment of clarity when I wondered if there was a condom in the vicinity, but glancing around the room, I doubted it. The man didn't even have coasters—how prepared could he be?

He positioned my hand like I was going to shift into a higher gear, but who knew who'd driven this thing before? "Maybe we should be taking precautions?" I said.

"You aren't on the pill?"

I shook my head.

"Don't worry, I know how to handle it. Just keep doing what you're doing."

In fact, I wasn't doing much of anything. Just lying flat on my back, shell-shocked, wondering what I'd gotten myself into. I'd always envied the spontaneous, the free-spirited, but now I was second-guessing the whole situation.

My thoughts were interrupted by noises from outside—voices and hurried footsteps and what sounded like the static and squawking of walkie-talkies. "What's that?" I asked, pulling my hand away.

"I don't know. Just ignore it." He'd moved down and was grinding against my thighs, his hand on my breast. "Feels great, doesn't it, Lola?"

One of Ryan's windows was definitely open. Outside the voices were louder, reminding me of the mob scene in the *Frankenstein* movie. I couldn't ignore it. Even Ryan seemed a little distracted, pausing to look at the window. He finally said, "God, I wish they'd stop whatever it is they're doing."

And then I heard it—Belinda calling, "Baxter, Baxter. Come on boy, come to Mommy." She sounded like she was right in front of the house.

"Lost dog," I said.

"Dammit," Ryan said, rearing up. "I'm closing that window." He dismounted and crossed the room, giving me a good view of him from the back. Before he reached the window, a bright beam of light shone into the room through the gaps in the blinds. "Shit," he said, dropping onto all fours. "What the hell are they doing out there?"

The beam of light swung in circles. Good God, it looked like an invasion. I sat up and pulled my halter top in place, snapped it securely, and then walked over to the window to peek between the slats. Gathered on the sidewalk I recognized Belinda, Brother Jasper, a few of the Chos, and two of the college girls who rented the house down the block. Belinda held a flashlight, one of those big industrial jobs that could have been used to direct plane landings. The group conferred for a minute or so and then broke into pairs, scattering down the sidewalk. "They're going away," I said, turning back to Ryan, who was still crouched on the floor.

"Too late now," he said sourly. He stood up and I could see that, luckily for me, it really was too late.

35

"So he couldn't get it up?" Piper asked. We were walking the mall, and she was pushing Brandon in his stroller. I'd just finished giving her the lowdown on the previous night.

"No, it was up at one point. Standing proud. It just didn't stay up. There was this commotion outside. The neighbors were looking for a lost dog." I stopped to pick up a board book Brandon had dropped over the side. Piper took it from me and stuck it in the diaper bag. "They were yelling and shining a flashlight. It broke his concentration."

"That's not all it broke." She laughed and made a grunting noise.

"Oh stop, please," I said, but I had to smile. Some things were a lot funnier in retrospect.

"So what did it look like?"

"What?"

She took a sip from her water bottle. "Don't be so coy. You know what I'm talking about. What did his thing look like?"

"You know the button mushrooms they spear and serve in drinks? A lot like that."

"I meant before it shrunk."

"Sort of like a Dodger dog."

"Oh, one of those."

We stopped at a bench, and she handed Brandon a chunk of soft pretzel, which he chewed on enthusiastically.

"So what then?" Piper said. "You just went home?"

"Yeah, but get this. Just before I'm out the door he stops me and takes my hands, and I think he's going to say he's sorry for how things went or whatever, but instead he pulls up my left hand—" here I illustrated by raising my hand like stopping traffic "—and jerks the ring off my finger and says, 'I better hold onto this.'"

"Really?" Piper looked fascinated. "Did he think you wouldn't give it back?"

"Apparently. So then I just slunk home, talked to Hubert for a while, and went to bed."

"Hubert wasn't part of the dog search party?"

"No, he didn't know anything about it." I rubbed my forehead. Despite a liberal dose of Excedrin, I still had a killer wine headache. "He'd gotten back from playing racquetball and spent most of the evening in the kitchen reading my aunt's diaries. He's addicted to them."

* * *

I'd only given Piper the bare bones of the Hubert situation. When I came home, he was sitting at the table reading. I must have looked pretty terrible after my ordeal at Ryan's—all bleary-eyed and rumpled. Lacking a comb, I'd raked through my hair with my fingers during the walk across the street. I had a feeling it didn't help much. When I walked into the kitchen, I was about to apologize for my appearance when he looked up and said, "How was the date?"

"A bit of a letdown, if you must know."

"Ah, too bad." But he didn't look like he meant it. "But you look great anyway. Really beautiful."

"It's the dress. It's a good color for me, or so I've been told."

"No, it's not the dress. I mean the dress is nice, but it's you I was referring to."

"Thanks." I stood for a second. He looked so familiar and welcoming in his T-shirt and jeans with my aunt's diary open in front of him. "Still reading that, huh?"

He grinned. "Your aunt was awesome. I wish I could have met her. I have about a hundred questions I'd love to ask her."

"Like what?" I pulled out a chair and sat down, glad to have something else to think about.

"Just about her life and her travels and the people she knew. Did you know that Myra was a young woman with a husband and a baby when she moved into the house next door? Your aunt was the first neighbor to greet them. She took a cake. Wasn't that nice? People used to do those kinds of things."

I thought guiltily of my own King Street moving experience. That day, and for the rest of the week, at least half a dozen neighbors had stopped by, bearing everything from flowers to homemade pickles. I'd thought they were a nuisance.

"And then," he continued, "I was reading one of her later diaries, and she wrote about Myra's baby getting killed. That's what she called her, 'Myra's baby,' even thought the little girl was almost four at the time. It's the saddest story. Myra was off visiting her sick sister for the day, and her husband was supposed to be watching their daughter, Janie. Janie ran out into the street and was hit by a car. They took her to the hospital, but it was no use. May said that Myra never forgave her husband for not being more attentive. She doted on that girl. She was their only child." He looked away, as if he'd been there and was remembering it himself. "And then two years later, Myra's husband took sick and died. At the funeral Myra kept saying, 'I didn't really mean it, I didn't really mean it,' and when your aunt asked what she was talking about, she said, 'I wished him dead, but I really didn't mean it.'"

"Hubert, you're depressing the hell out of me." I slid my feet out of my shoes and wiggled my toes. "Why read it if it's so sad?"

"It's not all sad," he said. "Your aunt had a very complete life—good and bad—but sad times are part of life too, you know."

"You can say that again," I said glumly. I turned sideways in my chair to give myself some room, and then I reached under my dress to take off my stockings. I pulled each one off in turn and draped them over the back of my chair. What a relief. The elastic cuff that had held them in place had left ridges around my thighs like the edge of a dime. I rubbed at the indents with my fingers, but nothing changed. Just my luck to be permanently disfigured as a result of an elegant evening out on the town. I massaged the marks, which had the unfortunate effect of making them more pronounced. I looked up to see Hubert staring at me in fascination.

"Do you need some help?"

"No, I—" I realized then that I'd hoisted my dress nearly to my crotch. "I just had to get these stockings off. They were driving me crazy."

"Lola, are you drunk?"

"Just a little bit." I lowered my skirt over my knees.

Hubert regarded me carefully. "A little bit?"

"I had some wine."

"How much wine? A lot?"

"I don't know. I lost count."

"That's a lot."

"I think it's mostly worn off by now." Why did he look so amused?

"So what went wrong with the date?"

"If you don't mind, I'd rather not talk about it."

"Not even a hint? The food was bad, the car broke down, the guy was a jerk? That was it, wasn't it? The guy was a jerk."

"I said I really don't want to talk about it."

"Come on, it couldn't have been that bad, could it?"

And that's when I began crying. At first I thought I was just blinking a lot, a sort of psychological impulse, like trying to blink away the image of Ryan's angry face when he told me it was too late. Or trying to blink away the thought that next week I would be thirty and the only diamond engagement ring I'd ever gotten was on loan and would soon be traded in for cheap cufflinks. Maybe moisture was forming in my eyes because I was tired and drank too much wine and my aunt was dead and I never really knew her and Hubert would have loved her. There were a lot of good reasons why my eyes might be getting so emotional. Whatever it was, though, once it started, I couldn't seem to stop.

Hubert looked stricken. "Oh no, Lola, don't cry. I'm sorry, I didn't mean to push it. I won't talk about it anymore."

I wiped my face with the back of my hand. "It's not your fault," I said, trying to choke back sobs.

"You're being nice. It *is* my fault. I'm sorry."

I could tell by his face we were entering that weird cycle where he felt awful because I felt terrible, and then I'd feel terrible about making him feel awful. Round and round it would go. "Just forget about it. It's nothing." I sniffed.

He leaned forward in his chair with a sad look on his face. "It's certainly not nothing if you're this upset." He held out his arms. "Come here." And then it was the easiest thing in the world to get up from my chair and crawl into his lap. "There now," he said, stroking my back. I settled against his chest and closed my eyes. The feel of his hand between my shoulder blades was almost hypnotic. My breathing slowed, and I found myself relaxing into him. Such a good man. "See," he said after a few minutes, "everything's going to be fine." Such a comfortable, reassuring man. I could see why the fourth graders loved having him as a teacher. "Are you sure you don't want to tell me what's wrong? You never know, I might be able to help."

"It's too complicated." His fingertips were making a circular motion on my back. I hoped he wouldn't stop.

"Try me."

"It's just…" I exhaled wearily. "I'm just so tired of everyone. I'm really starting to hate people."

"Not all people, I hope."

"Well, not you," I admitted. "And not Piper or my parents." I tried to think of other exceptions, without success. "But pretty much everybody else."

"I'm glad I'm on the short list, anyway."

"And I'll be so glad when Mindy's wedding is over next week. I'm really dreading it."

"Why?"

Wasn't it obvious? "Because it's all about Mindy and how beautiful she is and how in love she and Chad are and how they've been together forever. And then, compare and contrast, there's me." I stopped to sniff; Hubert handed me a paper napkin. "Me, the older unmarried sister, all big and frumpy."

"Oh stop. You've got to be kidding. You don't really think that."

"Mindy will look stunning. And my dress—" I hadn't actually seen my dress yet. She and Jessica had selected it, and I was picking it up from the mall the next day. "My dress will probably be hideous. Or very unflattering, anyway." I blew my nose into the napkin. "It'll probably make my ass look like it has a life of its own."

I waited for Hubert to contradict me, to say there's no way my ass could look like that. Instead he said, "Don't worry about it, Lola. Mindy's got nothing on you. And anybody who can't see that is a complete idiot."

OK, that was a good thing to say. "Remind me of that at the reception, would you?"

"I would if I was going to be there."

I lifted my head. "You aren't coming to the wedding?"

"No, Lola. For one, I wasn't invited. And secondly, I'm helping with the block party that day."

That damn block party again. "Can't you skip it? Tell them something came up?"

"I promised Brother Jasper I'd be available all day. The proceeds this year are going to help a family whose little boy has leukemia. The mom has to take off work a lot, and they're barely making it."

"Oh, but I wish you were going to be at the wedding." I could handle it if he were there.

His brow furrowed. "Piper told me Ryan was going to be your date."

"That might not be the case anymore."

"I see." He kneaded my shoulder with his thumb. "Well, normally I'd love to stand in for Ryan, but I'm unavailable on the seventh. Sorry."

I sighed. "I'd rather have you there than him any day." I hadn't realized it was true until I'd said it.

"There you go—if nothing else, you always have me. Small consolation I know, but at least it's something."

"That's no small consolation. It's huge."

We sat for a little while, him massaging my shoulders like I was headed into the boxing ring, me feeling better. After a few minutes he said, "Lola, you better get up. My legs are falling asleep."

I got up as requested, but we both knew it wasn't his legs causing the problem. Another part of him was now wide-awake and standing at attention.

* * *

What I'd told Piper was basically true: I came home, talked to Hubert, and then went to bed. I just left out that one little sexually charged detail. It wasn't like me not to tell Piper all, but I knew if I did this time she'd ask questions, probing questions that I wasn't sure I knew the answers to. I'd tell her about it at some point—just not now, sitting on a bench in the mall.

"So your date ended badly," Piper said, jarring me from my thoughts. "Does this mean he's not going to be your fiancé at the wedding?"

"I'm not counting on it," I said.

"But if he wants to, you will, right? You'll say you're engaged?"

"I guess." At least Ryan made good arm candy. And we had the proposal story ready. The ring was gorgeous. Maybe I'd go through with it after all.

Piper broke off another piece of soft pretzel, handed it to the baby, and then glanced at her watch. "You know it's almost two o'clock, don't you? Isn't that when you're supposed to meet Jessica?"

Ah, Jessica. The real reason for my trip to the mall. "Yes, two o'clock. Are you coming along?"

"No, I better get Brandon home before he has a meltdown. Have fun."

"Thanks.

Jessica was waiting for me when I arrived at Windsor, a mall store featuring a banner over the door that read, "Prom season is here!"

"You're late," she said as I walked in the door.

I had a headache and wasn't in the mood. "Whatever. I'm here now, so let's take care of this thing."

Ten minutes later I stood before a three-way mirror in a silvery, off-the-shoulder gown that fit like it was made for me. The fabric was iridescent, and when I moved from side to side it shimmered like dragonfly wings. "I can't believe how much I like this dress," I said to Jessica, who sat watching, her purse in her lap. I picked up the fabric like a princess in a movie and moved the folds of the material to reflect the light.

"I picked it out," Jessica said grumpily. "I've been doing a lot of your sister's decision making lately. What's up with that? She was all over this wedding at first. We were doing it together, but lately she never has time for me. Suddenly it's like you two are best friends."

I turned to her. "What?"

"Not that I'm jealous or anything, you are sisters, but she's kind of being rude about it."

"Rude about what?"

"All week she gave me the brush-off. She was either at your house or you two were going somewhere."

"Jessica, I don't know what you're talking about. I haven't seen Mindy at all this week."

She looked confused. "No, on Wednesday and Thursday she took off work so the two of you—"

"I haven't even *talked* to Mindy this week, and I worked Wednesday and Thursday."

"But Chad even said she was with you."

I shook my head, and we stared at each other.

"So where was she?" Jessica asked.

"I don't know." I thought of Mindy's fascination with Ryan. If he hadn't been out of town, I would have suspected something between them. But Ryan wasn't even home this week, and he had stopped in at my office on Friday, straight from the airport. Or at least that's what he said. My head still hurt from the previous night's wine, and thinking too hard made it worse. "I just don't know," I repeated.

"I'm going to ask her," Jessica said. "That's bullshit that she can't even tell me the truth. I'm her best friend and maid of honor, for God's sake."

"When you find out what's actually going on, I'd love to hear it," I said. Jessica said she'd let me know, but I wasn't holding my breath.

I drove home with the bridesmaid gown hanging off a hook in my backseat. Where in the hell had Mindy been all this week? I would ask her, I decided. If she was going to use me as an alibi, I deserved an explanation.

36

The next night Hubert and I were playing Scrabble in the kitchen when Chad burst in on us. Yes, the front door was open and the screen door unlocked, but I wasn't expecting any visitors, much less my sister's fiancé barging in red-faced and angry. "Where is she, Lola?" he yelled.

I'd just added "fire" to Hubert's "fly," landing on a double word score. A most excellent move on my part. Chad's appearance detracted from my achievement and startled me. "You're looking for Mindy?" I asked.

"You know I'm looking for her," he said. "Don't bother trying to cover for her. Just tell me where she is."

"I haven't seen Mindy or talked to her for a week now. I have no idea where she is."

"Mindy's missing?" Hubert said.

I filled him in. "She's been letting Chad and Jessica think she's with me the past week, but I haven't seen her."

"Aha, you *did* know." Chad pointed at me. "And you didn't tell me."

"Jessica and I figured it out yesterday at the mall. I called Mindy's cell today, but she didn't answer."

"But you weren't going to tell me?"

"I was giving her the benefit of the doubt. Maybe there's a good explanation."

"Like what?"

"I don't know," I said. "Maybe she's off planning some big surprise for you, a wedding gift or something." I could tell that neither Hubert nor Chad thought that was likely. Mindy wasn't much of a giver.

"You know something you're not telling me," he said accusingly. "She's been coming here and you've been driving her somewhere or something."

"What are you talking about? Why would I do that?"

"I know it because—" He snapped his fingers. "Come outside and I'll show you." He turned and disappeared from the kitchen.

Hubert pushed back his chair and got up. "Don't tell me you're not curious, Lola. Let's go out and see what the man's talking about."

I followed Hubert out onto the porch, down the front walkway, and over to Chad, who stood next to his car.

"Right here," Chad said, pointing to the curb. "Right here it's twenty-two point two miles from our condo. Twenty-two point two."

Three twos in a row had a nice symmetry, but I didn't get his meaning. "So?"

"Twenty-two point two," he said. "So doubled that's forty-four point four, right?"

I looked to Hubert, who nodded. In fourth grade they covered decimals. Chad continued. "And that's exactly how many miles Mindy drove each time this week when she said she was visiting you. I checked her odometer, and then I compared it by driving over here. The same twenty-two point two each way."

He checked the odometer and the distance to my house, but it didn't occur to him to actually follow her? Poor Chad.

Hubert clapped a hand on Chad's shoulder. "Man to man, I have to tell you," he said, "I've been here all week and I haven't seen Mindy. Trust me when I tell you Lola's not covering anything up."

"But odometers don't lie," Chad protested. "The mileage is the same."

"Coincidence maybe?" Hubert said. Chad looked crestfallen. Ready for a confrontation and not getting it—how frustrating.

"You need to talk to Mindy and ask her what's going on," I said. I'd love to know myself, for that matter.

"I've tried talking to her. She just says she's running errands for the wedding." He leaned back against his car like John Travolta in *Grease*, if John had been short and really depressed. His despondent expression turned to alarm when a flash of light reflected off the car. "What the hell is that?" Chad asked, glancing down the block at the source of the light.

Before we could answer, we heard Belinda off in the distance cooing, "Baxter, Baxter, come here, boy."

"My neighbor looking for her dog again," I said. For the first time ever, I was glad of a King Street distraction.

"Yoo-hoo," Belinda called out to us, oblivious to the fact that nobody outside of Mayberry said "yoo-hoo" anymore. She was heading our way. "Have you seen my little Baxter? He keeps sneaking out, the stinker."

Hubert said, "No, we haven't seen him, but we can help you look if you like." In the past I would have begged off, but I felt generous tonight and glad for a distraction. If Hubert was up for it, I'd go along.

"That would be great," she said, coming up alongside us. "OK, here's our strategy. We fan out over the neighborhood. He never goes more than a block or so away. Just call him like this, OK?" She cupped her hand around her mouth. "Baxter, *Bax*ter." For some reason she was looking right at me, as if I was the one who needed dog-calling lessons. "Then listen for his barking. Sometimes he gets his little collar caught on something. One time he found an opening in a fence but couldn't find his way back out."

Baxter didn't sound too bright. Not that I knew much about dogs, but weren't they supposed to find us when *we* were lost?

"Hubert and I can cover this block." She waved her flashlight at my house. "And you two can do across the street. Make sure you do both the front and backyards. People don't mind."

"I think Chad here was just about to leave," I said.

"No, it's OK," he said. "I'll help."

As Chad and I crossed the street, I heard Hubert say, "That's quite a flashlight."

"Two million candle power," she said proudly. "I got it at Sears."

"Sorry you got roped into this," I said to Chad when we reached the corner. I decided we'd work from one end of the block to the other.

"It's OK," he said glumly.

"Baxter," I called out as we walked.

"Baxter," Chad repeated. His heart wasn't in it. I could tell.

We walked behind the houses first. When we got halfway down the block, Chad said, "Wait," and held out an arm to stop me. "Do you hear that?"

I heard it—the faint barking of a very small dog.

"Is that him?"

"Maybe."

We followed the noise to Ryan's backyard. I hadn't heard from him since I'd last seen him in his button mushroom stage. The house had looked empty from the front, but from here I could see a dim light in one of the upstairs bedrooms.

"It's coming from over there," Chad said, pointing.

"That's Ryan's garage."

"Ryan—the guy from the Thai restaurant?"

"That's the one." If only it wasn't so dark. I'd thought Belinda's mega-flashlight was overkill, but I could have used it now.

"I couldn't stand that guy," Chad said. "Does he have a dog?"

"No." Or at least not that I knew of.

He went ahead of me, circling the garage until he reached the side entrance. "Baxter," he said, pushing the door open. He flipped on the light switch, and I followed him. Just as my eyes adjusted to the brightness, I felt fur brush past my feet and out the door. I didn't look down, though, because my eyes were too busy processing what else was in the garage. Parked right beside Ryan's indigo Jaguar was Mindy's Ford GT.

37

Turns out I had a good time at Mindy's wedding reception after all. Maybe because she wasn't there.

After we found Mindy's car in Ryan's garage, Chad wanted to storm the house, and I wanted to smash the car windows, but when Hubert showed up he had a more sensible idea. He thought we should *take* Mindy's car. Chad had a copy of her car keys, so I wrote a note, which I left on the windshield of the Jag— "Mindy and Ryan, come on over and visit when you get a chance! Love, Lola"—and then Hubert drove the Ford GT across the street and into my garage. Since we were none too quiet about the whole thing, it didn't take long for Mindy to come marching up my driveway, pulling Ryan behind her. She decided, apparently, to act like the wronged party. Sizing up the situation, she screamed at Chad that he had no business follow-ing her. How dare he. Didn't he trust her? Then she yelled at me for taking her car. She threatened to call the police and have me arrested. "That's a felony, you know."

No, I was not aware that moving a car across a street was a felony.

Through all of this, Ryan stood next to her without saying a word. I kept looking at him for signs of guilt or embarrass-ment or recognition or *something*, but there was nothing there.

You'd think he didn't know me at all. I felt humiliation and anger rising in my throat like bile, but it was tempered by a sort of relief. Looking at Chad's face made me realize how much worse it could be. All I could think was, *Thank God, he wasn't really my fiancé. Thank God, I never had sex with him.* I'd dodged that bullet.

After Mindy calmed down, she claimed that the whole situation was completely innocent. The story was that she was interested in Ryan's line of work and he was teaching her the ropes. All business. But none of us believed it. All you had to do was look at their faces and it was obvious—they'd been doing it.

"No way I'm marrying you now, Mindy," Chad said. "Just forget about it."

"We'll discuss this later at home," she said, flipping back her hair.

"Nothing to discuss," he said before getting in his car and driving away. It seemed I'd underestimated him.

As much as I admired him that evening, I admired him even more later on when he stood his ground. Mindy had to move back in with our parents, who in turn had to call all the guests to tell them the wedding was off. My mother was able to cancel the photographer, the band, and the caterer, but the hall wouldn't budge, and neither would the baker.

When the long-range forecast for the wedding weekend showed rain, rain, and more rain, Hubert got the bright idea to have the block party indoors at Mindy's hall and turn it into a dinner and dance. A sort of wedding reception without a bride and groom. My parents, who'd been footing the bill for the wedding, agreed to his plan when they heard they'd get their deposit back.

* * *

Brother Jasper sought me out when the party began. He had to lean toward me so I could hear him above the music. "Miss Lola, I can't thank you and Hubert enough for hosting tonight."

"No problem," I said. "As it turns out, I wasn't busy after all."

"Hubert said it was your idea to have a DJ and a cover charge."

"I thought of it, but I really didn't do anything. Ben Cho was the one who came up with a DJ who'd work for free."

"And you brought food." He gestured to a banquet table covered with various dishes and platters. One end was snack food—chips and salsa, pretzels, cheese, and sausage. The middle of the table consisted of slow cookers containing meatballs and chicken wings, while desserts dominated the other side—primarily cookie bars and brownies. A three-tiered wedding cake stood at the end, next to a sheet cake that was chocolate on chocolate. I'd smeared out the "Happy Birthday, Lola" on the sheet cake. The party was really for a sick little boy and his family. I could turn thirty anytime.

"Just a few platters. Everyone else in the neighborhood brought food too."

"You decorated as well, I heard."

I waved my hand. "It was nothing. Just some balloons and a banner." Hubert had helped with the banner. It said, "King Street Block Party." And underneath that was written, "Get well soon, Derek!" We hung it over the entrance to the hall. Belinda said she'd give it to Derek when she visited him at the hospital on Sunday. "I did want to tell you, Brother Jasper, that I'm sorry I never got back to you this week."

"What's that?" He smiled and cupped his hand over his ear.

I raised my voice. "I never got back to you this week." He still looked puzzled, so I tried again. "You had some cautionary tales to tell me?"

"Oh." His face registered comprehension. "I was going to warn you about Mr. Moriarty. But I heard you figured him out on your own."

Oh yes, I'm sure everyone on King Street had heard by now. "What in particular did you want to tell me?"

Brother Jasper put his hand on my shoulder and leaned in. "I don't want to muddy the man's name, but I did hear he's a player."

"He dates a lot of women?" The song was over now, and the DJ was taking a request from two little girls I'd never seen before. From the church, I guessed.

He nodded. "Also he doesn't have a job, from what I hear. His family has some sort of trust fund set up for him, but he's always running out of money." I was feeling better about this all the time. Sometimes events that seem devastating turn out for the best. Well, maybe devastating wasn't quite accurate. Disappointing, anyway. Brother Jasper added, "And when he borrows from people, he doesn't pay them back. I wanted to warn you."

"But he said he's a consultant and travels all over the world for work."

"People say lots of things, Lola."

I nodded thoughtfully.

"But wasn't it odd," Brother Jasper said, speaking into my ear now that the music started up again, "the way Belinda's little dog was in that closed garage?" He shook his head as if puzzled. Before I could say anything, he smiled and excused himself to help a large woman who'd just walked in carrying a platter of ham sandwiches.

* * *

We had a good turnout. Over the next several hours, I refilled the pretzel and chip bowls, helped reunite a lost toddler with his mother, restocked napkins, and still managed to dance so much my feet hurt. In between all that I greeted people I knew, some of whom I'd told about the party and others that Hubert had invited. Several of Hubert's fourth graders came with their parents. I wondered if inviting students violated some kind of teacher code, but Hubert waved away my concerns. "It's open to the public," he said. "And we're not serving alcohol."

Even though I'd encouraged them to come, I was surprised and pleased when Mrs. Kinkaid and Drew showed up. They came together but weren't "together," Drew assured me. Mrs. Kinkaid had me point out Hubert, who at that moment was dancing in the middle of a group of nine-year-olds. "Oh, he's *very* cute," she said. "You never said he was tall. And look at him with those kids." She gave me an accusing look, as if I'd been withholding valuable information. "Since it didn't work out with that other fellow, I think you should go out with this Hubert."

"You think so?"

"Without a doubt. Did I ever tell you how Mr. Kinkaid and I started out as just friends? I had no interest in him romantically at all, until one day I did. And we had a very happy marriage."

I promised I'd consider it.

Toward the end of the evening, Piper and Mike came up to tell me they were leaving and that they'd had a great time. She'd confided in me earlier that Mike hadn't wanted to come at all, so the fact that they'd stayed was telling.

"You throw a good party, Lola," Mike said, shaking my hand. He'd always been weirdly formal with me.

"Thanks, but it's really not my party—it's a neighborhood shindig. I'm just helping."

Piper gave me a hug. "Happy birthday," she said quietly. "Are your folks upset you're not spending it with them?"

Earlier in the week my mom and I agreed to celebrate my big three-oh the following weekend. They were still busy with my sister, who tearfully insisted the whole thing was a misunderstanding. I could have set my parents straight, but after hashing it out with Hubert, I decided against it. One-upping my sister didn't seem like that much fun anymore. "I think they're pretty busy consoling Mindy, and I've been busy planning the block party. My birthday is taking a backseat for now." My birthday was the least of anyone's worries. Turned out that right after the garage incident Ryan took off for an extended business trip and still wasn't back. Mindy tried to make amends with Chad, but he wasn't caving. She even apologized to me, which was a first. Not that she admitted to anything specific. Actually, what she said was, "I'm sorry if I've caused you pain." Not the greatest apology, but I gratefully accepted it anyway. She was new to the concept, and I could tell she was doing her best.

"Now all we have to do is track down our kid, and we can leave," Mike said, looking around.

"Where *is* Brandon?" I asked. Piper had been holding him when they walked in the door, and I'd seen him earlier toddling around on the dance floor. Piper's arms looked strangely empty without him.

"Mrs. Olson has had him for most of the night," Piper said. "She insisted."

"She's the best babysitter. We can't thank you enough, Lola, for helping us find her." Mike gestured toward the opposite side of the room.

I looked where he pointed to see Myra sitting on a chair next to the wall, Brandon perched on her lap. Despite the noise, the baby was asleep in her arms. "*Myra's* been babysitting for you?"

"I told you that," Piper said.

"She's been great," Mike said, putting his arm around Piper. "And Brandon loves her. Maybe now that we have someone reliable, I'll actually get to spend some time with my wife."

Would wonders never cease?

The party was officially over at eleven thirty, but at midnight there were a few stragglers left. Brother Jasper, who was the chauffeur of the evening, had driven two carloads home already and was back for a senior couple who didn't drive at night but still liked to stay out late.

"Thanks again, you two," Brother Jasper called out to Hubert and me. I was folding up the tablecloth from the food table while Hubert stood on a chair taking down the banner.

"No problem. Good night," I said.

"See you later," Hubert added.

We were the last two left, if you didn't count the three young guys who were stacking chairs and moving tables.

"Can we be done?" I asked, sinking into a seat. My feet throbbed. If anyone wanted the chair, they'd have to lift me with it.

"Almost," Hubert said, pulling up a chair next to me. "We just have to wait for the manager. I gave him the money for the bar bill, and he's off printing up a receipt."

"A bar bill? That sounds expensive. I hope it doesn't eat up all our profits."

"Nah, it's all soft drinks. Plus, just between the two of us, I covered it myself. My little contribution for the evening."

I gave him a studied look. Maybe I stared for too long, because he looked uncomfortable and said, "What?"

"You're really something else, Hubert Holmes. You know that, right?"

"I'll take that as a compliment."

"You should. By the way, Mrs. Kinkaid thought you were very cute. She thinks you and I should be dating."

"Would that be *the* Mrs. Kinkaid, the smartest woman in the entire world?"

He made me laugh. "That's the one," I said, returning his grin.

"Oh, almost forgot." He tapped his forehead. "I've been meaning to give this to you all night." He reached into his pocket and handed me a package the size of a deck of playing cards wrapped in aluminum foil. "Happy birthday."

"Am I supposed to open it or heat it up?"

"Ha ha—I couldn't find any wrapping paper."

Beneath the foil was a square of yellowed tissue paper with a small bulge in the middle.

"It's from your aunt May, actually. She wanted you to have it."

My dead aunt sent me a gift? I unfolded the paper to find an antique ring in a silver setting. The square diamond in the center was set high and surrounded by delicate filigree. "Oh, how pretty."

"It was her engagement ring. In her last diary she mentioned wanting to give it to you the next time she saw you. She was going to explain about leaving you the house too, but she didn't get a chance, obviously."

I slid the ring on my third finger, left hand. It was a perfect fit. "So why *did* she leave the house to me?"

He hesitated; from the look on his face I knew there was something.

"What?"

"You don't want to hear it from me. It would be better for you to read her explanation when we get home."

"No, tell me now."

"Well, her reasoning isn't all that flattering, but I really do think her heart was in the right place."

"She thought I was a despicable loser who'd never own a house otherwise?"

"Oh no, nothing like that," he said. "She just watched you at family gatherings ever since you were a little girl and noticed how you set yourself apart from other people. She thought the neighbors on King Street would be good for you. They'd take you into their fold, she thought."

"She was right about that." I held my hand out to look at the ring on my finger. Beautiful, in an understated way. "King Street is like a Venus flytrap. But in a good way, I guess."

One of the young guys who'd been stacking chairs had been watching us. When he walked toward us, I thought for sure he was going to make us get up.

"Can I ask…" he said and hesitated, giving me a second to read his nametag. Ralph had the lanky build of a teenager. He wore a white button-down shirt and black pants that would never have stayed up without his belt. "Did you guys just get engaged?"

I exchanged an amused look with Hubert and said, "Well, he gave me the ring, but he hasn't actually asked me yet."

Ralph's eyes got big. "Do you want us to leave the room? Give you some privacy?"

"No, it's OK," Hubert said. "I *am* going to ask her, but I want to wait until the time is right."

"OK," Ralph said dubiously. He started to walk away and then turned back. "Congratulations, I guess."

After he was out of earshot, I turned to Hubert and asked, "Did you mean that? About asking me later?"

"It's a distinct possibility," he said, "but I think we're getting ahead of ourselves. How about we get to know each other a little better and then decide?" He raised his eyebrows playfully, making me laugh.

I looked at the ring on my finger and then at Hubert, who'd been at every one of my birthdays since I was thirteen. I wanted him to be there for every one from now on, and not just as a friend. I said, "Sounds like a plan."

"Good." He grinned. "Now I have something to look forward to."

"Me too," I said. "Let's go home."

Acknowledgments

A novel isn't created in a vacuum (which is a good thing because it's awfully dusty in there). This book, in particular, benefitted from the support and expertise of many people.

Every writer should be lucky enough to have an editor like Terry Goodman. Truly, he's the best. And his e-mails make me laugh, which is no small thing.

Besides being a marketing genius, I appreciate Sarah Tomashek because she's always gracious when I'm completely clueless. Thanks, Sarah!

My gratitude to everyone on the AmazonEncore team for their work on this book. Please know your efforts and talents are valued by me.

Copyeditor Jessica Smith saved me from myself and taught me a few things along the way. I appreciate her keen eye and willingness to explain the craft.

A shout-out to Betty Dorst, who shares funny stories about her life, one of which made it into my previous book, *A Scattered Life*. After blatantly using her anecdote for my own means, I *forgot* to mention it in the acknowledgements of the novel. What kind of friend does that, I ask you? Betty, please accept my belated thanks.

Zach Trecker, a big thank you for describing my son Charlie as "easily amused." It's very true, and I stole your phrase. So sue me.

I'd also like to acknowledge the following folks, many of them excellent writers, and all of them wonderful people: Vickie Coats, Kay Ehlers, Geri Erickson, Kimberly Einiger, Alice L. Kent, Judi Littlefield, Joyce McGee, and Judy Bridges and the members of her Tuesday Roundtable at Redbird Studios.

Special thanks to Felicity Librie, Jeannée Sacken, and Robert Vaughan. This group of talented writers read every word of this book in manuscript form and offered insightful feedback and critique.

And to my kids, Charlie, Maria, and Jack, you've made my life richer and fuller than I could have ever imagined. Hugs and smoochies!

And most of all, to Greg. I'm glad it was you.

About the Author

Author photo by Greg McQuestion

Karen McQuestion has written fiction for years, but it wasn't until she self-published her first novel on Kindle that she found her readers. Her amazing success in this endeavor has earned a movie option and publishing deal for her first novel, *A Scattered Life*. She lives in Hartland, Wisconsin, with her husband and their three children.

1. In the beginning of the novel, Lola is reluctant to let Hubert stay the night because she's not set up for guests. Can you relate to her hesitation, and what does this say about her personality?

2. Lola seems awfully critical of her sister, Mindy. Do you think her attitude is justified? Is this, as she said, a sister thing?

3. Lola's neighbors appear to genuinely care for one another. Is this level of involvement unusual today? And what are the pros and cons of neighbors who know so much about each others' lives?

4. Did you notice that the main characters' last names were Watson, Holmes, and Moriarty, and did you make the connection to the books featuring Sherlock Holmes by Sir Arthur Conan Doyle?

5. Lola is so taken with Ryan's good looks and suave personality that she initially discounts the warning signs that all is not as it seems. Have you or a friend ever experienced a similar situation?

6. Piper is described as a take-charge person. How does this work against her when it comes to allowing her husband Mike to help with the care of their son?

7. Does Hubert's easygoing personality and willingness to clean Lola's house make him the perfect man? Discuss amongst yourselves.

8. How do you think Belinda's dog Baxter got into Ryan's closed garage?

9. Great-Aunt May bequeathed the house to Lola knowing that the neighbors would watch out for her. Do you think May discussed this idea with her neighbors at the time her will was drafted?

10. Do you believe Lola and Hubert will end up getting married, and if so, are they a good match?